THE
FORBIDDEN
ALPHA

JP SINA

The Forbidden Alpha

Author: Jp Sina

To Lima and B.

Thank you for teaching Mommy that
I should do what I love and love what I do.
Because of you, my loves, I was able to start writing.

And to you, the reader.

Without you, this wouldn't have been possible.

ACKNOWLEDGMENTS

Thanks to:

Amy for her unwavering belief in me.
Without you, I would be lost.

Joseph for his love and support.

Georgina for encouraging me and always being honest
with how insane my ideas sound.
My number one fan, you are amazing.

Jon for always answering the phone to
listen to my insane ideas.

Becca for her five-minute breathing calls to help me calm
down and for amazing advice. For all the encouragement
when I struggled to write after those one-star reviews.

Mom for nurturing my reading ability. Growing up,
Barnes & Nobles was better than Disneyland.

And last but not least, to all of the authors that kept me up
until 3 a.m., for the gift of book boyfriends, to scaring my
family with my random squealing and crying, thank you.
Thank you for the books that helped me escape when
facing reality was too difficult to bear.

TABLE OF CONTENTS

A DREAM

Adea

I feel like I've been running forever. I get to the bottom of the stairs and push with everything I have on the door. Please please please, I think to myself. I step back and push my shoulder into the door and it opens for me.

I'm blinded. All I can hear is the ringing in my ears. The wolf's bane grenade had gone off. I squint as the fog clears. Everything is moving in slow-mo as I try to find him; to smell him.

I can't hear Mavy. I stumble over a body and stare in shock as I find the head of my dearest friend, Gabriel. I fumble as I rush past the arms, legs, and heads of familiar faces, trying to find him.

In the corner of my eye, I see movement. I turn and see a pile rise and fall as a shape pushes up through the bodies. I can see his black hair and my heart swells as I watch him search for me. When his eyes lock on mine, I see the relief flood his face.

He stands up and I can feel the need to touch him grow and almost explode as he starts to come towards me. I can feel his need and his relief. I feel his shock... Shock fills his eyes and I frantically try to see what's wrong. I look at his chest.. his beautiful chest...

1

The mate bond snaps and my world is cold and I'm all alone. All I can feel is a numbing pain as I fall to the ground. I can't look away from my mate but I can hear his footsteps coming closer. He drops something near my head and grabs my hair. He starts dragging me and I hit my head on a rock.

The last thing I see is the empty eyes of my mate before I lose consciousness. The last coherent thought I have is knowing that I'm alone.

Beep beep beep beep beep beep beep

I groan as I hear my alarm go off. I feel a migraine splitting my head apart as I reach around for my phone. Where did I put it? I feel around for it and grab it from the floor next to the bed.

I roll over and groan. Fuck, I have to get up. The Alpha and his family get up at seven and I need to make sure that breakfast is prepared by the time they head to the kitchen.

The Moon Goddess must have been watching out for me because normally when a rogue stumbles onto pack land. They are killed when found. I'm lucky that Alpha Joshua gave me a job at the packhouse and provided a room for me to stay in.

I've been here at the Half Moon pack for the last four years. My parents died when I was young and Alpha Joshua and his Luna Rose didn't have to help me but they did. I'm thankful for the roof over my head and the warm bed I can sleep in.

I mentally push myself to get up and throw on one of the two jeans I own, a white t-shirt, and a hoodie. I have a bag of clothes Mavy had bought me but I haven't had the heart to open them yet.

I'm putting my hair up when I hear a quiet knock at the door. I look at my reflection in my small mirror and groan. "My brown hair looks stringy and frizzy; the only nice thing is its length. My brown eyes are dull and bloodshot.

There's nothing I can do to make myself look better. Oh well. "Come in", I whisper, knowing it's just Gabe coming to grab me for work. He's 5'11", has blonde hair, and a crooked smile. Not the tallest man in the pack but compared to my 5'3", he towers over me.

I turn around and Gabe whistles.

"Morning, Ady. You look like shit," he chuckles, looking down at my frizzy brown hair.

One time, some clothes went missing the day Gabe and I were working in the kitchen together. Some of the pack members blamed me for the missing clothes.

Gabe stood up for me and told them that I was with him the entire time preparing their food. Since then, he's been a great friend but sometimes he overshares his opinion.

I roll my eyes, "Morning Gabe." Tactfulness isn't his strong suit, but at least I could rely on him to tell me the truth.

"Have that dream again?" He asks.

The dreams started after my 17th birthday and have been haunting me for a year now.

When I first had the dream, I woke up with tears running down my face. They were so vivid they had me questioning reality. The next night I had another dream and it continued. I would get them once a month until I was having them every other week. Nightmares have become a normal part of life.

"Like clockwork", I sigh as we head down the hall.

We close my door and I lock it. As we walk down the hallway, I look at the tall white walls. They always make me feel so small. When I first moved into the packhouse, I fell in love with the old-fashioned vintage 19th-century European feel. Alpha Joshua is a little OCD so everything has a place and there's a place for everything. It keeps everything clean and organized so I guess it works.

"I had an amazing night with this she-wolf Ady, you don't even know. Goddess! You should have seen the tits on her. I had her in-" I cut him off before he can finish.

"Please spare me the details, Gabe. I do NOT want to hear where, how, or what positions you had her in. I'll take your word for it. Now please shut uuup", I groan. Gabe is one of my closest friends but I swear he's a man whore.

After every sexcapade, he insists on telling me every detail like I care. He swings an arm around my shoulder and leans in. "Come on Ady, if I don't tell you who else will I tell?" he whines. I can imagine his wolf pouting and I have to stifle a laugh. "Oh, my virgin ears," I say as I cover my ears. He continues to pout while we make our way to the kitchen.

I feel like I've been running forever. I get to the bottom of the stairs and push with everything I have on the door. Please please please, I think to myself. I step back and push my shoulder into the door and it opens for me.

GABE

Gabe turns on the light and snaps me out of my daydream. Alpha Joshua and Luna Rose were very considerate of me. They took me in and gave me a place to stay. I was a rogue and they could have killed me for trespassing on their territory.

Instead, they welcomed me into the pack, gave me an initiation party, and gave me a home. Without them I would have been a rogue and most likely would have lost myself.

After I recovered, I started working in the Half Moon packhouse where the Alpha, his Beta, Gamma, and their spouses stayed. I've been here ever since. We enter the kitchen and it's wide and open. There's a long wooden table with black leather chairs. The kitchen sink and marble counter tops are on the right. Instead of pantries, there are long wooden shelves on the wall that hold the plates, bowls, and cups.

I put on some music while Gabe and I start making breakfast. Later, Gabe will make lunch while I go to school. We see each other again for dinner and we work as a team to make the food.

Music makes the work go faster. I enjoy my early routine with Gabe. As we're setting the table, Mavy comes running in and wraps her arms around my waist. "Good morning Adea! Thanks for breakfast!" She kisses me and takes a seat.

"No problem Mave. I made your favorite!" I sing. She giggles as I grab her a plate. "How'd you sleep?" She sighs, "When I got home last night, I was so tired I slept like a log!"

Alpha Joshua and Luna Rose had twins which are rare for werewolves. Mavy and Shane are polar opposites. The top of Mavy's head lines up with my chest while Shane towers over me at 6 feet and they both have black wavy hair. Mavy has gray eyes while Shane has brown eyes like Luna Rose.

Shane walks in and stares at me, smirks, and sits down. Gabe elbows me, reminding me to get their trifecta breakfast onto their plates. Today, we went for a simple breakfast. I fill their plates with scrambled eggs, buttered toast, and bacon and excuse myself as Alpha and Luna walk through the door.

Alpha Joshua looks exactly the same and Luna Rose hasn't aged a day. Alpha is tall like Shane and has black wavy hair and gray eyes, while Luna Rose has pencil straight brown hair and brown eyes.

"You don't need to leave, Adea. You're more than welcome to sit with us for breakfast." Alpha smiles at me. I can't leave now so I grab a plate and Gabe fills my plate with scrambled eggs, crispy bacon, and buttered toast, and smiles. I swat his arm and take a seat in between Shane and Mavy.

Shane eats his food quietly while Mavy turns to me, "Trent is coming over before school if you wanna hitch a ride with us Adea." My mouth is full and before I can chew my toast, I swallow my toast making my eyes water, "It's okay Mavy. I've got to get some stuff done before school but you can go ahead."

Trent and Mavy aren't dating but his feelings were obvious. I did not want to be the third wheel and have Trent give me the stink eye the whole way to school. "Oh okay, Adea," she smiles looking a little sad. Turning back to her plate, she picks at her food.

Shane scoffs, "What've you got to do Ady? Scrub the toilets?" Alpha Joshua glares at Shane, "Shane", he warns. Shane tilts his head and stares at his dad, "Yes, Alpha?" he asks with a smirk on his face. His eyes have started glowing.

Mavy reaches over me and slaps Shane's shoulder, "Shane don't be such an ass. She's not a slave!" She sits down and looks at me, "I'm sorry, Adea. Excuse my idiot brother." She rolls her eyes and checks her phone.

Shane reaches over and touches my lower back. I sit straight up as chills crawl up my back. Shane looks down at his plate, "You know I'm just joking around, don't you Ady?" he lifts his head and turns to look at me.

Gabe stops and stares at us. "Yeah, I knew you were joking…" I tell the table. His hand slides lower on my back. "Shane's sense of humor is oh so funny." "Daddy, have you guys decided where the Crescent Ball is going to be this year?" Mavy asks.

"We have a meeting this afternoon to vote on where the ball is going to be. " Alpha tells her. "Out of all the packs, it comes down to the Silver pack and the Desert Moon pack. Where will our vote go, Josh?" Luna asks Alpha Joshua.

"We know that the Silver pack isn't well off so it might be a burden financially for them if we vote to have them host the Crescent Ball. But if we don't have the ball at the Desert Moon pack then we only have one other choice…" he says lost in thought.

"Wouldn't the best choice be the Desert Moon pack then?" Mavy asks. "Is the Desert Moon a safe place to visit?" Luna asks. "It's safe we just don't have an alliance with their new Alpha." Alpha Joshua says. "Desert Moon would be the better of the two because they can afford to throw the ball and it could be a good opportunity for our packs to get to know each other. We'd have a chance to talk about an alliance."

Mavy squeals, "Adea, maybe we can find our mates at the Crescent Ball if it's held at the Desert Moon pack!" I internally groan as I look at my best friend, "Visiting other packs raises the chances of finding your Goddess chosen mate…"

"Me? You mean WE can find our mates at Crescent Moon this year." She elbows me and gives me the side-eye. Her eyes are telling me I'm not going to escape this year.

"Daddy, can Adea and I go shopping this weekend for dresses? Please?" she asks with doe eyes. Alpha looks at us with a thoughtful expression and before I can tell them there's no need, he says, "That sounds like a good idea. Nothing inappropriate, Mavy, you hear me?"

"YES! Thank you, Daddy".

Ding! Ding-Ding!

"Trent's here! Gotta go." She stands up and gives her dad a kiss and her mom a hug. "Adea, we have plans tomorrow night! I'll see you at school." She glares at Shane as she runs out of the kitchen.

I stand up and grab all of the dishes and put them into the sink. Gabe cleans up after breakfast so I can get ready for school. "See you later, Alpha Joshua and Luna. I'll see you guys after school." "See you after school" they smile.

"See you Ady" Shane calls after me. I don't know what is going on with Shane but he's been slowly getting more and more aggressive towards me. Thankfully pack slaves were banned here at Half Moon. Shivers run up my back as I remember his fingers on my lower back.

I grab my bag and run out the back door. My favorite time of the day is my morning run before school. I haven't heard my wolf yet but I think she's going to show up soon. My sense of smell is heightened and I love the smell of the woods in the back of the packhouse.

I pull my hair out of my bun as I run. I keep running until I get to the clearing where the grass meets the small creek. I take a deep breath and enjoy the smell of the woods. This creek is my safe haven.

I take off my backpack and lay down on the grass. The sounds of the grass swaying in the wind, the sunlight peeking through the woods a mix of orange, blue, and yellow. The birds sing their song, and the cheerfulness in their voices brightens my day.

The light pounding of rabbits hopping along the ground brings a smile to my face. I could lay here all day if I could. Being out here makes me happy.

I hear a bell out in the distance and grab my bag. Time for school.

MAVY

I can tell you the exact moment my life changed. Everything I knew was turned upside down. Being a kid left in the world without parents is haunting.

It all started the day after I turned 13 and my little sister Ava, was 8. My father was the Alpha of the Ice Moon pack and my mother, his Luna. The Ice Moon pack wasn't the largest pack, but when my dad was the Alpha, we had 400 pack members.

One day, my father was challenged and he had no choice but to accept. I remember how worried my mom was. The wolf that challenged my father was Davien Stockholm. He wasn't from our pack but he was massive in size even before he transformed. His dark hair fell to his shoulders and his body was muscular.

He lunged at my dad but one thing my dad had on him was speed. My dad ducked and punched him in the stomach. "Yes!" I fist-pumped the air. Ava copied me while screaming, "Go Daddy!"

Davien grabbed his stomach and his head came down and my dad uppercut him in the face. There was a crunch as Davien's nose broke and blood gushed out. "Ew Mom!" I said in disgust. I looked at my mom to see her worried expression.

"Don't worry, Mom. Daddy can't lose," I reassured her.

She smiled but her eyes never left my dad. Davien fell to the ground and put his hand on the ground. My dad looked up and saw me staring at him. He smiled and winked at me and Ava.

I smiled back and my mom let out a scream. I looked up at her and then looked back at my dad. Davien had lunged at my dad and had pinned him to the ground.

My dad struggled against his hold but couldn't break through it. Davien cocked an arm back and punched my dad in the face. Over and over again. I stared in shock as my dad's face became unrecognizable.

I screamed, "Stop it! Stop it, please!" Ava was crying hysterically. Davien stopped and turned to me and my mother. He looked down at my dad and said, "Give me the title and I will spare you and your family."

My dad's eyes were covered with blood as he said, "I, Eduard Biscoff, step down as Alpha from the Ice Moon pack and declare Davien Stockhom as the new Alpha. In exchange, Davien Stockholm has promised my family and I, our lives."

After that day, my parents and I were cast out from our pack. We were declared rogues. I'd never lived anywhere but with the pack and the same could be said for my parents. My father didn't know how the human world worked but he grew up building the pack up along with his father.

He was determined to save us from going rabid. So, he decided to move us to a human city where they both could try to get jobs. It wasn't easy but with what we were able to salvage. They bought a small house.

We had a roof over our head and they both searched for jobs and put me and Ava into human school. It was hard for all four of us to adapt. We weren't used to the eerie silence now that we weren't a part of the pack.

We couldn't even link each other. I honestly think if we didn't have each other, we would have gone insane, or rabid like other rogues. Thankfully, we could almost fill the void with our little family.

It was quiet without a pack but we made it work. My dad got a good job as a contractor and my mom eventually got a job as an accountant for a small company.

He'd come home and tell us about the newest house or business he was working on. Mom would be cooking in the kitchen and I'd listen to him go on and on. When he finished a project, he'd drag us out of there and we'd marvel at his work. Every day went by filled with dad's stories and mom's food.

We couldn't go for runs or be a part of the forest because we lived in the city. I think that killed mom and dad the most. Their wolves suffered and they were easily irritated but we were able to make it work.

"Just wait until you see this one!" he told us one day after work. We were going out to check dad's latest project. He'd been working on an internet cafe packed with the latest PCs and equipped with a small coffee section where baristas would make beverages.. He was excited to show us the section where customers would order fresh hot sandwiches when they would get hungry. He was excited to be working with something tech-related.

On the way to finally see this new place in person, we were hit by a semi-truck and I woke up to a room with machines beeping and an oxygen tube down my throat.

"She's coming to, hey, honey?" I reached for the tubes and yanked them from my nose and mouth. Every breath I inhaled was painful and tore at my throat, tears welled in my eyes.

Looking around, I saw the nurse running towards me from across the room. She noticed me pull out the tubes. She grabbed my hands and I croaked, "Where's my mom?"

A look I could only identify as pity flashed in her eyes before she grabbed both of my arms. She looked me in the eyes and explained that there had been an accident.

"Okay…" I said and waited for the rest.

"Honey, your parents, and your sister… they all died on impact. You're the only one who survived."

I couldn't hear anything. I-what? They… they died? My mom? My dad? Ava? I was too cold to cry. I couldn't believe it. This couldn't be true. How… how could they just be gone?

I reached out, I screamed, I thrashed. Two more nurses were called in and held me down. The first nurse injected something into my arm and I slowly lost control of my body. I went limp and they laid me down slowly on the bed.

"It'll be alright, it's going to be okay," she said soothingly. "It's going to be okay," she said again as she looked into my eyes.

"The accident happened on Half Moon pack territory. Alpha Joshua and Luna Rose have taken care of everything. You've been out for a couple of weeks and we weren't sure you were going to ever come too."

My world crashed around me and I felt like my breath had been stolen from me. I hadn't had any control of my body as I laid there. Dead? Gone?

The nurses left me and a few hours later when whatever they gave me wore off, she came back again.

"What am I going to do now?" I whispered when I saw her.

"Oh honey, Alpha Joshua has informed us that you are to be cared for as a pack member. Don't you worry yourself! He has taken care of your medical bills and I'll let him know you're finally awake!"

Her eyes glossed over as she mind-linked someone. I hadn't seen a mind-link since I was a kid and it was almost weird to witness. Her pupils were covered by a white fog. I looked around the room and noticed flowers on my bedside.

When the nurse ended the mind-link, "Who bought me flowers, Nurse?" I asked.

"Oh! Alpha and Luna have twins. They just turned 14 and her daughter Mavy has been visiting you. I think the two of you will get along."

As if we conjured her, the door opened and a black-haired girl peered in. "Hey! You're awake. Thank goodness, I was worried you'd sleep for the rest of the year" She bounced in with a big smile on her face like we had known each other for years. She's got black hair and gray eyes and dimples poke both sides of her cheeks.

I didn't have the strength to smile or reply. I look away from her and stare at the wall. I didn't know what I'd do back then, where I'd go… I was just a kid. The lump in my throat was too hard to swallow.

The girl didn't say anything more until she left but then she came back. Day after day until I had grown used to her visits.

One day she had brought more flowers, and was talking about her day again.

"…. Thanks for the flowers," I said.

She looked around the room, not knowing who was talking. She turned back to me, "Was that you?!"

I nodded.

"Oh my gosh! So you can talk! I'm glad you like them! I wanted to bring something to brighten your room up. Shane helped pick them out. He's my brother." She smiled.

"So mom and dad say you'll be staying at the packhouse with us! I'm so excited to show you around. You'll most likely be going to school with us too."

Mavy and I sat and she talked for the rest of the afternoon where she filled me in on herself. This time, I listened.

She told me she was in the 8th grade and will be going to Trenton High next year. The Half Moon pack had been peaceful and had alliances with most of the surrounding packs.

She told me about the packhouse and how big it is but warned about her dad's OCD. "Fair warning, everything has to be perfect 100% of the time. My room is my own but the packhouse doesn't have a speck of dust.

The other pack members are okay. When we initiate you into the pack, you'll be able to talk to everyone. Was it hard being a rogue?" She asked.

I thought of my parents and felt sad again. I thought I would cry but nothing came out, "No…"

She stared at me and decided it's better to move on. "Did you like anyone where you came from?"

"No... we stayed to ourselves. I didn't have time… to think about boys." I told her.

"Well, I've been friends with Trent, he's my next-door neighbor since we were in diapers. He's my dad's Betas son and puberty has treated him well." She blushed, "He's just a friend but he's pretty, like prettier than me."

"We grew up making mud pies together. He's obviously just a friend..." she said super fast. I smiled at her and nodded.

I made a note to myself, Trent is off-limits. She smiled and grabbed my hand, "I know that you're not in a good place right now but just know that I've got your back." Her words made tears come to my eyes and I smiled and nodded. I felt a little better knowing I'm not completely alone in the world.

TRENTON HIGH

I slowed to a stop before I walked onto campus. Everyone's still waiting for the doors to open. I pulled out my cell phone and sent Mavy a quick text.

Made it. Where are you? I'm thankful I have the first period with Mavy. I can start the day off right every day. I glance down at my phone as the screen lights up.

I'm waiting in the quad with Trent. Come over!

Ugh, she's still with him.

I step onto campus and look at the Trenton High mascot statue. It's a huge wolf standing on two legs with ripped jeans and a six-pack. When Trenton High was built it was built by a human with a werewolf kink. I spot Mavy standing on a ledge waving at me and head over.

I see Trent and nod at him, "Hey Trent, how's it?" "Morning," he says. The bell rings and saves the day. "Time for class!" Mavy bounces and grabs my arm. "Later Trent!" she waves. We head to Chemistry when I see Shane and a few of his friends at the door. I avoid eye contact as we walk towards the door.

Shane's closest friend Liam is the oldest and the nicest out of the group. He doesn't pay attention to me and doesn't join in when

Shane torments me. He's the shortest at 5'11" but with his blonde hair and blue eyes, he's easy on the eyes. Devin is Shane's right-hand man but he's got a nasty temper. He's got inches on his friends and he's built like a rock. He's sporting a brown-haired Mohawk and has dimples when he smirks. I think Shane is going to appoint him as his Beta when he takes over.

Shane spots us and hands Mavy her backpack. "Thank you brother," Mavy says as she kisses his cheek. I shudder and look away. It's been four years that I've known Mavy and Shane and I still can't get used to how close they are. Mavy heads into class as Shane steps in front of me blocking the door with his hand. I look up at him as he cocks his head to the side.

"What did you do before school?" I look at his friends and they're watching us quietly. "I just had to grab some stuff and I ran here." "Hmm…" he murmurs as he moves his hand from the door.

Mavy caught me looking at the door and yelled for them to go to class. I head in and see she's already bustling with excitement talking to Nikki about the ball. I like to keep to myself at school but Mavy's friend Nikki was in our first period too. She always talks to her and she comes to the packhouse sometimes so I don't mind her.

Nikki loved that I didn't seem to have any sense of fashion. She was always trying to get me to wear something she thought I'd look good in but I always declined. Mavy would turn to Nikki to help dress me and would pair me with cute skirts and the occasional dress. So I knew what was coming with this ball.

No matter how hard I tried to focus, Shane enjoyed pestering me. I wasn't sure how I should react to his attention. We have assigned seats in calculus, and I sit next to him. "Are you avoiding me, Ady?" He said Gabe's nickname for me, enunciating every letter.

"No, Shane. I didn't have time to do my homework last night." I whispered as Becka glared at me.

"Are you excited to go to the ball?" he grabs a strand of my hair and tucks it behind my ear. He wasn't this handsy around Mavy.

"No, I just know that I don't have a choice when it comes to your sister," I smile. He chuckles and I still as I feel his finger sliding down my neck. I shudder and he mistakes it and thinks I like it.

He leans in and inhales, "You smell divine Ady." I close my eyes as I feel his breath on my neck. I move away from him and I can feel the knives in my back as I avoid Becka's gaze.

"Let's talk after class," he murmurs.

"I can't, I'm going home with Mavy."

"I only need a few minutes. I have a pack meeting so it won't take too long Ady," he says as he sits back.

I'm not sure when Shane started having an interest in me.

When I first moved into the packhouse we would spend time together because of Mavy. We weren't friends. He would make that clear when it was just the two of us. Recently he's been more physical with me.

He doesn't usually do anything when Mavy's around but after this morning at breakfast, I'm worried. The bell rings and I run for the door. Becka trips me and all of my books fly across the floor. I feel pain and look at my hand. I look up at her as I pick up my books.

"Whoops! I didn't see you Ady," she snickers and heads out. Everyone at Trenton High knows that Becka has the hugest crush on him. I pick up my books and head to lunch. "Don't forget Ady," Shane calls after me.

Like I could forget.

***

At lunch I find Mavy and Nikki sitting with Shane and his friends. "Adea here! I saved you a seat!" Mavy sings. I smile as I head over with my cafeteria pizza. I sit on her left and Nikki on her right.

"So we were talking…" Mavy says slyly. "About shopping tomorrow after school for the ball. You need a dress Chika!" Nikki is not going to let an opportunity to play barbie with me slide by. She isn't a werewolf but she's been close to Mavy since they were kids. She's the exception to the no telling our secret to outsiders rule.

"I'm tagging along to help find something poppin' and you can bet that I'm doing your makeup!"

"I don't—" I start.

Mavy cuts me off, "You don't have to worry about it. Daddy's buying our clothes for us. So don't use the ' I don't have any money ' excuse. I got you." She leans in and bumps my shoulder.

I roll my eyes, "I was prepared for this. I know I don't have a choice. Just promise me you won't make me wear something too flashy." "No promises!" She scrunches up her nose and beams. "Seriously though. We were thinking of something simple yet elegant for you Adea. You're already a natural beauty but I was thinking of something that could highlight your curves and make your eyes pop."

I look over and see Shane smiling at my discomfort. I've never been one to dress up and he knows it. "You can put makeup on a pig but will it be pretty?" he jokes and his friends howl with laughter.

"Har har. You're soooo funny." Mavy rolls her eyes and folds her arms across her chest. "Sike. That wasn't nice Shane." "It's fine Mavy, I know he's just kidding," I told her, trying to defuse the situation. "Why are you such an asshole, Shane?" Nikki says as she gives Shane a death glare.

If I could only have a pinch of Nikki's attitude I think I'd be able to tell Shane to shove it. "Come one guys, it's almost time for class."

"Sorry, sorry, I took it too far. I'm sorry Ady," he says as he blinks fast three times.

"Mmm, I'm sure. See girls? It was just a joke." Mavy and Nikki pout and glare at the boys. We decide to meet at the packhouse after I make dinner for Alpha and the rest of the house. Then we'll head out.

The last half of school goes by extremely slowly. I let my mind wander to the trail in the woods, to the creek hidden in the woods. My thoughts drifted to my wolf and what she would look like. Would her hair be the same color as mine or would she have her own physical characteristics?

I was pulled from my daydreaming when the bell rang and I felt my phone vibrate. I've got a message from Shane.

Gym. Now.

GOOD GIRL

TRIGGER WARNING
This chapter contains sexual assault and/or violence
that may be triggering to survivors.

Gym. Now.

I grabbed my books and stuffed them into my backpack. I pulled my hair up into a bun and headed for the gym. Breathing deeply, I tried to calm myself. The gym wasn't connected to the school so I had to leave the building and walk under the walkway until I got to the big blue doors.

I wished to be able to hear my wolf. I'm sure she'd know what to say or do. I pulled open the door and stepped into the gymnasium. It was empty and it felt eery without kids to fill the space. It was too late to turn back.

"Adea Danielle Biscoff." Shane said my full name, a sly smile pulling up at the corners of his lips.

My heart hammered in my chest, the hair on my arms standing up on end. I turned around and saw his eyes begin to wander. I could feel the heat from his gaze as they ran down the length of my face, traveling my neck, and down my body.

His eyes went up to my neck again, and they lingered there for longer than I would have liked. "Thanks for coming, Adea." he murmured thoughtfully. Shane was a very controlled man and over the last four years, I didn't see much emotion from him.

My voice wouldn't come out, I tried to but couldn't find the words. His eyes twinkled as he stepped towards me and without thinking I took a step back. This made him smile and he closed the distance between us.

I couldn't scream. I looked up at him, swallowing down my fear and discomfort. Why did I come here? The thought crossed my mind as Shane's fingers reached for my neck until they grazed my skin. His fingers pressed lightly on my neck and ran up and down causing me to shiver.

"What's going on Shane?" I asked once I could trust my voice not to crack. The cold air in the gym made goosebumps break out across my skin. I was mesmerized by him. "I've got to meet Mavy soon… Why did you want to meet up?" I said my voice betraying the fear I felt.

He was wearing shorts and a tank top and I was shocked when I could feel something hard against my belly. I looked down and my eyes widened in shock. I looked up at him, "You always smell so fucking good Adea." He murmured as he leaned down to my neck.

The neck of a werewolf was a sensitive area. When you find your mate, you mark each other on the neck while completing the mating process. I wouldn't know who my mate was until I turned 18. While I didn't know who my mate was I couldn't just let Shane mark me.

Before I could pull away his lips kissed my neck. His warm tongue on my neck made my knees weak. "Please… don't," I begged. He closed his eyes and leaned back, inhaling deeply. His jaw tensed as he fought for control.

Shane's voice was soft, when his eyes opened they were burning into my own with the intensity of his words. "Let me escort you to the ball." He said as his hand cupped my face. "I'm going with Mavy and Nikki, Shane. I'm going to help her find her mate."

Anger flashed in his eyes and I shook with fear. "You're going to help her find her mate? Or yours?" He leaned in and I could feel his breath on my neck. "I'm going to help her find her mate, Shane." His question and this whole situation confused me.

"I'll escort you into the ball. We're voting today at the pack meeting and I have a feeling it'll be at Desert Moon." I felt his hand caress my neck and slide down my chest to my waist. "Shane, I don't know what you're—" I couldn't finish my words as his lips came crashing down on my own.

His lips were warm but rough as he searched for a way in. My lips parted as his tongue dipped into my mouth. I was shocked that Shane was kissing me. I put my hands up to push him away. He let out a growl and pushed me against the wall. My head slammed against the wall as he pinned both of my wrists above my head.

Shane had me restrained against the wall and I was at his mercy. I looked up at him and his eyes were swirling. His obsidian eyes weren't pitch black anymore, there were flecks of gold in his eyes. He was breathing heavily as he stared down at me.

I felt sick as I tried to break free from his hold. "Please, Shane. I don't want this." I whimpered. He leaned down and kissed my neck. "Sshh, Adea." His other hand wandered down to the hem of my shirt. He reached under my shirt and I could feel his finger trail up closer to my breast.

My breath caught as I stared at him. His lips moved to my cheek and then to my lips searching for my tongue. He sucked on my tongue, feeling his hot breath made me nauseous. His hand squeezed my breast and his fingers pinched my nipple. My body was getting hot as he twirled my nipple in between his fingers. He pushed against me and I could feel his hard length on my stomach.

He moaned and reached for my jeans. His kisses became more fervent as his hand unbuttoned my jeans. I started to panic and thrashed against him. I bit his lip tasting blood and moved my mouth from his lips. "No! Get off of me. Please, Shane."

He stared down at me in surprise "You're mine Adea. I want to feel you writhing under me screaming my name." He closed his eyes and when he opened them the gold flecks were gone. "I'll stop if you agree to me escorting you." His hand fingered the band of my underwear.

He's never been this way with me. "Let's talk Shane. Please, let me go." I needed to get control of the situation. "Agree to go with me, Ady," he murmured.

"Okay," I cried. "Okay, just please stop." I made sure people knew I wasn't interested in dating. Not that anyone ever asked but deep down inside I knew I was saving myself for my mate. "I'll go with you."

Instead of letting go, his grip on my wrists tightened as his other hand slipped into my underwear. My eyes widened and I looked up at him. "I said I'd go with you. You said you'd stop if I said I'd go… you can escort me, Shane. You don't —" His finger slid against my slit until he inserted a finger. My body jolted with the intrusion. I closed my eyes fighting back tears.

"That's right, feel what I do to you." He whispered as his finger pushed deeper into my pussy. I couldn't find my voice. His finger pulled out and pushed into me. He groaned, "You're so tight Ady." I feel disgusted with myself as I feel my wetness coat his fingers.

He leans his head against my neck and moves his fingers faster and faster. My breathing hitches as I feel something growing inside of me. He sucks on my neck and pumps his fingers harder.

He inserts another finger and I can't help it when a moan escapes my lips. He nips at my neck and my pussy clenches around his fingers. He lifts his head and stares at me as a tear runs down my cheek. Shane leans in and kisses my tears as I close my eyes and turn away.

"Look at me." He says gruffly as his fingers continue to assault my pussy. "I want to watch you cum on my fingers, Ady." The feeling has grown stronger as my pussy clenches around his fingers. "Look at me." His voice stern. I moan as I cum all over his fingers.

"Good girl." He kisses my neck as he lets go of my wrists. He stares down at me as he brings his fingers to his lips and laps at my juices. I'm panting as I look away from him. He grabs my chin and brings my lips to his. "This'll be our little secret, Ady. I'll see you at home." He readjusts himself and steps back and walks out of the gym doors.

Leaving me shocked at what just happened. I pull up my jeans and button them. Falling to the floor, I tuck my legs into my chest and sob. Cries fill the gym as I realize what just happened.

My stomach clenched painfully at the thought of what Mavy would think if she found out. I wiped the tears from my face and feel pain as I stand up. This didn't happen.

The thought causes me to freeze. I can't lose her. I wipe my face and stand up. This didn't happen. This never happened. I turn and push on the doors.

PRETTY PLEASE?

"Chika! Where have you been?" Nikki screamed as I walked towards her car.

"Mavy and I have been waiting for you for over half an hour." She eyed my messy bun and heated face. "You look like you had fun," she purred.

Mavy stepped closer to me, "Have you been crying Adea?" she asked as she looked at my puffy eyes.

"Yeah, I'm just all over the place. School's been stressful." I grab her arm and smile. She looked at me doubtfully as I pulled her into the car.

Nikki blasted the car and played Cardi B the whole way home. Mavy and I singing "Be careful with me" with the wind in our hair. Nothing like a bit of girl time to brighten a shitty day. "I love this song!" Nikki screamed as "Press" came on next. I laughed as I watched Mavy twerk against Nikki's face.

My smile dropped when we pulled up to the packhouse gates. One of the guards walked up to the car and inspected the vehicle before he nodded for the other guard to let us in. "Thanks, Papi," Nikki said as she blew the guard a kiss. I laughed at Nikki's confidence. For a human, she had no fear whatsoever.

26

We pulled into the packhouse driveway and she dropped us off with a few minutes to spare before dinner. The packhouse was quiet so I mentally fist-pumped the air knowing everyone was out.

"Are you sure you're okay Adea?" Mavy's concerned look almost brought the tears back.

"I'm really okay Mave, I've just got a lot on my mind," I reassured her. I bite my lip as guilt hits me in waves.

"Well, I cannot wait to watch Nikki do your makeup for the ball. Maybe we can practice tomorrow before we go shopping?" She seemed to believe me and dropped the subject. She batted her lashes and gave me doe eyes.

"Nope. No way." I laughed.

"Please?" she begged.

"No."

"Pretty please with a cherry on top?" she asked.

"Nope."

"With sparkly sprinkles too?"

"Still no," I repeated.

"What if we walk down memory lane?" she bargained. "Chance to jump on Daddy's couch?"

I stayed quiet pretending to think it over, "Okay fine," I agreed, her face transforming into a goofy smile as she pulled me over to the sofa.

We had a good solid 5 minutes of jumping up and down before we heard the door open. "Mavy and Adea, get off my couch," Alpha Joshua's voice ordered as he walked into the living room.

"Aren't you two too old to be jumping on the couch?" he says as his eyes twinkle.

"You always spoil the fun, Daddy," Mavy grumbled, getting off the couch and crossing her arms like a child.

Alpha Joshua was over 6 feet and had beautiful brown hair. His face hadn't aged a day since I got here. "I got you chocolates from the pack meeting Mavy. You could share them with Adea," he told us as he walked closer with the chocolates in his hands.

"Sweet! I was wondering what snacks they'd have at the meet for the Alphas. I love these meetings." She squealed, rushing up to him as he embraced her in a hug.

Whenever there's an Alpha meeting we know there are always sweet treats and amazing food. When we were younger Alpha Joshua would bring us a plate of goodies.

"Thank you, Alpha."

At this point, I was standing next to the couch. He reached over and gave me a hug. "You girls smell like unmated males," he says as he scrunches up his nose.

He looks at me knowingly, and I purse my lips and avoid eye contact.

"Both of us?" Mavy asks and shoots me a glance.

"Mavy must have rubbed off on me Alpha."

Alpha's are bigger, better, and their senses are 10 times stronger than the average wolf. I know he could see through my lie.

"Hmm…" Alpha Joshua murmurs. He seemed to be mulling something over as Mavy ripped open the bag of chocolates.

"Well, I'm going to get started on dinner. We just got home and got distracted by the couch." I laugh nervously itching. to get away from his knowing stare.

"You don't want any chocolates?" Mavy's gray eyes grew wide with disbelief.

"I can have some later if you save any!" I laugh.

I start making my way towards the kitchen when Mavy asks her dad where the ball will be held. "The ball will be held at … Desert Moon," he says.

She squeals and grabs onto my arm, "We have a chance at finding our mates Adea!" My body becomes stiff, worried she'll smell Shane on me.

"We never get to see the unmated males at Desert Moon. They got a new Alpha about 2 years ago and Daddy hasn't had a chance to speak to their Alpha about an alliance."

Everyone's heard of the Desert Moon pack's new Alpha. His father took Desert Moon by force and

"So, we're going to practice and do your makeup when Nikki picks us up tomorrow." I give her a side glance.

"Don't even Adea, we made a deal," she smiles as we walk down the hall. She turns her head towards me and comes to a stop.

"Adea?" I can hear the caution in her voice and I hold my breath.

"Yes, Mavy." I whisper quietly.

"Why…" she shakes her head and grabs onto my arm tighter.

"Nevermind. I wish tomorrow night was here already!"

I let out a breath I didn't know I was holding. "It'll be nice to have some girl time," I say honestly. It's been a while since I've gotten out of the house for something other than school.

"Adyy," Gabe says as he sees me enter the kitchen. "I've already started cooking the chicken, do you mind cutting up the vegetables for me?"

I give him a side hug, "Of course, I got this! Sorry, I'm late!" I tell him as I grab the potatoes that are next to the sink. Gabe takes a deep breath and he stops stirring the chicken around. He turns and looks at me as I start peeling the potatoes.

Gabe turns to Mavy, "How's Trent treating you Mave?" Mavy giggles and blushes.

"We're just friends, Gabe."

"From what I've seen, the feelings are mutual. The two of you just need to admit it now." He gives her a knowing smile.

"Shane was saying I should see if Trent can escort me but I want him to ask me first." She turns to me, "He also said he could escort you in if you didn't have someone to walk you in Adea."

I stare intensely at the potatoes as I start cutting them. "If it isn't weird for my brother to escort you that is. No pressure."

I turn to her and smile, "I'd appreciate it." Gabe stares at me as I turn back to the potatoes.

The rest of the evening goes on like any other night. With Gabe singing to whatever is playing on his wireless speaker and Mavy laughing from the table. We made chicken, potatoes, and sauteed vegetables. I set the table and slipped out before anyone could show up for dinner.

EARTHQUAKE!!

As I headed to my room, I could smell his scent all over me. My body craved a shower. I made it to my room and grabbed what I needed. My room was on the small side but thankfully I had my own bathroom.

I turn on the hot water and put my stuff in the sink. Pulling my hair out of its bun and taking my clothes off I quickly hop into the shower. The hot water burned on my skin as I recalled what happened in the gym.

I scrubbed my neck and my chest trying to wash the memory away. What was that and why did I let it happen? Did I like it?

Tears fell down my face and mixed with the water. I squeezed my legs to my chest and let myself cry. Letting the water wash it all away.

***

I've loved reading ever since I was little. I first came across the library a few weeks after I moved in. The smell of the books piqued my curiosity and I've found a safe space to escape to.

"I knew I'd find you here." I look up and see Shane standing by the door. His hair is wet, and he's wearing a new pair of shorts. His tight white T-shirt left little to the imagination.

Mavy's head peeks in, "We were looking for you!"

Devin walks through the door next, ducking his head down to get in. At 6'6" he was not only tall but massive, his hair was brown and his eyes were a deep chocolate brown.

He spots me and sneaks a glance at Mavy. "We found her, thanks for your help Devin," Shane says.

Mavy comes and sits down next to me, "Beka wanted me to tell you to answer your phone, Shane," she shoots him a glare.

"You really need to watch who you stick your dick into. What if you get someone pregnant?" she wrinkles her nose at the thought of Beka as a sister-in-law.

Shane laughs and Devin looks at me. "I don't plan on producing an heir just yet, little sister." He glances at me and I feel a wave of nausea hit.

"I did want to tell you that I'm going to be announcing Devin as my Beta on our birthday Mavy."

"Gasp!" she covers her mouth and looks at Devin.

"That's great news! You've always been good to us Devin," Mavy says as she leans into Devin giving him a big hug. Devin wraps his arms around her waist.

"Thanks Mave," he smiles down at her.

Shane clears his throat and Devin steps away from her. "Congrats Devin. I'm not surprised he chose you as his Beta," I smile at him.

"Yeah?" he gives me a sly grin. "It's not official yet but I've already started helping our future Alpha with little tasks. Just today I guarded the gym door as he played with his new toy."

I blanch. "Ew gross, Devin! I did not need to know that. Ugh." Mavy covers her ears with her hands.

I swallow and look at Shane. "My beta knows everything," he says.

Great I think to myself. I watch Shane laugh and reach over to Mavy, grabbing her hands down from her ears. "Okay okay, he's stopped now."

She shoots Devin a glare. "Could you please keep my brothers shagging to yourself? I do not want to know who he's banging."

Shane shrugs, "Men have needs, little sister." He laughs and dodges her slap.

"Whatever. Just please at least wrap it up." she pleads.

I watched as Devin lightly flirts with Mavy and laughed at their cuteness. It was clear that Devin had a soft spot for her. If it wasn't for Trent I think there could have been something there. When Mavy and I started to yawn the group dispersed and we all headed to our rooms.

***

I bumped into Gabe on the way back to my room. "Ady!" he bellowed, wrapping his arms around me.

I stiffened, "Hey Gabe," I replied before he finally released me from his bear hug.

"Where have you been? You disappeared before dinner." He slurred. He was clearly a little buzzed.

"Sorry Gabe, I needed to escape reality for a few hours. I got lost in a few books."

Gabe wrapped his arm around my neck as he walked with me towards my room.

"Do you want to tell me why you smell like Shane, Ady?" he asked in a hushed whisper.

I hoped he hadn't caught Shane's scent on me when we were cooking. "I'm surprised you didn't ask me earlier, Gabe." He smiled as we entered my room. "You've had a little too much to drink," I laugh as he jumps on the bed.

Gabe sits up and pulls Smirnoff mini bottles from his pockets. "If you don't want to talk about it, let's drink about it," he says with a mischievous smile.

A couple of hours and many rounds of shots later, I was tipsy. Gabe was laying flat on his back as I downed the last bottle. I got up to turn off the lights before jumping back into bed. Gabe screams, "EARTHQUAKE!"

Sitting cross-legged next to him I laugh. "No Gabe, it's just me." I slap his arm. The room is swirling and I'm feeling light-headed. I lay back on the bed next to him in the dark.

My room was small but with the lights off I could see my glow-in-the-dark stars up on the ceiling. I feel my body relax and my mind getting fuzzy.

The room is quiet except for the sounds of our breathing. "Are you okay, Ady?" Gabe whispers as he turns his eyes to me. I turn my head to him and look into his eyes.

I can never hide anything from him. Gabe has always been there and he knows me more than I know myself.

A tear escapes and drips onto my pillow. "Shh, shh," he whispers and turns to me. "It's okay baby. It's okay."

He pulls me into another bear hug, this time it doesn't make me shiver, it feels warm as he strokes my hair. I let the darkness take over as I listen to his comforting whispers.

MINE

Adea

The air in my lungs feels like ice as I struggle to keep running. "Run, Adea," my wolf encourages weakly. I get to the end of the hall when I swerve down the stairs scraping my shoulder against the stone wall.

I wince in pain but all I can do is propel my feet forward. The sound of growls and meat ripping can be heard from outside. I reach the bottom of the step and I can feel my wolf's urgency.

Feeling the wolfsbane still in my system, draining my wolf's strength, I push my feet to move faster to fight the vomit from coming up.

Bracing myself for the locked door I crouch down and notice the white of my dress getting dirty on the floor. I charge for the door and smack into the tall wooden door pain erupting through my shoulder.

"Please, please, please," my wolf and I say at the same time. I turn around and walk back to the stairs. Stealing my resolve, I inhale deeply as I face the door, gathering what little strength I have left. I charge for the door.

To my relief, the door smashes open. I was blinded. All I could hear was the ringing in my ears. A wolf's bane grenade must have gone off as the door opened. Squinting through the fog, everything was moving in slow-mo.

"Find him," my wolf pleaded. "I'm trying Korra, I'm trying," I whined. I lifted my nose into the air but the wolfsbane still lingering in my system dulls my senses. I try to mind-link Mavy but I couldn't hear her.

My heart drops knowing that means she was either knocked out or... I stumbled over a body and stared in shock at familiar eyes.

I realize the eyes belong to Gabriel and my wolf howls in agony at the loss of a dear friend. I opened my mouth to scream but nothing came out.

"Leave him, Adea. There's no time to mourn right now. We must find our mate." Pulling myself away, I rushed past the arms, legs, and heads of more familiar faces. Fumbling in my weakened human state, I tried to find him.

In the corner of my eye, I saw movement. I turned and saw a pile rise up and fall as a shape I recognized pushed up through the bodies. Seeing his black hair my heart swells.

He pulls himself through and I do a quick once over and notice he's naked. His body is painted in blood, his chest and abs beautiful as ever and unharmed. His eyes lock on mine and I can see the relief flood his face.

He stands up and I can feel the need to touch him grow and almost explode as he starts towards me. I can feel his need and his relief. Korra is mentally wagging her tail and urging me to run to him when I feel his shock... Shock fills his eyes and we frantically try to see what's wrong. I look down at his chest... he's ripped open...

There's fresh blood seeping from his chest and my heart grows cold when the mate bond snaps. Korra howls in agony. Pain. I feel a gut-wrenching pain as I fall to the ground. I can't rip my eyes away from my mate. He falls to the ground as I crawl to him.

I hear footsteps moving away from him. Korra is whining in my head. We're too engrossed to notice when the footsteps get closer. There's a sound near my head as he drops something. I feel a slight tear as he grabs my hair wrenching me along with him.

He drops something near my head and grabs my hair wrenching me along with him. Korra retreats to the farthest part of my mind.

The world is quiet and still. My mate is just out of reach when he starts dragging me away. Goddess knows where to. I can't pull my eyes from the empty eyes of my mate. I hit my head and welcome the cold consciousness that takes me.

***

!! AUTHOR WARNING: THE FOLLOWING SECTION HAS MATURE CONTENT THAT MAY BE A TRIGGER FOR SOME PEOPLE. !!

My body is moving back and forth. I strain against the darkness that's trying to keep me under. My hands are restrained and I try to open my eyes. I can hear heavy breathing and feel a hot breath against my cheek.

I'm being pressed back and released. Something wet along my neck. I start to panic when I hear grunting. "Adea," he moans.

Sharp teeth clamp down on my bottom lip drawing blood. My body is still keeping that rhythmic motion.

"I've waited too long for you." My eyes open and I see long black hair above me, his eyes aren't looking at me. They're focused down on something between us.

As my eyes trail down his bare chest, his abs flexing, and his hips thrusting. I watch as his hard cock pulls out of me.

His eyes close and he moans as he thrusts into me to the hilt making my body jerk back. Repeating the movements he starts moving faster. A loud ringing in my ears threatens to split my head open.

My hands are still restrained. "Korra?" I whispered as I called her. I can't hear or feel my wolf. I whimper when I feel his hard cock thrust into my warmth causing pain. His eyes snap open and I feel his hand clench my throat as his cold lust-filled eyes locked onto mine. The warmth I once saw there was completely gone.

"I chose you then and I choose you now." He murmurs. He leans down, trailing his lips along my neck.

Having no fight left in me I close my eyes, his grip on me tightening as he continues ravaging me. I hear his canines extend and feel them poised at my neck.

Sinking his canines deep into my neck, I scream, as his thrusts quicken. He comes undone and licks my wound to seal his mark. I feel his seed fill me as he growls, "Mine."

I AM YOUR ALPHA

AUTHOR WARNING: THE FOLLOWING SECTION HAS MATURE CONTENT THAT MAY BE A TRIGGER FOR SOME PEOPLE. !!

Shane

I woke up that morning to a she-wolf under my sheets. "Mmm fuck." I let out a quiet moan. Her lips were wrapped around my already hardened cock. She lay in between my legs and I watched as her head bobbed up and down.

"Good morning, Alpha." she purrs with her mouth full. I didn't bother removing the sheets to look at her. I closed my eyes and imagined Adea's long brown hair in my hands, her soft lips wrapped around my dick, my dick hitting the back of her throat.

I groan as I feel her tongue sliding up the side of my shaft. "Fuck." She removes my dick from her mouth and takes my balls in her mouth. She wraps her hand around my cock and I almost cum when I feel her warm tongue on my balls.

She's licking me like she can't get enough. My toes curl as she continues licking my balls like melting ice cream. She grips my cock in her hand and slurps on my tip before moving back down to my balls.

Her hand slides up and down my shaft and at the same time, she sucks on my sack. Her movements speed up a little and I lay there and let her lead for a few minutes. I can feel myself getting closer so I grab her hair pulling her mouth open. I thrust my hips into her mouth and sigh when I feel her throat tighten around my cock.

"Yes," I hissed as I thrust up into her mouth. "Mmm," she cries in pleasure. Taking advantage of my need she grips my cock and starts twisting her mouth in circular motions. My thrusts become faster as I chase my orgasm. I push her up and down as she sucks and licks my shaft.

"Adea." I moan as I hit the back of her throat and feel her swallow as my cum slides down her throat.

She pushes the sheet off and glares at me. "Are you fucking serious right now?" She's clearly upset as her hazel eyes burn holes into my head.

"What?" I shrug trying not to laugh. "You moaned Adea's name as you fucked my throat!" She sits up and crosses her arms in front of her chest. "Such a dick move, Shane."

I sigh and sit up before brushing the loose strands of hair off of her face. I've been fucking Beka for 2 years now, I know she's got feelings for me but she's a good lay. She's pretty but I just needed a quick fix.

Adea's cheekbones are so perfectly defined, imagining her cheeks sucking my cock drives me insane. She's got these plump lips and she's got this cute button nose. Beka's got short blonde hair and she's tiny. The top of her head barely reaches my chest and her body has just the right curves.

She's an easy lay and I'll do the bare minimum to keep her around. "You've pleased your Alpha Beka, now get out." She huffs and sticks out her bottom lip. She gets off of the bed and picks up her dress, shimming as she pulls it up over her tits.

She reaches over the dresser to grab her bag and phone, flashing me her plump wet pussy. I feel my cock twitch as I watch her slowly lay on the dresser and pop her ass up to give me a good view.

"Are you disobeying me, Beka?" I murmur as she lays her head down and shows me her neck. I jump up and slowly walk over to her. Looking down I see her eyes closed and her neck offered up to me. Grabbing her hip I hold her down and lean back so I can watch as I slide my finger down her slit. She's wet and ready for me.

"No, Alpha. I only—" I lick her pussy to clit and she squirms under my touch. "You've been a bad girl." She whimpers, as I slide two fingers into her and watch as my fingers disappear inside of her wet warmth. She moans, "I only mean to please you Alpha. I've been a good girl."

"Do you want a reward?" I say as I watch my fingers pump in and out of her pussy fast and hard. I watch as her arousal seeps down her clit. The sounds of my fingers sliding in and out of her make my cock harden. I growled in approval as she clenched around my fingers. I lean down, stick my tongue into her pussy, and continue finger fucking her.

She's wriggling and moaning under my touch and I lap up her juices. I continue finger fucking her tight cunt as I stand up. I position my tip at her clit and remove my fingers.

"Beka," I murmur.

"Yes, Alpha," she pants. Beka tries pushing her ass against me and I grab her waist to keep her still.

"I am your Alpha," I murmur.

"You are my Alpha," she moans, gyrating her hips as she searches for some relief.

"I will call you what I want," I tell her.

I slide my tip up and down her open slit and she moans. "Be obedient, and take what I give you. Can you do that for me Beka?"

She's quiet as I slide my tip up and down her wet opening. When I stop she groans, "Yes, Alpha. Just please, fuck me."

"Good girl," I say and in one hard thrust, I've buried my cock into her warm cunt. She screams out in pleasure and lifts her hips up offering herself to me.

I pull myself out of her and look down as I thrust deep and hard into her pussy. She moves forward with each thrust. I don't even care that the dresser is banging against the wall. "This pussy is mine, Adea," I moan as I fuck her pussy.

"All yours," she pants as I thrust in and out of her. I can feel her clenching on my cock and I thrust into her over and over again. Watching as her body bounces off of me.

The sound of my skin slapping against hers is only adding to the fire. "Fuck, Adea." I moan as she cums on my dick. I keep fucking her as she continues squeezing my cock.

I thrust into her a few more times before I reach my climax emptying my seed into her cunt. Stepping back I pull out of her and grab a towel. She's out of breath on the dresser.

"I'm going to shower, see yourself out. Make sure no one sees you." I command as I open the bathroom door.

I hear a sob as the door closes.

MY HEART SKIPPED

Shane

4 years ago

I hated hospitals. The beeping noises, the smell of medicine, the sound of high heels click-clacking on the floor. Mavy was pulling on my arm, "Hurry up Shane! You're not even trying to walk fast." "I'm coming I'm coming," I grumbled. "It's not like she's going to be awake, we've been visiting all week." She turned her head and glared at me. Pulling on my arm again.

There was an accident that left two rogues dead and their daughter in a coma. There was a pack meeting where our father saved this pup from being killed. Most packs would kill rogues when they stumble onto their territory but my father, Alpha Joshua, was kind and compassionate.

He saw Mavy when he looked at this girl and couldn't give the order to kill her. Mavy's made it her personal duty to visit her every day since. Mavy pushes the door open and gasps, I stick my head in and see her.

She's not laying lifeless like she normally is. She's sitting up looking around like a scared little mouse. Her brown hair is messy and her chocolate brown eyes are filled with fear. I sit in the corner and watch Mavy bounce over to her oozing excitement.

"What's your name?" Mavy asks with a huge smile on her face.

The girl drops her head and looks up at her shyly, "My name's Adea," she whispers in a quiet voice.

"Will you have to enroll at our school? How old are you? What grade are you in?"

"Slow down child, she literally just woke up," the Nurse laughs. Mavy blushes and looks back at Adea.

"I'm 13 and I'm in the 8th grade." She smiles, showing a dimple in both cheeks. "I'm Mavy and this is my twin brother, Shane."

I look out the window as her head turns. I feel her eyes roam my face. She doesn't stop so I turn and look at her. "Hi," I smirk.

She blushes, turning back to Mavy. Hmm.. interesting. My wolf murmurs. 'What is it Max?' I ask him. "Something draws me to her," he says. 'What about her?' I probe. "I'm not sure." He says before retreating to the back of my mind.

We're not supposed to get our wolves until we're 18 but I've been able to hear mine for a year now. I haven't told anyone about it because I know it's not normal. I'm not sure how my parents would react. I haven't told Mavy either.

I shuffle my feet. We tell each other everything but Maximus thinks I should keep it a secret for a few more years. It's unheard of to hear your wolf early and I don't want to have to explain what happened when I first heard him.

Maximus first spoke to me when I kissed a girl after school. We were sitting on the stairs to the cafeteria. She was pretty and wanted to talk to me after school. She leaned in and gave me a hug. She kissed my neck and I started feeling a wave of different feelings wash over me.

She looked up at me and I leaned down until our lips met. "She's not our mate. You shouldn't be doing this." He growled. I was so shocked I pushed her away and she hit the wall.

She looked at me, got up, and ran away. "What the fuck? Who are you? Am I going crazy?" He had a low voice and laughed. I'm the other half of your soul. My name is Maximus."

"You'll be staying in our packhouse so you'll have me and Shane!" Mavy said happily, breaking me from my daydream.

***

Adea has been living with us for two weeks. She's clumsy and has started making the packhouse meals. Her food isn't bad but I avoid her unless Mavy forces me to.

I'm sitting in my room throwing my basketball up in the air and catching it when Mom knocks on my door. She opens the door and peeks her head in. "Your father and I need to speak with you."

Dad mind-links me, "Come to my office, son." "Yes, sir." The link cuts and I get up. "Behave, Shane," Max says to me. I get up and make my way to the end of the hall and knock twice before entering.

My dad is sitting at his desk when I walk in. Mom is standing next to him with her hand on his shoulder. Dad gets up, grabs Mom's hand, and comes around the table. "Have a seat," he says gruffly.

My dad was strong, humble, and always did what he thought was right. He was a good Alpha and as a young pup, I looked up to him. "We received a call from the school today notifying us of you pushing Beka down."

Mom sits down next to me, "Is this true?" she asks quietly. I feel panic rush through my body and I refuse to look at her. "What do you have to say for yourself, Shane?" My father asks. "Look at me, son." He uses his Alpha force to make me meet his eye.

"She was kissing me when I-" "Don't tell them about me," Maximus says, cutting me off. "It's not what it looks like. I didn't mean to use that much force. I wasn't thinking. She got up and ran away."

"We don't hit girls, Shane. Ever. Men shouldn't ever use their strength against the weaker sex." My dad says, I can see the restraint in his eyes. His wolf is also angry at me.

I cower under his gaze, "I wasn't trying to hurt her-" "I thought I raised you better." He looks down at the ground, "I'm disappointed in you." My mom sobs.

"You are grounded until next week. No practice, no games, no friends. You are to stay in this house and I'll assign you chores to do."

"But dad, I have a game-" "DON'T CUT ME OFF!" He yells, his eyes glowing, his wolf fighting for control.

"You're dismissed." He stands up and walks to his desk. I stand up and leave. As soon as I close the door behind me, the tears fall. I've never disappointed my parents before... I've never been the golden child but I've always tried my best to please them.

I walk down the hall and turn down the stairs. They didn't even try to hear me out, "Father is right," Maximus says. "I don't want to hear it from you. This is all your fault!" I scream aloud.

I run down the stairs bumping into someone, looking down I see Adea sprawled on the ground. "I'm sorry, I didn't mean-" she says, stopping when she looks up at me.

"Are you okay?" She asks. Standing up she reaches for me, "Yeah, I'm-" I say before she wraps her arms around my shoulders pulling me into a hug.

I try to move away but her arms tighten around me and I feel my wolf stir. I inhale and her scent pulls me in and I unconsciously wrap my arms around her. My heart skipped.

What the fuck.

NOW

Shane

After that day on the stairs, I kept my distance from Adea. Her scent, her smell, they drive me crazy. My plan to stay away from her worked for a few years. We saw each other every day but I made sure to avoid her.

My friends started to notice her as she started to grow up. Her tits came in, her hips curved, and her ass got fat. I took out my jealousy on her. This way I could speak to her without getting too close.

Deciding to make my way down to the kitchen, I put my AirPods in my ears. Rounding the corner I collide with Gabe, "Excuse me, Shane," he says as he moves to the side.

I stop and look at him, "Where are you headed?"

"I've got to wake Ady, I need to make sure she doesn't sleep in," he says, bowing his head.

I've always hated how close Gabe and Adea were. I met her first yet Gabe's close enough to go to her room. An image of Gabe over Adea makes me frown.

I continue walking down the stairs and sit in the living room while I wait for Mavy to come down. Pulling an AirPod out I hear

Mavy and Gabe come down the stairs. Hearing a bit of their conversation, I smile when I hear Adea tell him she doesn't want to hear anything about his sexcapades.

After waiting a few minutes, I make my way to the kitchen. Mavy's already sitting at the table watching Adea and Gabe cook. I walk in and give Adea a quick once over, she's wearing her usual jeans and hoodie combo. Her hair piled on top of her head in an effortless messy bun.

After setting the table, Adea sits down between Mavy and I. I watch as she pushes her food around on her plate while we discuss the upcoming ball. There was a pack meeting today after school that I had to attend. Half Moon hosted it last year as well as let the other packs know that I would be stepping up as Alpha when I turn 18.

"Trent is coming over before school if you wanna hitch a ride with us Adea." Mavy asks looking at Adea hopefully. "It's okay, Mavy. I've got to get some stuff done before school but you can go ahead."

What stuff does she need to do? Thinking about her alone with Gabe or any other man has me seeing red. "What've you got to do Ady? Scrub the toilets?" I spit. Shit, I said that out loud.

My father glares at me and shoots me a warning. "Yes, Alpha?" I ask with a smirk. My wolf is coming to the surface, fighting for control.

My sister reaches over Adea and slaps my shoulder. "Shane, don't be such a dick. She's not a slave!" Thinking of all the things I'd do to Adea if she was a slave has my cock pitching a tent. Thankfully Mavy apologizes to her and they don't notice.

Her hoodie is raised and I can see her exposed back. A smile pulls at the corner of my lips, and before I know what I'm doing, I reach over and caress her lower back. Her back stiffens as I pretend to be looking at my plate before facing her, "You know I'm just joking around don't you Ady?".

Gabe clenches his fists and gives me a side glance before turning his body to watch Ady. "Yeah, I knew you were joking…" she says quietly. I let my fingers trail down her back. Mavy mumbles something and their conversation drifts towards the ball.

Before I know it Adea is saying goodbye to my parents. I can't bite back the words, "See you, Ady!" I call after her. Watching her hips sway as she walks out of the kitchen. It's getting harder to stay away.

***

Before heading to school I pick up Liam and Devin. I've known these guys since the diaper days. "Mavy didn't need a ride?" Devin asks. His infatuation with my sister peeved me.

"Trent got her," I say with my eyes never leaving the road. He's never acted on it but I know he likes her. In all honesty, I wouldn't mind them together but my sister has her heart set on finding her mate.

She thinks her mate is Trent but she's not the Moon Goddess. No one knows who she's chosen for us until we meet them.

We make our way to Mavy and Adea's first-period class. She forgets her shit all the time. If she didn't have her head attached she'd probably lose it.

We're waiting outside the classroom for a couple of minutes when they show up. My little sister thanks me and gives me a peck on the cheek.

She heads into class with Adea when I quickly block her path. "What did you do before school?" I ask Adea inhaling and smelling the woods on her.

"I just had to grab some stuff," she quickly replies. "Hmmm.." I murmur as I move my hand. She stays still waiting for permission when Mavy yells at me to go to class. I laugh as I head out with the boys.

"Do you like her?" Liam asks, nudging my shoulder. Devin is looking the other way but I know he's listening. I look at Liam, his blue eyes sparkling with interest.

I shrug as we head to class. "You've been paying more and more attention to her. If I didn't know better I'd say you want something from her." He presses.

Devin's opening his locker and shoving his books in. "Are we going to the gym after school, Alpha?" Devin asks.

I smirk and nod my head, "Of course, I gotta keep this physique somehow don't I?" I let my hands roam slowly down my body.

Devin laughs and Liam pouts, "Can't we do something else after school? I hate going to the gym right after. Let's go to the movies or something."

Devin rolls his eyes, "We're trying to bulk up Liam. You should come." Liam sighs, "Naah, I'm just going to go home. I can't go to the gym every day like you guys. I need some downtime."

***

I couldn't keep my eyes off of her at lunch. Beka tried talking to me and I ignored her. Following my gaze, she scowled when she saw what caught my attention. Leaning on the table to block my view, her fingers caressed my shirt.

"Not now Beka," I growled, pushing her hand away. She sat up and folded her arms across her chest. Pouting like a fucking child, such a turn-on.

When the girls left the table I noticed a few guys checking out Adea's ass. I got their attention when I kicked the table.

"What the fuck are you looking at?" My voice was low and menacing. Hearing the threat, they lowered their eyes.

She stayed on my mind the rest of the day. Sensing my mood, Devin stayed quiet. Thoughts of her with another man ate at me.

What if someone makes a move? What if someone asks her to the ball? What if she gets a boyfriend? Trying to calm down, I closed my eyes and took deep breaths.

By the end of the day, I had zero fight in me. Reaching into my shorts pocket, I pulled out my phone. As the bell rang I sent her a text.

Gym. Now.

CLAIM HER

TRIGGER WARNING
This chapter contains sexual assault and/or violence
that may be triggering to survivors.

Shane

Gym. Now.

Before I could stop myself, I sent the message. Grabbing my stuff, I signaled Devin while I headed out. "What's up?" he mind-linked me. "I have to make a stop before we head out." I linked back.

I shoved my stuff into my locker and he did the same. "Something wrong?" He asked. "I just need you to come with me." "Yes, Alpha." He nodded and followed me as I walked out of the building.

We walked in silence on our way to the gym. In the distance I see Adea disappear in the gym. As we get closer I turn to him, "Keep watch. I don't want anyone interfering with our talk." I don't need to use my Alpha blood to command him. Devin always listens to me.

As we pull up to the gym doors, he bows his head in understanding. I open one of the blue doors and step into the gym. "We're just going to have a talk," I try to convince Max.

I call out her name and she looks like a deer stuck in the headlights. I can't hold back the smile that breaks out across my face. "She looks cute even when she's frightened," my wolf murmured.

I can't help checking her out, I'm free to do what I want since there's no one around. She's gorgeous as always. Her jeans can't hide her curves, her neck bare. I look away as the thought of marking her crosses my mind.

"Thanks for coming, Adea," I murmured, trying not to let her hear the lust in my voice. She was silent. I took a step towards her and she took a step back, making me smile. The next thing I knew, I was right in front of her.

I finally had her all to myself. The thoughts of being with her wore down my ability to stay away. Reaching for her neck, I couldn't help it when my fingers trailed her skin.

"So soft," my wolf sighs almost painfully. I trail my fingers up and down her neck, stopping when she shivered. "What's going on, Shane?" She asked. Her eyes focused on me, not looking away. "I've got to meet Mavy soon… Why did you want to meet up?" She asked, fearfully.

"She's afraid," Maximus murmured. I could mentally see him focusing on her, feeling his need for her. Having her so close to us, inhaling her scent, is so intoxicating.

Maximus takes control. Breathing her scent in deeply, my dick hardens. Her eyes widen as she feels me, she looks down and looks up. "You always smell so fucking good Adea." We murmur.

He leans down to her neck. "Don't mark her Max, we can't do that," I say firmly. "She'd be ours if we made her ours." He growls at me. We're interrupted by her plea, "Please… don't."

Closing our eyes, I fight for control. "Let me escort you to the ball." I cup her face with my hand, "We need to slow down, Max. We want her to want us."

"I'm going with Mavy and Nikki, Shane. I'm going to help her find her mate." Max growls in anger, "She's going to find HER MATE. Take her now, Shane, or I will."

"You're going to help her find her mate? Or yours?" I ask. "I'm going to help her find her mate, Shane." She looked cute when she got mad. Her nose wrinkled up and her eyebrows furrowed together. She looked like a bunny.

"I'll escort you into the ball. We're voting today at the pack meeting and I have a feeling it'll be at Desert Moon." The image of someone else's arm around her waist brings me to the edge. I need to touch her, if I can just put my scent on her...

"Shane, I don't know what you're—" I bring my lips to her. I'm thirsty and her lips are water. I need her. I felt myself losing control, I needed more of her. She tried to push me away, growling. I pushed her against the wall. I need control.

Grabbing her hands, I held her wrists above her head. My breath catches as I look down at her, she's flawless. Her big brown eyes look up at me, I've got her in one place, under my control. "Take her," Max growls. "No," I rasp as I try to fight his control.

"Please, Shane. I don't want this." She whimpers. I lean down and kiss her neck. I don't want her to fear me. "Sshh, Adea." I soothe her. "She's pure. We can't take her yet." I tell Max. "Claim her Shane, or I'll take her," Max warns.

I let my hand slowly slide down her body. Reaching under her shirt, I move slowly up her stomach until I reach her breast. "She's enjoying it too," Max moans. "I need more of her," he demands.

My lips trail her cheek searching for her lips. When I find the entrance, my tongue brings her tongue out, and I suck on her tongue, hard. My hands caressing her breast, I roll her nipple between my fingers and pinch.

Her bottom lip trembles, and her body shudders. I pushed my cock against her stomach, needing to feel her against me. Max and I moan at the same time, and he reaches for her jeans.

"I need her now," he groans. I'm kissing her soft swollen lips, and unbuttoning her jeans. She's pushing against me and I taste blood as she bites me. "Fuck, I like when they put up a fight," Max groans.

"No! Get off of me. Please, Shane." "You're mine, Adea. I want to feel you writhing under me screaming my name." Reigning in control, taking a deep breath, I try to calm down. "I'll stop if you agree to me escorting you."

"We're not stopping yet, Shane." Max growls. "I know, calm down, if she can agree to go with us we can get another chance with her." I try to reassure him. "Okay," she cries. "Okay, just please stop." "I'll go with you."

Before I knew it, my hand slipped beneath the fabric. Her eyes widened, and she looked sexy as she looked up at me. "Let's talk Shane. Please, let me go." "I said I'd go with you. You said you'd stop if I said I'd go... you can escort me, Shane. You don't —"

She goes quiet as I slide my finger against her slit. "She's so soft," Max murmurs. We're both aroused and we're mesmerized as I insert a finger into her soft heat. She's so tight, and I groan internally.

Her body jolts upwards at the new intrusion. Closing her eyes, I whisper, "That's right, feel what I do to you." I push my finger deeper into her tight warmth. I pull my finger out and push into her again.

"You're so tight, Ady." I groan as her wetness drips down my finger. I lean against her neck and move my fingers faster and faster into her depths. Her body slowly moved up and down with the rhythm.

"She's enjoying it," Max moans. I suck on her neck when I feel her core tightening around my finger, so I add another finger and pump into her. She moans and I nip at her neck.

The feeling of her pussy clenching my fingers makes me think of what it would feel like if her tight pussy was wrapped around my cock.

Thinking of my cock replacing my fingers, I look up and see a tear run down her cheek. I kiss her, "Look at me." I say gruffly while my fingers speed up.

Imagining her pussy clenching around my hard cock as I fuck her has me tensing up. "I want to watch you cum on my fingers, Ady." She's close, "Look at me."

She raises her head and looks me in the eyes, as she cums on my fingers. "Fuck," Max groans. "She's fucking beautiful," he murmurs. "Good girl," I say appreciatively.

I kiss her neck and realize I'm still holding her wrists. I stare at her and bring my fingers to my lips. I lap her juices up as I watch her breathing heavily. She looks away shyly. Grabbing her chin, I pull her back to me and kiss her lips.

Can't have her telling Mavy about this. "This'll be our little secret, Ady. I'll see you at home." My cock is standing on end. I readjust myself and mind-link Devin, "Coming out."

He opens the door smirking. "Ready to work out?" He laughs. Shoving his shoulder, I smirk back. "I need to work this off." As soon as we were off-campus we shifted and ran to the gym to work out.

Two hours later, I let him know I needed to head to the packhouse. "I'll see you later man," I tell him. I'm feeling better after going ham. He bows and I wave to him over my shoulder before shifting and heading home.

"I can't wait to see her squirm," Maximus murmurs. I'm satisfied knowing she smells like us but as we run I can't help but agree. "She's cute when she's under us," I murmured. Thoughts of our time with her earlier stays on my mind.

The wind in our hair feels amazing, the ground under our paws as we thunder towards the packhouse. "I can't wait to see her," I whispered looking up at the night sky.

ANOTHER DAY

Adea

I woke up in the morning with the sun blazing through the window. Groaning as I drift out of sleep and back into the terrible hangover that was only worsening by the minute. I don't know which was worse, the drilling in my head or what I remembered from the dream.

Closing my eyes, I try to remember what I can. In my dream, my wolf's name was Korra, and the only difference between this dream and the last is that there was something bad that happened after I was dragged away.

Images of my mate's face were blurry but the emotions were all still strong. Who was that after? Who dragged me away? I couldn't see his face but I knew him.

I've never been with a man but everything felt so real. He even said my name… I wish there was a witch I could talk to. Witches aren't allowed on pack lands. I sigh, shaking my head in defeat, there goes that idea.

Pulling myself up, I stare out the window. What's the point of these dreams? Will they ever stop? Gabe tossed and turned next to me, "Ugh, who turned off the lights?" he groaned. I giggle as I watch him reaching aimlessly for an imaginary lamp by the bedside. I completely forgot he was here.

"It isn't light, it's the sun. And you're in my room. I don't have a lamp so you can stop reaching for it." I laugh.

"Remind me why we thought it would be a good idea to get hammered last night?" I try to wipe the tiredness from my face when I feel a sharp pain.

"Ugh! I'm a lightweight, Gabe, you shouldn't have let me keep going!" I grumble as I walk away but can't fight the smile. I sit there for a few minutes before I catch myself nodding off.

"Gabe?" I look over at him. He's not moving and I move closer to him.

Gabe is oddly silent, I nudge him. Assuming he went back to sleep I continued nudging him until he's at the edge of the bed. Eyeing his round butt, I use my foot and kick him over the edge of the bed. "Fuck!" he yells as he hits the floor. "Wake up Gabe!" I say as I roll over and stand above him.

"Okay okay, but why are you yelling?" he groans, turning away from me.

"It's time for Cinderella to get up and I can't do anything without my trusty mouse sidekick." I laugh and clap my hands, I shower quickly and come out to find Gabe isn't on the floor anymore.

Hopefully, he's in the kitchen already. Rushing downstairs I walk into a full kitchen. Alpha and Luna are sitting at the table, next to him are his Beta and his mate, even the Gamma is already here.

Mavy and Shane are busy talking about something in the corner. Alpha Joshua looks up at me, "You okay, dear?" He asks as Gabe signals me over.

"Good morning Alpha, Luna." I bow my head, "Yes, sorry, I'm late. I had a long night and my alarm didn't wake me up," I told him before putting my backpack away and heading over to Gabe.

He motions to the coffee jug, and I walk around the table and fill everyone's cups. When I reached Shane, I noticed he had his AirPods in and I wouldn't have to worry about his attention. I dropped my head and filled his cup quickly.

My hands were shaking, making me nearly spill the coffee on the table. Alpha Joshua smiled as I filled his cup. Luna looked up at me and reassured me there wasn't a rush and to take my time.

Mavy and her parents have always been kind people, what went wrong with Shane? Images of his eyes focused on fingering me make me blush. I'm gratefully distracted when Gabe comes over, holding a tray of dishes.

He picks up a plate and places them in front of the Alpha and the Luna first. Then hands their kids their plates. The smell of eggs, bacon, sausages, and pancakes makes my mouth water.

"You got to work quickly," I smirk at him. Gabe cocks his head to the side, hand on his hip, "Oh sugar, I got all the fixings," he says in a country accent.

After we placed everyone's plate on the table we happily walked to the counter and started making our plates. "Can you even eat right now Gabe?" I whisper to him.

Looking over at his plate he's grabbing 3 of everything. I placed what I wanted onto my plate, and sighed in pleasure. The best part of the day is good food. Nothing like a nice meal to fill the belly.

"I can always eat, Ady," he smiles at me. After we finished eating breakfast, everyone had their own side conversations going. I could feel their excitement about the Crescent Ball and the topic of all of the newly aged wolves finding their mate was heavy at the table.

After Gabe and I cleaned up we got ready for school, I asked Gabe for a ride to school. "Mind taking me before you crash?" I ask while trying to give my best puppy dog eyes.

"I got you, girl. I'll meet you in my car at 10, don't be late."

The ride to school was relaxing. We had the windows down and the cool breeze was welcome on this hot day. Gabe dropped me off at school with a few minutes for me to run to class.

"Thanks, Gabe!" I say while hopping out. "Don't forget I'm going dress shopping with Mavy and Nikki before dinner so I won't be helping prep today," I say apologetically.

He rolls his eyes, "I think I can manage without you, Ady," he smiles. "Let me know how it goes, and send me pics of the dresses you try out in a batch," he says in a very convincing, overly feminine voice.

School goes by quickly. I make sure to keep my nose in my books, listen to the teacher, and avoid Shane and his friends as much as possible.

It was Friday so the teachers made sure they assigned us something to do over the weekend. I groan as I remember Nikki is going to be doing my makeup today.

It's not that I don't like dressing up and letting them doll my face up. I just hate letting others buy me clothes with money I didn't earn… and I know how expensive makeup is.

Nikki only buys the best of the best. I remember seeing the price on the bottom of some of her stuff she brings to school and it makes me queasy. It's like putting her money on my face and I don't know if it even looks that good.

Speak the devil's name and she shall appear. Nikki pops her head into my last class wearing denim shorts, and a white v-neck t-shirt.

"Don't forget we're all going to the packhouse today after school. I need your face washed and ready. I'm creating art today," she sing-songs.

"Like I could forget," I say as I roll my eyes. "See you after class," I call after her as she walks away.

THANK YOU, DADDY!

After I ran home, I assumed Nikki and Mavy would have made it by now. I decided to call Mavy and see how much time I had before they arrived.

"Hey, Adea!" I could hear Mavy smiling through the phone.

"Heeeey, Chika! Are you ready for your makeup sesh?" Nikki yelled.

"I was calling to see where you guys are," I asked sheepishly.

"We're grabbing some snacks and then we'll be home in a bit," Mavy said.

"Do you want anything?" Nikki yells.

"I'm good, I don't want anything. I'll see you soon," I told her before hanging up.

Thanks to the run, I got some me time and wined down a bit. The sounds of the forest always worked to calm my nerves. The smell of the dirt and wind was like a sedative.

I had enough stress over what happened with Shane in the gym. I decided that tonight I'm going to go with the flow and enjoy some much-needed girl time.

I head into the packhouse and automatically go to the kitchen. It's too early for dinner prep so it's empty. Next, I run to the bathroom and wash my face clean for Nikki to work on.

***

The deafening music heard echoing through the halls alerted me to Nikki's arrival. The noise gets closer and the door bursts open. "The fun has arrived!" Nikki sings out loud.

"Turn the music down Nikki, I don't want my dad to come in here," she says. Mavy's carrying a ring light and bags of goodies while Nikki is carrying bags of makeup.

"Are you going to war? Why and how do you have so much makeup?" I laugh.

"Because I am," Nikki says matter of factly.

"You're so dramatic," I snort. "Hey, hey. Trust the process," she says confidently.

"Set the ring light up there Mave," Nikki orders. I love how Nikki doesn't let the werewolf rules control her. Nikki sets her bags down on my table and starts opening up her supplies.

"This is a primer, I also bought different colors of foundation to see what matches you. Your eyes are so pretty Adea, I can't wait to give you wings, gah!"

I look over at Mavy for help but she's ripping open a bag of gummy worms. She shrugs at me as she pops a few in her mouth.

Nikki gets started on my face and I feel like a doll being pampered. I wasn't allowed to look in the mirror but I felt like I was wearing a mask. "You don't need makeup but girl you did the assignment." She says proudly.

"Check it out!" She squeals to me and Mavy. I look in the mirror and am blown away. The girl staring back at me has wing-tipped wide eyes, my hair is framing my face, and she didn't go heavy on the makeup.

It doesn't look too different but she outlined my face and my lips look lush and pink. "You look amazing Adea!" Mavy says. "Let's get out of here, we have a lot to get done today," Mavy smiles as Nikki puts her ammo away.

***

Two hours later it's 6 o'clock and we've tried on almost every dress in this mall. "Try this one next, Adea, we have to find the perfect one!" Mavy says as she throws the dress on the bench. She's trying on a long white dress with a slit going almost all the way up to her hip. There are spaghetti straps and a low cut showing off the curves of her boobs.

"Oh, my gosh sis, that one is beautiful on you!" Nikki whispers with excitement. I reach over to look at the price and my jaw drops. She grabs the tag and looks at the price.

"Hey! We are not doing that! We are enjoying our hunt and the right dress is never too much." Mavy smiles.

"Who spends $2,000 on a dress?!" I ask in shock. She shoots me a glare, "I mean you look amazing in it," I tell her.

"Now I just need shoes," she says as she turns around and walks out of the dressing area.

I look at Nikki's dress and let out a whistle, "Oh my gosh, is that your dress?" I ask her in awe. It also has spaghetti straps, but her dress is black and so sheer it almost looks see-through.

She gives me a half-smile and does a spin, the slit is going up the back and stops right below her ass. The chest area cuts low below her tits and it's somehow keeping her chest pushed up and together even though there's nothing keeping the dress together.

"If you were a werewolf and your mate saw you at the ball, I wouldn't be surprised if they took you right there on the ballroom floor!" I laugh at her.

She smiles at me proudly, "Thank you, thank you. I try." She winks before sashaying into her dressing room.

I look down at the dress Mavy threw down for me to try. It's red and feels like silk, the cut in the front doesn't look too low. I think I might like this one. I slip off my jeans and hoodie, step into the dress, and pull it up and put my hands into the sleeves.

It's a perfect fit. I look at my reflection in the mirror, "Wow," I murmur. My shoulders are bare and the sleeves fall on my arm. The cut on my chest goes halfway down my boobs, and it hugs my curves. The slit goes up the front past my thigh and falls just below my ankles.

Nikki and Mavy walk into my dressing room at the same time. Mavy's jaw drops and Nikki's eyes grow wide with surprise. "Lord have mercy Adea. You look…" She stops clearly speechless.

I blush at their gaze, "I think this is the one," I tell them.

"You're damn right that's the one!" Nikki squeals. "Don't be shy, turn around and give us a twirl." I slowly turn around.

"It's perfect Adea! I think black heels would be the best to wear with it," Mavy says with a smile on her face.

"If you find your mate, he's going to thank the Goddess for blessing him with you," Nikki says. I change and Mavy helps me pick out the right heels to go with the dress.

"Nikki will do your makeup the same way too. I can't wait for the ball! I wish it was tomorrow." Mavy tells me. After we find our shoes, we go to check out and Mavy has me wait with Nikki at the door.

"All done!" She says as she walks to us with the bags. We both reach out and grab our stuff from her.

"Thank you Mavy," Nikki and I said at the same time.

"Oh it's not on me, it's on Daddy," Mavy says with a huge smile.

"Thank you Daddy!" We call out as we walk out of the store. We head to the Palisades restaurant for dinner and enjoy a posh meal on Alpha and I don't think about money and enjoy the rest of the night with my girls.

Later that night, after a nice cool shower. I lay my head down and have a dreamless sleep.

YOU ARE MINE

The next morning I woke up feeling light and bubbly. I love those girls. After a warm shower, I spent my morning prepping a light breakfast for the packhouse in case they stopped in for a small meal. I usually have the weekends to myself because everyone is usually doing their own thing.

I spent the rest of my morning in the library. The walls were decorated with tall shelves filled with books. My favorite spot was a soft white lounge chair by the window. The windows started from the floor and almost went all the way up to the ceiling.

It was always quiet in the library, not many of the she-wolves came in here to read. By 3 pm I had read 3 books, my body was feeling stiff so I sat up to stretch.

The door to the library swung open and Shane came walking into the room.

He scanned the library until he spotted me in the corner. "Good afternoon," he greeted me.

"Hi," I replied, not taking my eyes off the book as he walked closer and kneeled down beside me.

"Where have you been all day? I didn't see you around," he asked as I flicked through the book I couldn't focus on reading anymore.

"You're looking at it," I said, moving his hand off my leg. The library is silent while I ignore him but I can feel his gaze on me.

"Look at me," he said, grabbing my chin and turning my face to him. He looked amazing like usual. His dark eyes staring into my soul, his high cheekbones, and plump lips were enough to make any girl swoon.

Remembering what he did to me, I shake my head. "I'm trying to concentrate, Shane." I declared, pulling my face from his grasp.

I continue flipping through the book when I feel his hand on my leg again. I pluck up the courage and turn to him, "What the fuck was that?" His obsidian eyes search my face.

"Don't you have a lot of girls you can play around with?" I whisper yell at him. His eyes light up and the tips of his lips curl into a smile.

Everyone knows that Shane has been fooling around with girls for a few years now. He's basically a manwhore. I close my eyes trying to compose myself.

"This afternoon didn't happen," I say when I open my eyes.

"Are you mad about that?" he asks leaning in. I won't give him the satisfaction.

I still couldn't hear my wolf yet, but I know that I was hurt. He scares me and I can't have that happening again.

"Those girls were weeks ago, Adea. I used them to fulfill my natural impulse to mate. I have needs and they met them," he explains.

"You can do that, Shane, with someone else." I look him in the eyes. "I'm waiting for my mate."

Irritation flashed in his eyes, "I could be your mate," he says, his voice deepening.

"You're allowed to have a past, Shane. I'm not your mate." I say. "I—" His hand moves to my thigh. I grasp his hand and try to push it away.

"I can't help wanting you, Adea. I've wanted you for years and I did a terrible job of trying to show you I wanted more," he explains, putting his hand back on my thigh.

I look at him. He's looking at me earnestly. "I could be your mate," he says again.

I let out a sigh closing my eyes trying to make it make sense.

"Didn't you enjoy yourself?" he murmurs as he leans in.

His breath on my neck causes me to freeze up.

"I—" The thoughts of his fingers on me flash through my mind. Then I remember the guilt.

"I'm sorry." He cuts me off. "I'm sorry that I'm not sorry."

"I feel like I don't... I don't even know you." I stare at him in disbelief. "When was it okay to do that to somebody, Shane? This is not okay. You can't—"

He grabs me by the back of my neck and pushes himself in between my legs.

"I'm next in line to be Alpha of this pack Adea. I've got Alpha blood running through my fucking veins. I can do whatever the fuck I want to, and sleep with who I want to."

"I'm not just a pawn in your game, Shane." I look down when his gaze becomes too much. I want to do those things with my mate.

"It feels wrong, Shane," I whisper as I feel his Alpha aura falling onto me.

"Do I need to remind you of your place, Adea?" he says in a low voice. I can feel him trying to get me to submit. I will fight it.

"Please leave me alone," I hissed. Beads of sweat start forming on my skin.

"Leave you alone?" he leans into my neck. "Submit to me," he commands. He's so strong, I can't fight it.

I fell to my knees, my head bent, my neck offered in submission. Tears spring to my eyes, I can't believe he's using his alpha power on me.

"This is how you should be in front of me, down on your knees, offering yourself to me," he murmurs.

I hear him shuffle and I gasp when his shorts fall to the ground. He steps closer to me and trails a finger down my neck. "So beautiful," he says.

I close my eyes and fight back tears. His finger trails my neck and he grips a handful of my hair. He pulls my hair bringing my eyes up to meet him.

He pulls his cock out with his other hand and slides his hand up and down his shaft. His breathing picks up as I stare into his eyes.

"Now, please your Alpha," he commands. His eyes daring me to disobey. He pulls me towards his hardened length. "I've never done anything like this with anyone before," I whisper.

Not only do I not want to be doing this but I don't even know where to fucking start. I can barely move my body and his force on me is tiring me out.

"Lick it," he encourages me.

I stare at his cock, it's 8 inches at least three fingers thick. I open my mouth and slide my tongue across his tip. I look up at him and watch as his eyes close.

I lick halfway down his shaft up to his tip as precum drips from his tip. He groans as he looks down, losing his patience he shoves his cock past my lips. He pushes deep into my mouth, "lick it while I fuck your mouth."

Fighting the tears from falling, I lick his tip while he starts moving back and forth. His grip on my hair is starting to hurt as his cock fills my throat.

My throat is constricting and I feel pain as he continues to thrust into my mouth. I grip his waist to try and push him back but he slams into my throat and I cry out.

His moans fill the library, "Fuck, Adea. Your throat was made for me." His pace is quickening and his cock feels like it's getting harder. I shut my eyes to try and drown out the pain I'm feeling in my throat.

I watch as Shane's cock disappears completely and I try to relax my throat. He pulls all the way out and slams into my throat over and over again.

His waist is going back and forth and his movements turn into small jerks. His head tilts back and he groans as I feel his cum slide down my throat. "Swallow," he groans and he keeps moving as he finishes.

Shane lets go of my hair and leans down pulling up his shorts. "I just can't leave you alone Adea." I look up at him as his eyes burn into mine.

He reaches down and wipes my tears away. "You've pleased your Alpha," he says and I can feel his hold on me disappear.

He reaches down and touches my lips. "I'll leave right now but I'm not leaving you alone Adea. You are mine."

He kisses my forehead and turns on his heel. Leaving me on the library floor.

GUMMIES

Gabe

Some of the pack members have already left for Desert Moon. It's only a weekend trip yet I've been hauling bag after bag to trucks and jeeps all morning.

If it weren't for the AC in the packhouse I'd be sweating my ass off. Alpha Joshua helps load the cart while I see how many bags I can hold with one hand.

"This is the last bag I swear!" Mavy giggles. "Can't be too sure of what we're going to wear and what we might need," she blushes.

Alpha Joshua grabs it from her and puts it on the cart. "I'm sure you guys have everything you need. Be outside in 10 minutes Mavy." He tells her sternly.

We make our way downstairs and my hands are getting tired. "Excuse me Ady," I huffed.

She moves out of the way, "Sorry Gabe, I was daydreaming," she says deep in thought.

A heatwave hits me and I can feel myself sweating. "I'm ready to hit the road and get there," I tell Alpha.

"I know what you mean, it's not too far away so we will get there quickly," Alpha tells me.

"Can I ask you for a favor Gabe?" Alpha asks after we get all the suitcases and bags loaded.

"Of course, Alpha," I tell him.

"Could you keep an eye on Mavy this weekend? I'm going to be busy and with all the unmated males around," he says nervously.

"Yes, Alpha. She's like a little sister to me. I'll bug her this weekend," I reassure him.

"Thank you, Gabe. I can breathe a little better now." Alpha says while he shuts his jeep door.

"Morning Adea," Joshua says as we turn around.

"Women and their things," I groan.

Alpha throws his head back and laughs, "You think this is bad? This is just for a weekend trip."

"Morning Alpha," Ady nods as she greets Alpha.

"What're you going to do when you find your mate, Gabe?" Alpha asks and it's quiet until I realize he's asking me.

"I don't think I'll find her. It's been a year since I've turned 18 and I have yet to find her… Not that I've been looking," I say while trying to hide my embarrassment.

"Well, we are going to the biggest ball of the year. With so many packs in one territory, your chances are really high." Ady encourages me.

"Haha… yeah," I say, scratching my head. "Are your bags packed Ady?" She's not one for fashion and dressing up but I know she's got some stuff from shopping.

"Yeah, I'm all packed and ready to go." She says.

"My stuff is already in my car, I just have to grab some snacks for the road. I'll grab it and head to your room to help with your stuff." I told her.

She turns and heads to her room. While I'm packing my phone beeps.

Shane- We're heading out now. Let me know when you guys make it to Desert Moon.

I'm not friends with Shane and we don't hang out but after the way Ady cried, I'm definitely not fond of him.

Throwing my phone in my pocket, I grab the bags of snacks and head to the car. Time to get this show on the road.

***

Adea

I took off the scrunchie that was in my hair and let my hair loose. Driving in Gabe's red 1970 Dodge Challenger was a vibe. It was scorching outside but with the windows down and the wind in my hair. It was close to paradise.

I look down at the book I'm currently reading. As soon as I open it Gabe snatches it out of my hands. "No no no, we are not reading a book on this road trip. Save your book for when you're in your room before bed or something," he says as he tosses my book to the back seat.

I chew on my bottom lip, "Fineee. What've we got to snack on?" I unbuckle and reach into the back seat to look through the bags.

"We got everything you need. Chips, gummy bears, gummy worms, and chocolate." He says proudly.

I snag a bag of tropical flavored gummy bears and sit back. "Ready for the ball?" He asks while I pop a few yummy little gummies into my mouth.

I snort so hard I choke on them. "I'm ready for it to be over," I say as sweetly as possible. He runs his hand through his hair and chuckles.

"I know what you mean. Everyone wants to find their mate but I'm kind of resigned to the idea. I'm happy with how my life is right now," he says honestly.

"Do you think a mate would ruin your happy life?" I say as I grab a handful.

"I don't think they'd ruin it, I'm just content, you know?" I chew and think about what he said. "I think I know what you mean. I don't want much…" my voice trails off as I think of Shane.

"So, are you going to tell me what's going on between you and our future Alpha?" He asks. I don't hear any judgment in his voice. "He wanted me to let him know when we got there. Is there something I should know?"

It's not cold but I shiver when I think of Shane. I pull my legs up to my chest and cross my arms. "Honestly, I don't even know what's going on," I murmur.

Sensing my discomfort Gabe changes the subject and the rest of the drive goes by filled with laughs and ends with me throwing a handful of gummy bears at him.

The greenery has disappeared and has been replaced by farmlands. There's a small city area up ahead and Gabe lets out a low whistle when we realize we're staring at Desert Moon.

Tall buildings and shops welcome us to Desert Moon territory. I knew they were doing good but this is basically a small city.

We pass a big sign that says, "Welcome to Desert Moon".

ALPHA

Ethan

Being an Alpha means that I must do things on occasion that I don't want to do, hosting the Crescent Moon Ball is one of those things. I hate being surrounded by strangers, all of them flitting around my territory. I don't do chit chat and I don't pretend to like people. I prefer spending my time in the woods, patrolling my borders, training my warriors, and the occasional she-wolf or two.

Sadly, the packs have voted and the Crescent Moon Ball will be held here on my territory. I've been the Alpha of my pack since I took over and we haven't been to any functions unless 100% necessary. It's been scarce. I was one of the youngest Alphas and because of that other packs thought that I needed to prove myself. We are one of the strongest packs in the United States.

I do take pride in the fact that we are also one of the wealthiest. I push every pack member not only in training but also in their academics and because of that we have had a lot of new business start-ups in our territory.

Another reason I had to accept that the Crescent Ball was going to be held on my territory is that it's a part of the mating ritual. For werewolves, finding your mate is second to our natural instincts.

When we turn 18 years old we're expected to find our Goddess-given mate but for an Alpha, the pressure is on. When an Alpha finds his mate, he finds his Luna, and she not only makes him stronger but makes his pack stronger.

My mate either wasn't in my parklands or wasn't of mating age yet. It's been 2 years and I have yet to find her. The longer you go without your mate the antsier you'll get. As an Alpha, my pack members are afraid I'll lash out at them one day.

I'm not too focused on finding her but I know that finding my mate has been my pack's priority. My Beta has been trying to get me to go out for drinks again. He goes to other territories for a night out in hopes of finding his mate.

"The other packs will start arriving soon, Alpha. I'll be at your side to welcome them." My Beta Odis remarks. Looking around my office I know I have to get up soon. It's customary for Alphas and their Luna to welcome the incoming pack leaders.

"Olivia notified us that the first Alpha and Luna should be arriving in the next hour." Odis notifies me. Olivia is my Gamma, she is unmated and her duties always come first.

She's got short black hair and she's 5'6", she's tiny compared to me but she isn't someone you piss off. "Let her know I won't be late," I chuckle. Odis laughs and mind-links Olivia.

"Which pack is coming first?" I ask him. "The Half Moon pack Alpha and Luna will be here first," he replies. The Half Moon pack is the second largest pack in the US, they had a treaty in place with the previous Alpha.

I'll feel him out and see if we will be allies or enemies. Thinking of Olivia, I smile, but of course, I'll be on my best behavior.

***

I'm standing outside in 80-degree heat wearing a suit. My Beta at my side, we were told they would be pulling up soon, and I've got a suspicion that Olivia had us come out a few minutes earlier than the eta.

Odis is also wearing a suit and tie, he always looks professional, even when we're doing regular daily work. He stands at 6'3", blonde hair that's short on the sides, long on the top, sun-kissed tan, with a muscular build second to mine.

He's surprisingly celibate, despite all of the flirtatious advances he's received from women. A large red jeep pulls into my driveway. Thank God they've arrived. "Let's get this over with," I whisper to Odis.

They pull up and Alpha, Luna, and his kids jump out of the Jeep. "Alpha Ethan, may I present Alpha Joshua and his Luna Rose." These words are spoken by who I assume is his Beta.

Alpha Joshua smiles widely at me, steps forward, and reaches out his hand. "Alpha Ethan, I thank you for personally welcoming my family and me to your territory. We are excited to be here."

Odis looks back and forth from Alpha Joshua's hand to me, I chuckle as I reach for Alpha Joshua's hand. We shake and he's got a firm grip. So far so good. He's given a good first impression.

"Thank you for coming! I hope you enjoy your time here." I say gruffly before nodding at his Luna. "Let us know if you need anything during your stay." I hear a squeal behind them, I'm guessing these are his pups.

They look to be in their teens, twins. The male is tall, has wavy brown hair, and cold black eyes. His sister is short, has black wavy hair, and warm grey eyes.

The male one looks at me with discontent and the little one looks at me with wide eyes and blushed cheeks. "I welcome you to my home."

I can read people and I can tell she's kind and innocent. I give her a warm smile and her brother lightly growls.

"This is my son Shane and my daughter Mavy," Alpha Joshua says, introducing his pups. "They're still in High School but will finish this year." Shane nods at me and Mavy bows her head respectfully. I nod, acknowledging them.

Olivia appears from nowhere, "Please come in, follow me, we will get you settled." "I don't like the way the pup is looking at us," Elijah growls in my head. "He's a pup and a teenager. We will not start a war over a pup," I laugh.

"Thank you," Alpha Joshua says before he and his family follow Olivia into the packhouse. "She always appears out of thin air," Odis whispers. "She's a witch, I tell you," he says in mock shock.

"I heard that, you brute," Olivia mind-links us talking to Odis. "See? Witch," he mouths and I can't help but laugh.

BITCHES LOVE ME

I feel a tingle of excitement as I look out the window. The small city is full of werewolves walking around. I can taste the excitement in the air.

As we drive through the city, I see large brick buildings, one after the other blend with the city lights.

"You've got some drool, right there," Gabe says pointing at my mouth.

"Shut up," I laugh and wipe my face just in case.

We make a right and drive up and down a few treeless hills until it brings us to a driveway. The driveway looks like it goes on forever. The sun is still blazing mercilessly in the sky as we drive up the driveway.

At the end of the driveway, there's a massive house. I don't mean mansion big, I mean 10 mansions big. The concrete driveway turns into a red-tiled driveway and we're surrounded by tall stone buildings.

"We've made it," Gabe whispers. "And holy shit, it's nice." His black Audi pulls to a stop and someone appears from the door under the stone archway.

I look at the sasquatch of a man walking over to us. He's huge, he's got on a clean suit, and he's handsome. Like really handsome. He's got blonde hair that's a little messy, I'm guessing due to the heat. He's muscular like a bodybuilder.

Is this the Alpha? Gabe opens his door and runs over to open mine. "Thanks, Gabe," I say genuinely. Gabe's a manwhore but I swear his mate is going to be very lucky.

"Good evening," the blonde man says with a professional smile. "My name is Odis, I'm the Beta of Desert Moon. Welcome to our humble home."

"Hi, my name is Gabe and this is Adea, we're from Half Moon pack. Our Alpha arrived earlier this afternoon," Gabe says, reaching his hand to give the beta a handshake.

They shake hands and Odis gives me a nod. "If you head in, our Gamma Olivia will let you know where your room is."

"Oh, we're not together," I say quickly.

"We've shared a bed before Ady, don't be like that," Gabe says, putting his arm around my shoulders.

I push him hard and shake my head at him. "Our Gamma can help you with room arrangements," Odis says with a small smile on his lips.

When we walk through the door we're greeted by a busty girl with long red hair and green eyes. She eye-fucks Gabe as a wide smile spreads across her face. Gag.

"Hey, my name is Sasha, and I'll be helping you today," she purrs while staring at Gabe. "Where's Olivia?" Odis asks.

"She said Alpha needed to speak with her," Sasha says, never taking her eyes off of Gabe.

"Well, hi, my name is Adea and this is my friend Gabe," I told her.

"I've got your rooms on the second floor of the building behind this one. The fifth floor is where the Alphas and their Luna's are staying. The fourth floor is where the Betas and Gammas stay. On the third floor, we've put the children of the Alpha's."

"Please stay away from the fifth floor unless you're called up there. Our Alpha doesn't take rule-breaking lightly," she says firmly.

"Understood," Gabe says, pretending to be hanging on her every word.

"Thanks," I say while Gabe reaches for the keys. We turn to leave when she grabs Gabe's hand, putting a small card in his hand.

***

"What was that about?" I ask in a hushed voice when we get into our building.

"What can I say? The bitches love me," he says, earning him a scowl from me.

We made it to the second floor. "My room's a few doors down from yours. So make sure you let me know if you need anything," he says seriously.

"Mmhmm," I say as I open my door. Gabe follows me in and drops his suitcase by the door.

"Wow," I say in awe while I look around the room.

The room is decorated in a minimalist style that blends perfectly with the theme and setting. It's designed in an earth tone and furnished with wooden furniture.

It's beautiful. I inhale and smell that all of the amenities are made with organic products. There's a large queen-size bed and the pillows and blankets are pure white. The throw pillows are a beautiful deep red.

I walk over to the bathroom and love the curved doorway. Opening the door, I stare in awe at the large shower and a beautiful tub. I can't wait to soak in there.

'So, do you need help unpacking?' Gabe asks sarcastically looking at my one and only bag.

I breathe in and smell that the amenities are all organic products and the room has a queen-size bed that has a beautiful wooden headboard. The pillows are blankets are pure white and the throw pillows are a beautiful red.

"You can hang up the dress for me if you want," I say, unzipping my bag. I take the dress out and hand it to him.

He lets out a low whistle as he eyeballs my dress. "Damn son! You're going to have unmated wolves wagging their tails at you all night!"

I burst out laughing and swing at him, "Oh hush!"

"What time should I be here tonight?" Gabe asks while scrolling through his phone. "About that…" I say while avoiding eye contact.

He puts his phone down, looks at me, and his eyes hone in on me. "Ady…? Do you have something to tell me?"

"Shane is escorting me tonight." I rushed out. The room's quiet and I can feel his gaze on me.

"Hmm… well… I'll be here too. I've got someone I can bring," he says and I look at him as he flashes me with a crooked smile.

"Gabe! You shouldn't take a date to the Desert Ball! What if you meet your mate there! She'll be devastated," I say angrily, scowling at him.

"You can NOT take another girl to the ball," I say firmly. "But I would like it if you were there," I told him.

"I got you," he says while hanging up my dress.

Walking over to me he wraps me up in a big hug. "I'll be close by tonight," he says, and I can hear the sincerity in his voice. "Don't worry about me, Gabe," I murmur as I hug him back.

The Goddess blessed me with a good friend. I shoot her a thank you as he steps away and grabs his bags. "I'll meet you downstairs in 2 hours," he says as he walks out the door.

I jump on the bed when the door closes. "Finally," I sigh in content as I snuggle into my bed. "I could get used to this," I smile into my pillow before knocking out.

GET IN BITCHES

Giving my lashes one last coat of mascara, Nikki leans back to inspect my face. She hasn't let me look at myself yet and I'm kind of getting nervous. This was going to be a good night. This was going to be a good night. I kept repeating the mantra in my head like I was whispering a spell.

Nikki sighs, "So this is love," she sings as she twirls me around to look at myself at the full-length mirror on the wall. I was killing the smokey eye, my eyeliner was perfectly winged. My long brown hair had big loose curls in them and fell effortlessly down my back.

My lips were plump and pink. My chin came to a point, and my cheekbones weren't super high, but they were high enough. I've never thought of myself as attractive but the woman looking back at me was breathtaking.

A shriek broke me from my trance, I look to see that Mavy had come in and by the shriek, she loves the way I look. "Oh my gosh Adea, you look SO good. We chose the right dress!"

"Thanks, Mavy," I say with a blush. "I think you clean up really nice too!"

I turn back to my reflection and love how the dress hugs my curves. My c-cup looks amazing in this dress and somehow this dress lifts and squishes them without any support. The swoop is a little too low for me but when will I ever get the chance to dress up like Cinderella? I'll own it for tonight.

Nikki and Mavy are already dressed and ready. Nikki's hair is in a tight elegant bun and her dress leaves little to the imagination. Her chest is almost completely exposed, the dip in her dress cuts down to her ribcage. Her dress is sheer and if you look hard enough you can see through it in the light. She's gone for a sexy look and she showed up and showed out.

Mavy's dress is long and falls to her ankles. She's wearing black heels that could stab a man. The slit on her dress runs dangerously high. Subtle yet deadly.

"You guys are going to be the hottest girls there tonight!" I squeal.

They laugh and Nikki bats her eyes at me, "You mean WE are going to be the hottest girls at the ball tonight, Chika!" Making Mavy and I laugh.

A knock at the door pulls us from our squealing and Mavy fast walks to the door. "Well hello, there stud!" She says as Shane takes a step in and kisses her on the cheek. "Your escort is here Adea," she calls to me.

I look at Shane and he looks as handsome as always. He's towering over Mavy, he's wearing a black tux, his hair is gelled back, and his obsidian black eyes have flecks of gold in them as he looks at me.

His gaze slowly drops down the length of my body, pausing at my chest before continuing down my dress. His eyes snap back to mine, "You look hot," he murmurs.

Mavy slaps his shoulder, "Shane, manners! He means you look beautiful, Adea," she shoots him daggers which he smirks at.

"Don't be jealous. You look beautiful, Mavy. I hope you find your mate tonight, though, I might have to stop myself from ripping his head off," Shane huffs while he gives his sister a quick hug.

"I for one, am thankful that Shane can appreciate the hard work I put into Adea tonight," Nikki says proudly. "If you find your mate tonight, I wouldn't be surprised if he fucked you on the dance floor tonight!" Nikki laughs.

Shane growls and I jump in before the girls can say anything, "I'm here to help YOU TWO find your mates. I don't have any intention of finding my mate. And if ONE of us was going to be dragged out of the ballroom tonight by a mate it would be YOU, Nikki. Just look at your dress! I can see everything," I say with a laugh.

Shane saunters over to me and my body is on high alert. I try to swallow the lump forming in my throat. He reaches out and I have to try with everything in me not to flinch back. His arms wrap around my waist and he pulls me into him for an embrace.

I can smell his cologne as my face is pressed against his chest. Leaning down he whispers into my ear, "You look amazing tonight." I can feel his breath on my neck as he gives me a quick kiss on my earlobe.

His hand slides down my waist and squeezes me. "Thanks," I whisper quietly. "Hey hey, don't forget you're an unmated wolf, Shane. You need to keep your distance from unmated females. You'll give people the wrong idea," Mavy says with a hand on her hip.

"I think that's the point," Nikki mumbles.

"What was that, Nikki?" Mavy asks.

"What? I was saying how handsome Shane looks tonight," Nikki says with a bright smile that didn't meet her eyes.

Shane smirks, removing his hand from my hip, he takes a step away from me. Looking at Nikki, he cocks his head to the side, "Thanks Nikki, I aim to please."

My phone lights up and I see that I've got a text from Gabe.

Gabe - I'm heading out. I'll meet you guys in the hall.

Adea - We're ready. Be right out!

"Gabe is ready and he's going to meet us in the hall. Are you guys ready to head out?" I ask the girls. "As ready as I'm going to be," Nikki says before grabbing her clutch.

Shane opens the door for us as we leave my room. When we get into the hallway, Gabe steps out of his room followed by Sasha. She's wearing a waist-high pencil-thin red skirt and she's stuffing her blouse in when she looks up and sees us.

Her beautiful red hair is straight and her green eyes laugh as she smiles at us. "Hey, we met earlier. I'm Sasha, Gabe's date," she says with a wave.

Gabe's wearing a black tux with a red dress shirt. His hair is a little messy and he's wearing diamond earrings on his ears. He blushes as he presses the button on the elevator. When we all get into the elevator the girls introduce themselves to Sasha.

Shane stands right behind me pressing into me. I almost jump when I feel something hard press into my lower back. I gulp and look around to see if anyone notices.

The elevator door opens and one by one we step off of the elevator. We're welcomed by a black limo, "You didn't think we'd go to the ball separately, did you?" Nikki smiles mischievously. "Get in bitches!" She squeals. Mavy and I both look at each other and burst into laughter as we rush to get in.

A VOICE

Ethan

"We're done for the night, Alpha," Odis said with a smirk on his face.

"Are you sure? Because you said that a few packs ago," I asked, shaking my head.

After five hours of welcoming pack Alphas to my territory, I was ready for a break. If I have to shake another hand without rest, I swear I'll tear it clean off.

Odis could barely hold in his laughter. What an asshole. I headed towards my office and he followed me.

Walking through the doors, I went and sat on my chair, a sigh of relief as my back hit the seat.

"How many soldiers do we have stationed around the pack grounds?" I asked as I leaned my head back and closed my eyes.

"We've got groups of 5 scattered around the pack grounds. Desert Moon was werewolf country. There was one ruler and that was me. I have raised my packs standing and more than doubled my pack numbers since taking over.

Beta Odis had a few Deltas that helped him when he was overworked but most of the time he handled his own. Olivia, my

Gamma, took care of different sections of Desert Moon. Thankfully we were big enough that she had chosen leaders to run the three divisions.

We've detected small movements outside of our territory. It's nothing alarming but one can never be too cautious. I will not have any unnecessary issues arise. Especially while I have outsiders on my territory.

"Make sure the soldiers are on high alert, even those stationed inside during the Crescent Ball," I tell Odis.

"I've got a handle on it, Alpha. I won't disappoint you but if I may give you a suggestion?" He says with a chuckle.

Odis was the best Beta an Alpha could ask for but when I say that he does his job too well. I mean it.

"What?" I growl.

"You stink. You definitely need a shower before the Crescent Ball starts, which is in 30 minutes," he says holding his nose. "Can't have you scaring your mate off."

If it was anyone else I would have thrown something at him but I'm close with Odis. "Can't have the ladies smelling me like this now can I?" I joke back.

Odis scoffs and walks to the door. "If that's it, I need to freshen up myself." I wave him goodbye and he shuts the door on his way out.

Walking into my bathroom, I turn on the jetted tub. I need a quick relaxing soak before I go out there tonight. I'm running on zero fucks and I can't have Odis thinking I'm going to start a war.

I take off my jacket first, then unbutton my suit. Unfastening my belt, I let my pants and underwear drop. Stepping into the tub, the hot water causes my muscles to unwind and relax.

My cock twitches and I close my eyes trying to ignore it. "I don't have time for this," I say with a sigh.

"We need to find our mate," Elijah complains.

"I'm not too focused on finding her right now," I tell him as I finish washing.

"What we need to focus on tonight, is finding our mate and claiming her," Elijah growls.

Images of my last lay flashed across my mind.

"I'm tired of your quick lays. I want our mate," he bites at me. Grabbing a towel, I start to dry myself off. I scratch my head as I try to think about a mate.

"I wouldn't get your hopes up," I tell him.

"We will find her," he urges me.

"Fine, but if we don't find her, we're going to have to consider a chosen mate."

He growls but I cut him off, "The others will see us as weak, and as much as I love a good fight, I don't want to deal with a fight breaking out here with all of these visiting packs."

"And if we find her? What then?" He asks me and I can hear the pain in his voice. "Enough talking. I need to get ready," I say as I push him to the back of my mind.

***

Adea

Nikki cracks open a bottle and our night starts off by filling a few glasses. I'm sitting with Gabe on my right with Sasha, and Shane on my left with Nikki and Mavy. Passing our glasses one by one, she smiles and raises her glass, "Cheers to Desert Moon!"

I take a few small sips when Shane leans down and whispers in my ear, "I want you." Gabe stills next to me and I think he heard.

"So does Gabe have a girlfriend back home?" Sasha asks nonchalantly.

Mavy looks at her, "No, he doesn't. He's always busy so... no time for a girlfriend."

I feel Shane's hand on my thigh and I cringe internally. "I can't wait to check out the hotties from the other packs!" Nikki shrieks before throwing back the rest of her drink.

"Let's take a picture!" Nikki says, grabbing her phone. We all squish in and smile as she takes a few pictures.

"Yasss, we are killing it tonight girls! Oh and guys! Gabe, Shane, flawless as always," she says, blowing them kisses.

The ball is being held just fifteen minutes away, and we arrive at a beautiful open clearing that leads to the hall. Gabe and Sasha head in first, followed by Nikki and Mavy. As soon as they're in, Shane wraps his arm around my waist.

"Thanks for escorting me, Shane," I murmur as we walk in. I'm blinded by the beautiful lights and stare in awe at all of the werewolves gathered.

There are so many people, I don't know all of them but I recognize a few. The women and girls are dressed in beautiful different colored dresses and the men all look handsome.

The hall is tall and vast. The decorations are a light touch around the hall. The music is flowing but is low and beautiful. I'm sucked in by the beauty that is Desert Moon.

I feel Shane's grip tighten on my waist, "You look so fucking amazing tonight!" He leans down dangerously close to my neck.

The girls and Gabe huddled around us in a circle. "Look at all the fine men here tonight!" Nikki squealed.

"Right? I can't wait to dance with a few of them," Mavy giggled.

We wandered over to the pastry table and filled up on a few snacks. Nikki filled her glass and waited for Mavy to pop the last pastry in her hand into her mouth.

Grabbing Gabe and Mavy, she leads her to the dance floor and starts dancing. "Do you mind if I steal your date?" She asked me, batting her eyes promiscuously.

"Go for it, I'm going to eat a few more," I told them with a smile. The little cream puffs made my mouth water. I watch Sasha lead Shane to the dancefloor and start grinding on him.

What a relief. I get a break from Shane and get to indulge in my sinful pleasures. I smile as I bite off half of a cream puff. The chocolate melted in my mouth.

Pure bliss. A sweet smell fills my nose and I look down at my plate. "What is that smell?" I say aloud. After searching my plate, I realize that the smell isn't coming from my plate. I freeze.

"Mate!" A voice calls out in my head.

MATE

Alpha Ethan

I didn't want the ball here in the first place so of course, I didn't want to attend. I didn't search for my mate over the years and I didn't want to search for her tonight.

After years of Olivia reminding me that the Goddess had a mate for me out there, she planted a seed in my head. I have to admit the seed has started to grow.

Did I want to scour the country for my mate? No. But would I be lying if I said I didn't wonder if she was going to be here tonight? Yes.

Outside of Odis and Olivia, I keep no one close and I preferred it that way. For an Alpha, having a mate is crucial. Having a mate makes you stronger, don't ask me how but it just does.

Since I was hosting the ball, I had to be there first to greet the visiting Alpha's and their Luna. I couldn't help but smile when guests started flooding in. They couldn't help but shoot me frightening glances.

I sat at the head of the Alpha table. When Alpha Joshua and his Luna came in they greeted me and quickly took their place at their seats. Alpha Joshua was the only one tonight who didn't give me a scared look.

I went back to gazing over the guests as they mingled. Unmated males and females gave me more frightful looks but I did see that some had lust in their eyes.

"Do you think she's here, Alpha?" A deep yet lighthearted voice called out to me. My Beta, Odis, was itching to know.

"Maybe," I said in a short tone. He knew that I wasn't looking for my mate nor would I be disappointed if this weekend ended without finding her.

"Would you claim her if you found her?" I could hear the curiosity in his voice. I looked at him with mock shock.

I could feel my head start throbbing. He was shuffling around and mentally pacing. I could feel his anxiety like it was my own.

"What is it, Elijah?" I asked, trying to mask my annoyance and irritation.

"I'm not sure…" Elijah whined, his agitation only growing by the second.

I was not going to be able to deal with this and guests at this rate. Elijah and I both froze as a sweet aroma caught our attention. The smell only got stronger. I've never felt a smell but this smell felt warm and I could almost taste it on my tongue. Vanilla and honey filled my senses and calmed our irritation.

I couldn't help but scan the crowd, I needed to find the smell. Before I knew it, I was following the smell into the crowd.

My wolf and I needed to find her. I froze when I saw her. She bit into a chocolate-covered cream puff and the moan that left her lips had my wolf want to claim her.

My gaze lowered as I took her in. Elijah and I searched her body with a fervent need. Her chest scooped low and her dress outlined her silhouette beautifully. Her hair fell softly down her back.

A need to touch her took me by force. She froze and looked through her plate. I couldn't hold back a smile when she knew the smell didn't come from her pastries.

"Mate!" Elijah and I said at the same time. A feeling spread through my body as I stared at her face. Her eyes widened in surprise as she locked eyes with me.

"Mate," I said aloud. I don't know how or when but I stood in front of her. I watched her as her chocolate brown eyes slowly looked down my body.

I watched in interest as her eyes froze at the tattoos peeking out from my wrist. Her eyes made their way back up to my face. She looked at my hair and her eyes stopped at my lips. Lust flashes through her features before she quickly puts the thoughts aside.

Being closer to her now, I let my eyes roam her face, her cheekbones are flushed. She has a cute button nose. My eyes roam to her neck and my wolf is itching to mark her.

I've never given a woman so much attention. She had our undivided attention and I smiled knowing she already had Elijah wrapped around her little fingers.

I reach out and wipe the chocolate from the side of her mouth. I'm shocked by the sparks that erupt from my fingers and spread throughout my body.

"Do you know who I am?" I ask my little mate. I didn't see her earlier when I greeted Alphas so she couldn't be an Alpha's daughter.

"Other than the fact that I am yours… I don't know who you are," she whispered and I smiled as I watched a pink blush spread across her features.

Elijah urged me to grab her hand and hold her. "What's your name, little one?" I asked her, unable to focus on anything or anyone but her.

"Adea," she whispers. She looks up at me with those chocolate eyes. "My name is Ethan, the Alpha of Desert Moon."

Her brown eyes widen and a gasp leaves her lips. I should be worried about her being afraid of me but Elijah and I can't help but imagine her beneath us.

I needed her.

MORE OR LESS...

Adea

"My name is Ethan, the Alpha of the Desert Moon pack," he says like it isn't a big deal. He's the Alpha of this pack? Hearing him say Alpha, I automatically think of Shane.

Thinking of him watching us here together like this scares me to my core. Is he watching us? Is he angry? Pulling my hands together, I fold my hands to try and stop the shaking.

Think Adea, think! What should I do? He takes a step towards me and without thinking I take a step back.

"Don't be afraid of him Adea! He's ours. The Goddess made him for us," the voice whines, and I can see her mentally pacing.

I shake my head, "No, we don't know him. This comfort we feel from him and this pull to him is all the mate bond!" Why can't she see this? We can't trust whatever this is.

My wolf whines in my head, "That's not true!" I can feel her desperation like it was my own but I know that her feelings aren't mine. I can see this situation for what it is and I know... I just know I can't trust him. I can't trust her feelings.

"Look at him! He's huge, do you think such a man is going to be gentle with us? He's known throughout all of the pack territories to be ruthless.

He's conquered other packs and doubled his pack numbers. An Alpha doesn't get to his station by being kind," I try to knock some sense into her.

This tug-of-war of emotions between my wolf and me is exhausting. Her big white head drops and I can feel her hurt through our connection.

"Finding him only adds another self-absorbed, violent, giant of an Alpha to our worries. What do we do when Shane finds out? What do we do if he's watching us right now?" I cry and I know none of this is her fault but I can't hold back the words.

Ethan grabs my hand, and I'm pulled from my thoughts. I watch as he turns on his heel, and pulls me in the direction of the side door. I stare at the back of his head, trying to ignore the tingles shooting up my arm, trying to ignore her excitement. The music gets quieter as we get outside and walk farther from the hall.

We pass a tall beautiful water fountain but I don't get to look over its beauty as we come to a stop. In one swift motion, he pins me against a wall. I stand still and shut my eyes as I wait for what's going to happen next.

After a few moments, when nothing happens, I open my eyes slowly to look at him. I have to look up and when I do I lock eyes with lustful cold eyes.

His hair is drooping over his eyes and his lips are slightly open. His scent and warmth are stimulating my senses and I can feel goosebumps break out across my body.

"Are all men like this?" The thought crosses my mind and my wolf whines. "What's happened to you before isn't normal. Those things weren't supposed to happen to you Adea."

I feel a tear escape and run down my cheek and I bite my lip to stop it from quivering. I won't beg anyone ever again. It doesn't matter how I feel, he'll just take from me… like him.

He presses his head against the cement wall above me and in doing so his chest connects with my cheek. "Why do you smell of an unmated male?" He asks slowly in a low tone.

Shit. I forgot about that. Our sense of smell is strong but an Alpha's sense of smell must be 10 times stronger. "My… escort is male," I tell him. Unsure of what else to say about Shane.

"Are you seeing him?" He asks quietly. Am I in trouble? I know he can't be jealous… we just met. Be reasonable Adea, his new mate smells of an unmated male. Of course, he'd know what's going on.

How do I answer him? Should I tell him that I'm not seeing him? That's not entirely true. Do I tell him that he likes me? That he's possessive of me? Do I tell him that he's seeing me?

My wolf lets out a snort, "That would be more accurate."

"More or less…" I say quietly and I feel him tense and take a step back.

This time when I look up into his eyes, they're glowing. His hands grip my arms and he pulls me closer to his body.

"Are you testing my patience, little one? Do I look like I'm joking?" He growls. I can't help but melt. His husky voice is calming even when he's angry.

"I don't know what you want me to say."

His touch has calmed me and I can feel the mate bond working on soothing my fears. "He's … more than a friend," I tell him honestly, biting the insides of my cheeks.

Ethan lets go of me and punches the wall behind me. I still when he gets closer and leans into my neck.

He inhales deeply before asking, "Have you fucked him?"

I feel my body tense up and my hands start to shake again. I clench my hands into fists and look him in the eye, "No… we almost did but… it didn't happen."

He lets out a breath I didn't know he was holding and a small smile pulls at his lips. In a quick motion, he steps away from me and pats his hands together.

The smile on his face is gone as quick as it had appeared and his eyes are back to being cold. "After this weekend is over, you'll be staying here."

I close my mouth and clench my teeth together. Knowing that I have no choice in the matter and nothing I say will change his mind.

"Who you were seeing before doesn't concern me," he growls. "What does matter is that today you became mine." He straightens and lifts his chin.

"From today onward you are mine. You will never see this pup again, and you will tell me if he reaches out to you. Am I clear?" I nod and the thought of hurting him makes my heart clench.

"What pack are you from?" He asks me in a cold tone. I can feel him distancing himself from me.

"I'm from the Half Moon pack, my alpha is Alpha Joshua, and his Luna, Rose." Fear starts to eat at me as I wonder what's going to happen when Shane realizes I'm not going back.

"Don't worry about Shane, our mate will take care of us. My name is Korra by the way," Korra whispers, and I ignore her.

"Make sure to say your goodbyes. I'm going in first, come in when you're ready," he says before leaving me standing in the garden.

SUBMIT

I take a deep breath and let out a long and steady breath. I look up at the moon and feel Korra looking at it with me. It's a beautiful full moon tonight, it lights up the garden, showing the beauty of the garden.

I can't let myself get emotional right now. We still need to go in and act like everything's fine.

"We can explain everything to our friends tonight in the room," Korra reassures me. "I was dormant but I was by your side since you were young. I couldn't say anything or talk to you… but I've always been here."

Dabbing at my tears, careful not to ruin Nikki's masterpiece. I laugh, "We can't let her see us looking like a mess." I pull myself together and look at the water fountain.

Lifting my chin, I square my shoulders and steel my resolve to head in. That's when I see it, with the moon shining so bright. How did I miss it?

Out from the shadows, a figure steps into the light. My body starts shaking and I take a step back. I can't find my voice.

"Would you care to explain why I come out here and see you dry humping Alpha Ethan in the dark?" He asks me with a calmness that leaves me frozen in place.

I open my mouth but nothing comes out. "Run to our mate, Adea!" Korra yells at me. I can hear her but I can't move.

His eyes are a mix of black and gold and the look he's giving me looks murderous. He's by my side in a second and I can feel my eyes widen in shock.

He grabs my neck and slams me against the wall. I let out a gargled cry as I try to breathe. "Shane," I say in a raspy voice, raising my hands. I claw at his hand that's wrapped around my neck.

Shane's standing with his hand on my neck, his gaze leaves a trail of unease as he looks down my body. When his eyes are making their way back up they stop on my breast and he lets out a growl.

"Do you not remember what I said yesterday?" He says as he pulls my dress down and my spaghetti straps rip and my breasts fall out in front of him bare.

I feel myself going numb and I turn my feelings off. His warm tongue touches my chest and he takes my left nipple into his mouth. He sucks, hard and bites down on my hardened nipple.

I cry out, and he lets my tit go. "You're mine," he says and thoughts of Ethan flood my mind as Korra thinks about him.

"There's no point Korra," I say as I block her from my thoughts pushing her to the furthest part of my mind. This will hurt her more than it'll hurt me.

He leans over and takes my right tit into his mouth. Licking, sucking, and biting as it hardens. He stands up and stares down at my body.

Letting go of my neck, he cocks his hand back and my face explodes in pain when his hand connects with my cheek. He raises his hand and slaps me across the face a second time and this time my head snaps back and hits the wall.

"Look what you've made me do," he bites. " You've angered your Alpha," he growls at me and I lean against the wall for support. "Submit," he orders and I feel my body collapse to the floor, his power washing over me, and I bow my head, offering my neck to him.

I feel Shane's hand wrap around my arm and pull me up. "Good girl," he kisses my neck, sucking on me. His other hand grabs my tit and massages my nipple between his fingers.

His hand trails down to my dress and he yanks it up above my waist scrunching my dress around my waist. My tits and pussy are now bare to him and I try to focus on the moon.

The same moon that showed me the beauty of the garden now shines its light on my body for Shane to feast on.

He licks his lips and bends down in front of me. Even on his knees, his face is eye level with my belly button. His hands grip my waist and he growls when he sees my pussy.

He pulls my waist towards his face and I look at the moon when I feel his tongue lick my folds. My mind is blank as his tongue slips between my folds.

Closing my eyes, I shiver from the cold as his tongue pulls out and pushes into my pussy. This is my reality.

I ball my hands into fists to stop them from shaking while he assaults my pussy. "You are mine, this pussy is mine. No one is going to take you from me. Your place is at my side or under me."

Shane slips a finger into my pussy as he takes my clit into his mouth and sucks hard on it. His finger pumps into me and I can feel something build up inside of me.

"Cum," he demands and I feel an explosion and he growls. I can hear sucking noises as he laps up my juices. He stands up and looks down at me. His hand grabs my chin and drags my face a little lower so that my eyes are no longer on the moon but on his satisfied face.

"Look at me when I take you," he growls. He unbuttons his pants, unzips them, and drops them. "I've waited for this day, I should have taken you sooner," he murmurs as he fumbles trying to get his cock out.

I close my eyes and try to block out what's happening when a loud roar fills the air. The noise causes Shane to freeze and I open my eyes when I don't feel his body heat. What I see is Shane sprawled on the floor.

SLEEP LITTLE ONE

Someone steps in front of me, blocking my view, his eyes are filled with concern. A warm jacket drops around my shoulders and a shiver runs down my back when he embraces me but I don't feel scared.

I jump when a low growl snaps me out of it. Thoughts of what almost happened to me keep replaying in my head cause my throat to constrict. I'm gasping for breath when a soothing voice tells me I'm okay.

His hand slowly pats my back and his other hand holds my hair until my breathing slows. He pulls down my dress and dabs at my tears. I can hear a loud thud followed by another. Soon the thud makes a crunching noise.

"Give me my mate," my savior says in a low voice. "With all due respect, Alpha, I think my friend needs tending to. Her girlfriends and I will take her to her room, while you clean yourself up."

The voice belongs to Gabe and I lean into his embrace. "She's like my little sister and I think your appearance right now would scare her," he says protectively.

I move to search for the source of the voice and Gabe holds me closer. "Don't look, Ady," he murmurs to me. Looking up at him, his eyes are strained and his hair is messy.

"Odis, follow them to her room," the voice orders, and I realize someone else is with us. Gabe walks with me, pulling me into his side. I look at him as he leads me around the hall, he stares ahead and I can see his eyes are pained.

I open my mouth and close it again. I open it again when I find my voice, "I'm sorry for worrying you, Gabe." He stops and we're standing in the front of the hall now.

"You don't have to apologize, Ady. I told you I'd be by your side and I …" he says in a clipped tone. A car pulls up to us and Odis escorts us in.

Gabe rolls my window down and the drive is smooth and cool. The moon shines down on me and I find myself nodding off. A heavy cloud presses down on me and I can't fight it anymore. I let sleep take me.

***

Dream

Adea

"Wake up, Adea. We need to get up," my wolf whines.

My body is moving back and forth. I strain against the darkness that's trying to keep me under. My hands are restrained and I try to open my eyes. I can hear heavy breathing and feel a hot breath against my cheek.

I'm being pressed back and released. Something wet along my neck. I start to panic when I hear grunting. "Adea," he moans.

Sharp teeth clamp down on my bottom lip drawing blood. My body is still keeping that rhythmic motion.

"I've waited too long for you." My eyes open and I see long black hair above me, his eyes aren't looking at me. They're focused down on something between us.

As my eyes trail down his bare chest, his abs flexing, and his hips thrusting. I watch as his hard cock pulls out of me.

His eyes close and he moans as he thrusts into me to the hilt making my body jerk back. Repeating the movements he starts moving faster. A loud ringing in my ears threatens to split my head open.

My hands are still restrained. "Korra?" I whisper-call to her. I can't hear or feel my wolf. I whimper when I feel his hard cock thrust into my warmth causing pain. His eyes snap open and I feel his hand clench my throat as his cold lust-filled eyes locked onto mine. The warmth I once saw there was completely gone.

"I chose you then and I choose you now." He murmurs. He leans down, trailing his lips along my neck. Having no fight left in me I close my eyes, his grip on me tightening as he continues ravaging me. I hear his canines extend and feel them poised at my neck.

Sinking his canines deep into my neck, I scream, as his thrusts quicken. He comes undone and licks my wound to seal his mark. I feel his seed fill me as he growls, "Mine."

His grip on my throat lessens and I feel his body weight press down on me as he collapses on top of me. His length still fills me and I wince when he moves, and I feel his seed drip out of me.

Staying still, I feel his chest rise and fall and when I pluck up the courage I look at his face. His eyes are closed and I can hear light snores fall from his lips.

Moments pass and he rolls over on the bed. I stare at the ceiling and look at the window. The moonlight spills in. Does the Moon Goddess enjoy my pain?

I slip off of the bed and walk to the open window. Looking outside I look at the territory, the night is filled with an eerie silence.

Thoughts of escaping bring a smile to my face. No… I can't escape. Looking down, I feel the urge to jump. I could escape him in death but… that would be too easy.

I turn my head back to him on the bed, ass out, hair messy. I once considered him the closest thing I had to family.

I feel a warm liquid slowly sliding down my thigh. Looking down I realize the liquid is blood. Looking back at the bed I see his clothes on the floor, next to his sword.

My fingers twitch and my feet lead me to the bedside. Slowly, my hand reaches down and grips the blade. I wrap my other hand around the blade and call on strength I'm not sure I have.

I look down at him lying in bed and -

I'm being lifted into the cool air when I'm pulled from my dream. A sweet scent fills my nose and a calmness washes over me. My head feels heavy and I let go. My head lulls to the side where it stops against a hard chest.

Tingles break out against my cheek and spread to my toes. I try to fight the tiredness to no avail and keep my eyes closed.

My body melts when warm water swallows me whole. Strong arms hold me and start scrubbing me. I try to fight the tiredness and am able to lift my eyelids slightly when I see a tattooed arm scrubbing my thighs with a blue bath scrub.

Blinking, my eyelids get heavier as I try to open my eyes. A sweet cinnamon smell soothes my nerves, "Sleep little one, I won't touch you tonight," the voice coos. My head lulls to the side and I drift into oblivion while a strong yet soft hand gently washes me.

DON'T WORRY

When I wake, I'm in my room, there's a heaviness pressing me into the bed. Opening my eyes, the curtains are closed and the room is dim. I search for the object that woke me up when I see a muscular tan leg on my stomach.

His waist is covered by a thin white sheet and his chest is right next to my face. His arm is wrapped around my chest and I'm breathless as my eyes take in the sight in front of me.

There's a man in my bed! My eyes trail the length of his exposed ripped torso up to his chest and broad shoulders.

My eyes zoom in on his tattoo and I have to suppress the urge to trace it with my fingers. His chest rises and falls with each breath he takes.

Looking up, I see a chiseled chin and let my eyes take in his face. Ethan's hair is messy, his lips look soft and inviting.

Before I can examine him a little more his eyes snap open and he locks eyes with me. Closing his eyes again, his lips turn up in a small smile.

"Good morning little one, how'd you sleep?" He murmurs in a deep husky voice that has Korra's ears perking up.

"Good morning, Alpha," I blush and look away.

"He looks amazing," Korra purrs.

"We just slept together. You can call me Ethan," he says with a smirk. "You had a rough night. How are you feeling?" He asks with a hint of annoyance in his voice.

"I slept well… But umm, by any chance… Did you bathe me?" I've got to be out of mind. I must have dreamt it. I must h-

"Yes. You reeked of…" He takes a deep breath and inhales before continuing, "You needed a shower. We couldn't wake you, so I bathed you."

Korra sighs, "Didn't I tell you he'd take care of us?" She's literally swooning. He says it like it's totally normal to bathe someone you just met. I know my face is beet red but I have to know, I look down at my body to see I'm in a button-up dress shirt.

He must have noticed where I was looking and read my mind because the next words out of his mouth were, "Don't worry. I didn't do anything to you."

"Handsome AND a gentleman. You have to admit we don't meet many of those, Adea." She says and I can feel her melting.

Ethan's gaze lowers and I can feel his eyes on my cheek before they lock on my neck. His stare makes me nervous. Korra's basically salivating at the thought of him marking us. "It's way too soon for that, Korra!"

His hand reaches out and his fingers graze my neck. "I'll never let him touch you again," he murmurs as his touch sends tingles down my body. It feels so good that I have to suppress a moan from escaping my lips.

I raise my hand to my neck and notice it's tender to the touch. When his eyes lock onto mine I can see pain there.

"I may not be… a good lover but I'm a good Alpha. I don't know if I can love you, but I know that I will protect you," he says firmly.

His hand is on my cheek and he leans into me pressing his head against my forehead.

Ethan's breathing gets deeper and I feel something poking my hip. My eyes widen when I realize he's hard. He chuckles and moves his leg off of me. "Can't help it, you're beautiful," he says as he sits up.

My eyes bulge now that his back is facing me. His shoulders are wide and his back is muscular and tan. Korra scoffs and I smile to myself. "I'll admit he's gorgeous, Korra."

"This is the first time I've slept in," Ethan chuckles. He stands up and I realize he's only wearing briefs. Lord help me, I avert my eyes when he turns around to face me.

"Get ready little one, I want to take you to breakfast," he says before he heads to the bathroom. I can't help it when my eyes follow his ass on the way in.

With him gone, I get up and look around. His room is really big, for a man's room I'm surprised he has furniture. There's a dresser against the wall, I don't see any pictures anywhere. Thankfully there's a mirror above the dresser and I get a chance to look at myself.

My brown hair is a mess and my cheeks are a little flushed. My right cheek is swollen and my eyes are puffy from crying last night. His shirt is huge and it almost reaches my knees.

I grab it and inhale, I smell like him. I look at myself again and notice a large bruise on my neck. It's dark purple, I touch it, and thoughts of Shane threaten to take over.

Closing my eyes I turn away from the mirror and see a neatly folded pile of clothes on the dresser. There's a loose v-neck t-shirt, denim shorts, and matching bra and underwear set.

I slip off his t-shirt and dress quickly. The idea of him opening the door while I'm trying to pull the denim shorts over my butt has me moving with a speed I didn't know I had.

The bathroom door opens right after I button up my denim shorts and Ethan walks out. My jaw is on the floor as I give him a slow once over.

Ethan's wearing checkered shorts that hang dangerously low and a loose white t-shirt but even that can't hide his muscled body. I swallow the lump in my throat as I eye-fuck his tatted arms, a few of the veins in his arm visible as he pulls his shirt all the way down.

He catches me drooling and chuckles, "Are you ready little one?" He stops in front of me and puts a hand lightly on my waist. "Yes," I say, a little breathless.

THE SWEET NOTE

Adea

His hand is on my waist as we walk down the hall. Little tingles shooting up my side where his hand rests.

Gabe's door opens before we get to the elevator. When he steps out, I notice he looks tired, like he hasn't slept all night.

He walks over to me and gives me one of his big bear hugs. "You okay?"

"Y-" I'm cut off by a low menacing growl. Gabe and I both look behind me to see Ethan glaring at Gabe's arms around me.

Gabe's eyes widen in understanding and he lifts his hands in the air. Inhaling, Ethan cracks his neck, before closing his eyes.

"I've just found my mate and we have little restraint when it comes to … unmated males touching what is ours."

Opening his eyes, Ethan presses the button on the elevator. "I understand, Alpha," Gabe says with a bow.

Ethan gets into the elevator and pulls me in against him. "We're headed to breakfast, we can catch up later. Okay, Gabe?"

Gabe gives me a nod and flashes his crooked smile. Ethan drops his head low near my neck. His breath makes my insides clench and I wave to Gabe as the door closes.

Ethan's arm snakes around my waist.

"He's just a friend," I mumble and slowly lean back until my back touches muscle. "Gabe has been my good friend… you don't have to worry about him."

Ethan doesn't say anything else. When the elevator dings, his grip on my waist disappears, and before I can complain he grabs my hand.

When we walk into the lobby, we bump into a she-wolf.

"Good morning Alpha," she says with a quick bow before turning to me with a smile.

"Good morning Adea," she says as she leans in and gives me a tight hug. I don't remember meeting her.

"Oh right, we haven't met yet. My name is Olivia and I'm the Gamma of Desert Moon." "Good morning Gamma," I say, smiling at her. She's a few inches taller than me, and she's wearing a black shirt with a white snake and denim shorts. Her black hair is straightened and falls right above her shoulders and her grey eyes remind me of Mavy.

"I'm sorry about last night but don't worry, he'll be taken care of," she says and a hint of anger flashes in her eyes.

I hadn't even thought of Shane. I need to ask Ethan, "What-"

He pulls me into his side and his closeness has a calmness washing over me.

"That's the mate bond working," Korra coos. "Isn't he perfect?" She purrs.

"We need to ask about Shane, Korra," I mentally scolded her.

"Why? Our Alpha will take care of it," she says and I can feel her disdain for Shane.

"Where are you guys off to?" Olivia asks while looking between me and Ethan.

"I'm taking her to town for breakfast," Ethan says with a small smile.

"Going to miss out on Sasha's cooking today? She's making chicken and waffles," Olivia says.

"No, she can have Sasha's cooking next week. She'll be staying here from now on and I want to take her to The Sweet Note," he murmurs.

"Ooh, can I come?" She asks with excitement.

Her eyes widen and she blinks, "Silly me, three's a crowd," she says before we can answer.

Ethan chuckles before he leads us outside.

"I'll see you later, Adea," she calls after me.

"Bye," I say and wave back.

"Well that was a little weird," I mentally tell Korra.

"Hmm.. she smells funny, doesn't she?" She mumbles deep in thought.

"You'll have to excuse Olivia, she has a way of knowing things," Ethan says as we walk up to a white old-fashioned corvette.

"Wow," I let out a low whistle. She's flawless and has a beautiful deep red leather interior.

"Thanks, she's a 1953 corvette," he says beaming with pride. I watch him walk forward and open the door for me.

My heart warms and I get into the front seat. Comfy and soft, "Thank you," I tell him as he closes the door.

He runs over to the driver's side and hops over and into his seat. I smile as he revs the engine and we take off.

It takes about 20 minutes. before we get to town. I can't believe he's helped build this small city. It's bustling and businesses are full of people. Parents are walking with their children and couples are on dates. We pull up to the first free parking spot we see.

"I can't wait for you to try their waffles," he says with a small moan. He opens my door for me and I look up at the restaurant as I hop out.

It's got a little dining area outside, the building is a rustic off-white color, and long green branches are stretching along with the building. The shop has ceiling to floor windows and the door is a cute salmon color with a black quarter note on the front. There's a cute little sign that reads, 'The Sweet Note'.

When we get inside there's a cute backsplash that resembles grass. There's a neon sign that says 'Do what makes you happy. It's a quaint little shop with white booths on the left side and an open kitchen separated by a long counter.

The waitress behind the counter greets us, "Good morning! Have a seat anywhere you like, Alpha." Korra mentally growls and I have to bite my lip to stop my own growl. He grabs us a booth in the back corner.

When we sit, Ethan smiles at me. "My favorite thing to eat here is the Love Note. It's a thick and sweet waffle that's covered in fresh strawberries, blueberries, a drizzle of Nutella, and whipped cream. They don't have syrup here, they have their own special sauce. I don't know how to explain it other than to say it's pure bliss."

I can't help but laugh. It's the most I've heard him talk, and it's about a waffle. "I'll take your word for it. I'd like to try that."

"Kelsey, we'll take two of my usual." He says calling over to the waitress.

"Would you guys like anything to drink?" She asks us.

"Just water for me," I say with a smile.

"I'll have a glass of orange juice, please. Thanks." He tells her.

"I can't wait to try it," I say when my stomach lets out a loud growl.

"Nice," Korra laughs.

I grab my stomach and blush while Ethan laughs. "What do you think of Desert Moon?" He asks while leaning in.

Butterflies erupt in my stomach as his grey eyes stare at me with curiosity. "It's got a small-town feel to it. I haven't had the chance to explore much of it yet but when I drove through with Gabe we were shocked to see that the town was almost as big as a city."

His smile slips a little, "How long have you known Gabe?"

"I've known him ever since I moved into the Halfmoon packhouse. So… about 4 years now."

He's silent for a few minutes before he takes a deep breath. "I wasn't sure what to think when he took you to your room last night. But after I cleaned up, I came up to your room and he was sitting in the chair by your bed."

Shit. I completely forgot that Gabe took me to my room last night. Ugh. I'm the worst friend ever. I should have stopped by his room this morning.

"Stop beating yourself up, he was probably sleeping in," Korra reassures me and I smile at that. We both know how much he loves his sleep.

Kelsey interrupts my thoughts when she puts our plates in front of us. "Enjoy!" She says, before heading back to the kitchen.

I look down at my plate, it looks too good to eat. The waffle is huge and the special sauce he was talking about is a thin white color. I cut a piece of the strawberry-covered waffle and took a bite.

I close my eyes and let out a moan as I savor the flavor. It's sweet and the waffle is thick and soft. The little drizzle of Nutella is like icing on the cake.

"This is amazing," I say, opening my eyes. Ethan is staring at me with lust-filled eyes. Korra's basically drooling and wagging her tail as we feel Ethan's gaze drop down to my lips.

"Told you," He says in a low voice.

I nod as I take another bite. "Can I ask you a question?"

"You can ask me whatever you'd like, little one," he says while he cuts up his waffle.

"Have you been with a lot of women?" He chokes a little before swallowing.

"I won't lie to you. I'm no saint."

Korra's head drops low and she growls as the thought of him in bed with someone else crosses my mind.

"You didn't think he'd stay pure for us did you?" I ask her.

"I don't know what I was expecting but I do know that the thought of him with some she-wolf doesn't sit right with me," Korra growls.

"Have you had many lovers?" I'm surprised by his question.

"Other than… Shane… there hasn't been anyone else," I say in a quiet whisper.

He clenches his jaw and nods his head before he continues eating.

We finish our food and he holds my hand as we walk downtown. He takes me into a few boutiques to pick out some clothes. He picks out a few of them and makes me choose what I want.

If I didn't he threatened to buy one of everything in the shop. By the time we're done shopping, we have more bags than we can carry.

"Let's head back to the packhouse. I think we've done well today," he says with a chuckle. After we've loaded the bags into the trunk he walks me to the passenger's side and opens the door for me.

Before I get in, I look up at him, and leaning onto my toes I reach up and kiss him on the cheek. "Thank you for the gifts," I tell him before getting in.

He smiles before closing the door. When he gets in, he grabs my hand and lifts it to his lips, "The pleasure was mine, Adea."

GOOD AFTERNOON, LUNA

The drive home passed by in a blur as I watched the treeless hills rush by. When we get back to the packhouse, Korra is itching to touch Ethan and I can feel it through our link.

"I've got a few issues to deal with, little one. Otherwise, I would stay with you," Ethan says looking a little down.

"Okay… Ethan. I'm just going to go up to my room."

He lets out a little growl and grabs my hand and pulls me in for a hug. Breathing in his smell as the tingles shoot up my arms.

Korra purrs, enjoying his embrace. "Hug him back!" She whines and her big white head drops to the ground.

"You do things to me," he murmurs in my ear. His breath sent shivers down my spine. Yummy shivers. Ethan's chest is pressed against my face and I'm so close to leaning into his embrace.

"Give me your phone," he says as he moves back and I let out a breath I didn't know I was holding.

I unlock my phone and hand it to him. He freezes for a minute when he sees my wallpaper. It's a picture of Gabe and me the night he slept in my room. I watch him as he starts typing into my phone. He's breath-taking… Korra puts thoughts of him bathing me into my mind… and I have to shake my head to clear the dirty thoughts from my mind. When he hands it back to me I see that he's added his phone number.

"Call me if you need anything," he says before heading back out and Korra whines like a lovesick pup. I also don't want him to leave but I'm not going to tell her that.

I head up to my room and spot Nikki when the elevator doors open. She's standing in front of my room. When she sees me she runs and gives me a big hug. "Oh my gosh, Chika! Are you okay? I heard the Alpha beat up Shane!" She says, looking at me with worried eyes.

"What happened after the ball? You disappeared on us! Mavy needed us last night," she whispers.

"Let's go inside," I tell her, grabbing her hand.

When we get inside we sit on the bed and Nikki starts tearing up. "No one's telling us anything. I was never a big fan of Shane but that doesn't mean I want him to die," Nikki tells me through tears.

I can't believe I haven't tried to reach out to Mavy. I've only been focused on my problems, the best friend of the year award doesn't go to me.

"How's Mavy?" I ask Nikki.

She wipes her tears, "She's not doing good. Shane was taken to the pack hospital last night. No one's allowed to see him and Mavy said they can't reach him through her wolfy link. His parents and Mavy have no idea what's going on."

She scooches in closer, "What happened last night? I saw you and Gabe get into a car and leave. Are you guys… seeing each other?"

I take a deep breath and exhale. "Nikki… I found my mate last night."

Her eyes widen in shock before a smile spreads across her face. "Oh my gosh!" She squeals. "You lucky dog! How was it? Who is he?"

Korra growls at the dog comment and I laugh. "Woah Woah, one question at a time! Honestly, it was overwhelming. His name is Ethan... and... he's the Alpha of Desert Moon."

Her jaw drops and her eyes move left and right as she tries to come to terms with what I just told her. "You're saying... that your Goddess-given mate is the Alpha of this pack? Girl, shut up! I think I saw him yesterday, he's fineeeeee!"

"Wait, I saw you leave with Gabe last night... and Shane is in the hospital right now... because of the Alpha..."

Realization crosses her face, "Oh my gosh... wait this isn't bad... you can talk to him to see what's going on... and why Shane isn't allowed to have visitors!"

"Tell her Adea, she's your friend," Korra encourages me through our bond.

"Nikki...." I say trying to gather the balls to tell her about last night.

A knock at my door has both of our heads turned. "It's me, open up!" Gabe calls from the other side.

Standing up, I rush over to the door and let him in. "Are you okay?" He asks with worried eyes. Gabe pulls me up in a bear hug and squeezes me tight.

"He's getting his scent all over you!" Korra whines. Her white fur swaying as she shakes her head. "I don't mind Gabe but Ethan and Elijah will."

Pushing Gabe away, I hold his hands, "I'm... okay Gabe." I give him the most convincing smile I can. "Ethan... took me to breakfast."

I walk him over to the bed and we both sit next to Nikki.

"As I was saying... maybe you could find out what's going on with Shane?"

A loud low growl comes from Gabe and we both look at him wide-eyed. Nikki jumps, "Gabe? What's wrong?"

Gabe closes his eyes and breaths deeply a few times before opening them again. "She will do no such thing. Ady...."

I squeeze his hand and turn to face Nikki. "You know that Shane and I haven't been getting along... Recently the verbal niceties have turned into... something physical. And last night... he... " Come on... just spit it out. "Last night he did it again at the ball and Alpha... Ethan found us."

Gabe squeezes my hand reassuringly and I feel a little better. "Alpha Ethan and I both went outside and found them at the same time. I couldn't help Shane... and I don't know if I wanted to."

Nikki's jaw drops and she seems at a loss for words. My tears are threatening to spill when there's another knock at the door.

I let go of Gabe's hand and walk over to the door. When I open it, I'm met with the man who escorted Gabe and I to my room last night, only today he's smiling.

"Good afternoon Luna, I've come to help you pack."

RUDE AWAKENING

Odis

Friendship is what kept me here, Ethan has never told me to stay but I've always known that he needs me. I've always loved him like a brother. Sometimes I wondered what made me feel this way. Deep down, I already knew. It was this friendship, this family that I found here at Desert Moon that kept me here. Ethan and I grew up the same way. Always alone, taking the grunt of life. When he rose up and took over, I knew I had nowhere else to be than by his side.

When he first started bedding women, I knew his wolf wasn't happy. I knew Alpha Ethan wasn't happy about it but he would never say it. He says they were just nameless faces used to scratch an itch... Alpha has ... particular tastes and I know he wasn't sure that his mate would be someone who could take what he had to give.

I know he says he doesn't want a mate and that she would just be used to strengthen the pack but I know that he wants a mate. We crave having a family of our own. I just hope he knows that.

When I walked out into the gardens behind Alpha... I knew he'd found her. When I saw her pushed against the wall with his hands on her. I felt a protectiveness swell in my chest that I've only felt for Alpha and Olivia.

I stood and watched as Alpha threw him to the ground and poured his hate into him. I watched and enjoyed as he made him bleed. I needed to see him dead but when I looked at her leaning into her friend.

I felt despair. Her eyes were void of emotion, her lips swollen, tears running down her face. She was beautiful. My future Luna was beautiful and I was breathless.

"It's just her pain that we find beautiful," Troy tells me trying to soothe the panic spreading through my mind. "Nothing else."

"Odis, follow them to her room," Alpha ordered. "I don't know him, watch them until I get there." Alpha mind-links me.

I mind-link our ride and look to her friend. He pulls her along with him. "I'm sorry for worrying you, Gabe," she whispers. He stops and I know he's struggling as much as I am.

"You don't have to apologize, Ady. I told you I'd be by your side and I…" he stops and I know he blames himself.

The car I called for arrives and we get in. I watch as she stares out the window until she falls asleep. Gabe catches her and holding her until we get to the hotel. I run out and open her door for him to come out. He reaches in and picks her up, carrying her up to her room. They're close but I don't see anything inappropriate in his eyes.

I watch as he puts her in bed and grabs a nearby chair to sit by her side. "This is my fault," he says more to himself than to me. "I knew… I fucking knew…" He clenches his jaw and tears spill.

I shift uncomfortably. "I'll be outside until Alpha comes," I tell him in a firm tone. I can't afford to show weakness. I don't know him and staying in here is making me… empathetic towards him.

Glancing at her, I steal a look before heading to the door. I guard the door, keeping an ear out for her. It's 2 am when Alpha shows up. He gives me a small bow and opens her door.

Gabe stands up and looks at him before looking at her. "Leave us," Alpha tells him. Gabe hesitates and I know Alpha doesn't like how close he is to her. "I won't hurt her, she belongs to me."

Gabe nods and moves away. Alpha strides until he's next to her and I know he's conflicted. "Take care of him until I'm able to deal with him," he orders me.

"Yes, Alpha," I bow and look at Gabe. He nods and follows me out. When we get outside we walk to the elevator.

He stops at the last door, "This is me."

"You won't be leaving when the other packs do. We may need you as a witness from your pack."

He nods. "I won't leave her."

"I'll call on you tomorrow," I say before I step onto the elevator.

When the elevator doors close Troy chuckles. "Maximus won't like how close they are."

I nod, "I know. That one's in for a rude awakening."

"I've had him taken to the hospital," Olivia mind-links me, distracting us from Gabe.

I cleaned up the blood with two of our trusted soldiers. They were pups but did a good job. Afterwards, I headed to the pack hospital to check if he was dead. Doctor James welcomed me when I walked in.

He was wearing a long white medical coat, brown eyes that were always scanning. He was 5'9" and had dark skin. "Beta, I'm assuming you're here to check on the new patient?"

When I nod, he continues, "He's got 4 broken ribs, his nose is going to need surgery, and his face is looking better. His Alpha blood is healing his face quickly. The rest of him isn't so lucky but if he wasn't an Alpha's son, he would have had a fractured skull. I think after a few weeks he will be all healed up." He looks at me, "But I'm guessing you don't care about his healing."

"No," I agree. "After he's healed enough, he will be moved to the pack dungeons. For now, I don't know if it'll be for torturing or until he stands trial."

Doctor James sighs and then nods. "Is he allowed any visitors?"

"No, he will be treated as a prisoner and can't talk or see anyone. This is an order doc."

"I understand, Beta, I'll notify the nurses."

"I'll be back tomorrow." I give him a nod before heading out.

I bump into his little sister when I get outside. "Beta Odis," she says with a bow. "Please, can you tell me why I can't see my brother?" She's tiny, barely reaching my chest. His little sister. I thought she was cute yesterday but after what her brothers did... I don't know if I can trust her innocent face.

"He's committed a severe crime and will stay in his room until he is healthy enough to stand trial," I tell her.

"Why didn't you mention the possible torture?" Troy asks. He's looking at her and I can feel his curiosity pouring through the link.

"She doesn't need to know," I reply and he chuckles.

"Sure," he says and I know he doesn't believe me.

"Please," she says and reaches out to me.

I shift and dodge her hand. "I am under orders. Now if you'll excuse me," I say before leaving her. When I look back, she's crumbled on the floor. I push back the guilt that tries to worm its way into my heart. We don't have the luxury.

I get back to the packhouse and sleep. When I wake up it's later in the afternoon and I know Olivia's going to be pissed. My dick is pitching a tent, "Shit." I stroke my length when she fills my thoughts. I stop, "No. I can't."

"We need to find our mate," Troy tells me. "It'll be easier after we find her."

Sighing, I decide to talk to Liv. "Liv, I slept in," I mind-link her.

"I know you did. I've taken care of your responsibilities, don't worry." She says through the link.

"I owe you one," I tell her, and I can feel her smile through the link.

"Just treat me to a nice meal and we'll call it even," her bubbly voice rings in my ears.

"Deal," I say, and stretch.

"Odis, I need you to help Adea pack and move her into my room when you're able," Alpha mind-links me.

"Yes, Alpha. I apologize for sleeping in."

"It's okay Beta, you were up late. I also slept in. I got up not too long ago," he chuckles.

"I'll head there right now, Alpha."

While I brush my teeth, I look at my reflection. My hair is getting longer and I note that I need a haircut soon. My arms and chest are covered in tattoos and my left nipple is pierced. Spitting the toothpaste into the sink, I turn on the faucet and wash my face. Thoughts of seeing her run through my mind. Shaking my head, I dry my face and go to my closet to pick out a suit. Maybe I should dress less professionally so she can be comfortable around me. "She's our future Luna, put on a suit," Troy growls. "You're right," I say and put my suit on. I grab my phone and walk out the door. She's just a couple of floors down.

The elevator doors open and I make my way to her door. I hear talking inside before I knock. When she opens the door, she looks tired and a little shocked when she sees me.

"Good morning, Luna, I've come to help you pack," I say. I attempt a smile.

OLIVIA

Adea

I'm standing holding the door open staring at the Beta. Did I hear him right? Korra squeals and bounces around my mind. "Why would I pack?" This can't be right.

He walks in and scans the room finding Gabe and Nikki on my bed. "I have orders to take you to your new room," Odis says politely. He's wearing a dark grey suit and it looks nice but out of place. It's the weekend and he's wearing a suit. Focus Adea, he's making you move rooms, now is not the time to be wondering why he's wearing a suit.

"Where are you taking her?" Nikki asks Odis. Her eyes are red from crying.

"Alpha Ethan wants her to move to her new room. Since she won't be going back, she will be staying here. This room is for guests."

I look at Gabe and his expression is calm like he knew this was going to happen. "I'll help Ady," he says standing up.

Gabe grabs my suitcase and starts pulling my clothes from hangers, my nerves are wreaking havoc with the idea of where I could be moving. If I'm not considered a guest anymore... and

Ethan's the Alpha... they wouldn't possibly... "But they would, wouldn't they?" Korra says unable to hide the excitement in her voice.

"Is he moving me to his room?" I ask Odis quietly.

Odis stares at me, contemplating his words before he speaks. "Yes, you will be his Luna. It's normal for mates to live together when they find each other," he says.

We had brunch this morning but I'm worried. I don't really know him or anything about him. We wait in awkward silence, and Nikki is still sitting on the bed deep in thought.

"Can't you see he won't hurt us?" Korra asks.

"It doesn't matter if he's our mate or that he was nice to us this morning. We don't know him, Korra. We don't know how he is when he's angry. So yes, I'm worried about sharing a room with a complete stranger," I say. I'm clearly upset and I don't see why she can't see where I'm coming from. She's supposed to be on my side but when it comes to him, she's definitely not.

When everything was packed, I looked at Nikki. "I'm going to take my stuff upstairs. I can come to you when I can..."

"If you need help, ring me. I may be human but I'll still kick some wolf ass if you need me," she says coming over to me. We hug and I hear her sniffle.

Gabe walks over and picks up my bags. "I'll help take her bags upstairs and be right back Nikki," Gabe tells her. She nods tearfully.

I turn to Odis and find him watching me. "Follow me, Luna." Gabe and I follow him out. When we get to the elevator, the doors open and he lets me and Gabe on first. When we get upstairs the hallway is wider and there are fewer rooms. We walk to the end of the hall where Odis pulls out a key.

When he opens the door, we walk in and the huge is breathtaking. I thought my room was big. This room is at least 3 times the size. There's a king-size California bed next to these beautiful ceiling to floor windows. In the middle of these windows, there's a wooden curved double door leading to a beautiful deck. His walls are plain except that the walls across from his bed are covered in tall white shelves filled with books. There is a giant chair in front of the bookshelves and a beautiful gold light next to the chair. The floor is covered by a fluffy white rug. As we walk in, I peek at the bathroom, it's about the size of my last room.

"Everyone will be leaving tomorrow but I'll be staying behind with you," Gabe tells me with a smile.

This comforts me. "You are? Why?"

"I was a witness to what happened and I can be of help to you and Alpha," Gabe confesses.

I'm putting him between me and Mavy. I let out a sigh, "I'm sorry to put you in this position Gabe."

"What? No, Ady. I screwed up. Alpha Ethan has given me a way to make amends. Of course, I'll stand as a witness to what's happened. I'll always have your back."

Before I can let the tears run, I walk to Gabe and hug him. "Thanks, Gabe. I don't know what I'd do without you."

Odis clears his throat behind us, "We have things to talk about." Gabe nods and steps back.

"I love you Ady. Link me if you need anything," Gabe says.

"Excuse me, Luna. Here is my card, call me if you need my assistance," Odis says and hands me a card from the inside of his suit.

Knowing that they're both going to leave me here in Ethan's room and realizing I'm going to be alone now scares me. "Okay," I squeak. "I'll see you guys later."

They head to the door, "Wait... let me come with you." Odis freezes and turns back to me. "I don't know if that's a good idea, Luna. I had orders to help you pack and bring you here."

I cross my arms and stare at him, "Yes, and you've done that. Did he say I couldn't leave this room?" I can feel the anger bubbling up.

"No, Luna. He didn't…" Odis stops talking. "Forgive me." He bows. When he looks up his eyes are clouded. "Follow me," he says before opening the door.

When we get into the elevator he presses the 1st-floor button. "Where are we going?" I ask him.

"There's a meeting hall. We're going to meet Li.. Gamma Olivia. So we can discuss where to go from here." His eyes cloud over and I look at Gabe. He gives me one of his crooked smiles, "Don't worry, bestie. It'll be fine."

The elevator doors open and we walk into the lobby and Sasha is standing behind the desk. She smiles at us as we head down a hallway. I haven't been down yet.

Odis stops at a door and we follow him in. I see Gamma Olivia sitting down at the end of the table. I look back at Gabe but he's stopped walking. When I look back to Gamma Olivia her grey eyes have turned to a glowing yellow.

She lets out a low growl, "MATE."

WHERE WERE YOU?

A smile spreads across Olivia's face and her glowing eyes look past me locked on Gabe. Her eyes trail down his body and slowly drag up to his face. Looking back at Gabe I see a look of utter shock in his eyes. His crooked smile is nowhere to be found and he's surprisingly quiet and doesn't move.

Olivia stands up and glides over to Gabe hesitantly. Her head cocks to the right as she stares up at him curiously. Gabe blinks and I think realization finally dawns on him because in a flash he's got Olivia pinned up against the opposite wall.

He's got her body pinned against his own and her hands up above her head. He leans his head down to her neck and inhales deeply. Olivia offers him her neck and Gabe's tongue comes out and licks up her neck.

At that moment a cough behind us has us turning around. Alpha Ethan is standing in the doorway looking at the scene in front of us. I look over to Odis and see a look on his face that I can't quite read.

Gabe and Olivia are still in their own world oblivious or uncaring of Ethan. I can't help but feel giddy that Gabe has found his mate. He's always made it seem like women were just for fun but I know he wanted to find her.

Ethan coughs a little louder, "Gamma." Gamma Olivia's eyes open wide and she looks around Gabe to Ethan. A light blush spreads on her cheeks and she looks back up at Gabe.

"As hard as it is for me to say this," she motions between the two of them, "will have to wait until later." She lets out a little giggle and Gabe lets go of her. Her feet touching the ground she pats her hair down and smoothes out her clothes.

A firm arm wraps around my waist, "What are you doing here?" Ethan asks as he pulls me into his side.

Beta Odis steps forward, "She said she needed to be here, as future Luna." He gives Ethan a small bow. "If you don't want her here, I can escort her out, Alpha."

Leaning my head up we lock eyes. "Please let me stay for Gabe," I try to say firmly but it comes out as a small plea. A small growl has us turning to face Gamma Olivia and Gabe.

Gabe turns to look at her and she blushes. "Sorry, I don't know what came over me," she says with a shaky voice.

Ethan turns to Odis, "It's okay, she'll stay."

"Shall we begin?" Beta Odis asks with hooded eyes.

We all find our seats except for Alpha Ethan. Odis is seated by the head of the table and he looks at Olivia as if waiting for her to take her seat. Gabe is sitting across from them at another table.

Ethan whispers in my ear, "You can stay as long as you stay quiet." He doesn't look for reassurance or ask if I agree before he takes his seat at the head of the table. Olivia walks over and takes a seat by Odis, her eyes never leaving Gabe.

I walk over and sit next to Ethan, trying to calm my nerves. Alpha Ethan looks at Gabe, "I asked you here today as a witness of what happened last night," Ethan says without looking at me. I drop my head in shame. "Alpha Joshua and his Luna will be here in a few minutes with their Beta and their pup." My eyes search Ethan's face for answers but I don't get any.

Gabe looks Ethan in the eyes, "I will tell them the truth of what happened. I have to do something to help Ady." Gabe's eyes flit to me and he gives me a small smile. "I knew… something was going on between them and I didn't say anything. I'm partially to blame for what happened last night, Alpha. When the trial is over, I will take whatever punishment you see fit."

I can't stop the gasp that tumbles from my lips and I look to Ethan. I would think him uncaring if I didn't see the muscles in his jaw twitch. He's upset and I'm scared of what that means for Gabe.

"It wasn't-" I start but am cut off when Ethan shoots me a look. When I look at Beta Odis he shakes his head. I swallow the painful lump in my throat and look at Gabe.

"I think that we should ask him what happened," Olivia says. There's a tremor in her voice, fear for her newfound mate. "Or go over what he plans to say," she says a little more firmly.

Ethan looks to Gabe, "Where were you?"

Gabe's eyes drop to the desk and he lets out a breath. "I was with Sasha," he says, his eyes focused on Alpha Ethan. I hear a pained cry coming from Olivia but I can't stop looking at Gabe.

"We snuck into one of the bathroom stalls and she was giving me head. When we were finished, we walked back to the dance floor. That's when I noticed that I couldn't find Ady," Gabe says. His voice cracks a little towards the end when he says my name. "I promised her I would be by her side tonight but I let temptation sway me."

He closes his eyes before continuing, "I searched for her when I saw Alpha Ethan going outside so I followed him. When we got outside, I found us in the gardens, and I scanned the area… That's when I saw Ady looking at the moon and Alp-Shane was on the floor. He stood up and grabbed her chin, when he pulled his cock out,

Alpha Ethan roared and pulled him off. I went straight for Ady, she was almost completely naked, and I ripped my jacket off. I called her name and it was like she didn't hear me… didn't see me."

Gabe stops talking but keeps his eyes on the desk. My eyes flicker to Ethan, he isn't looking at me. I didn't notice that tears were falling from my chin. "I plan on saying the same thing when Alpha Joshua gets here and I'll repeat the same thing when Shane is put on trial."

The door opens and in walks Alpha Joshua and Luna Rose followed by Mavy. She looks up and when our eyes lock my heart drops.

COME HERE

Adea

Alpha Joshua spotted Alpha Ethan first. He walks over to Ethan. Ethan stands to greet him. Alpha Joshua looks tired. Bags hang under his eyes and there's no smile on his face. Alpha Rose looked worn out, her hair frizzy, her nose red from running, her eyes bloodshot from lack of sleep, and puffy from crying.

I glance at Mavy and see that her eyes are locked on me, she isn't sure if she should be thankful, angry, or upset. Her eyes go back and forth between me and Alpha Ethan. When Alpha Joshua notices me, I give a short bow, and he takes a seat at another table across from where Gabe sits. Luna Rose nods to me and sits by Alpha Joshua's side. His Beta on his other side. Mavy walks over and sits beside her mom but her eyes are still on me.

"I've called you here today so we can discuss what has happened and what the consequences are going to be," Ethan says addressing my pack leaders. "Do you know what he's done?" Ethan asks Alpha Joshua.

"I don't know what my son has done to deserve such a beating, Alpha Ethan. We came here as guests hoping to enjoy the ball. My son has been in the hospital for 2 days now and I would like to know what he possibly could have done to warrant being treated as a prisoner when he's injured," Alpha Joshua says. There's anger in his tone but I can tell he's trying to keep it under wraps. I've never seen him this way and I can feel the guilt spreading in my chest.

Alpha Ethan cracks his neck before answering, "Your son has attempted to rape my mate." Alpha Ethan's voice is calm but dripping with controlled anger.

Alpha Joshua and Luna Rose's eyes go wide. Disrespecting an Alpha's mate can lead to death or war but they just found out their son attempted to rape an Alpha's mate. Mavy lets out a pained cry.

"Alpha… I know my son… he may be… difficult at times… and headstrong but he… he wouldn't-" Alpha Joshua chokes out before Ethan cuts him off.

"He would and he did attempt to," Ethan tells him. "My Beta and I both witnessed it but I know it can be hard to believe people who aren't from your own family. Thankfully, we have a witness who happens to be from your pack."

That's when all eyes turn to Gabe sitting alone at his own table. Gabe squares his shoulders and looks at Alpha Joshua and Luna Rose. Before he speaks, he gives them a low bow when he lifts his head, his eyes are hard.

"I witnessed it, Alpha. I promised Ady I would be by her side tonight because she had been having issues with Shane. She was afraid of being alone with him and since Mavy set her and Shane up, she had no choice," Shane says and Mavy lets out a sob.

"Last week during breakfast, I saw Shane touching Ady under the table and that night I made a mental note to ask Ady about it but changed my mind because I figured she would talk to me about it. That night at dinner she was a mess," Gabe pauses glancing at Alpha Ethan.

He swallows before beginning, "I went to her room that night to check on her. I took liquid courage so she would hopefully feel relaxed enough to tell me what was going on. She didn't say anything about what happened and instead cried in my arms."

"We made plans for me to escort her to the Ball here at Desert Moon but Mavy set her up with Shane somehow and she let me know when we arrived here. I ignored my gut feeling and escorted Sasha instead. I didn't notice when Ady disappeared because... because I was in the bathroom stall with Sasha. When we went to the dance floor, I couldn't find Ady," Gabe says.

"I let temptation sway me. I searched for her and joined Alpha Ethan when I saw him go outside. I followed him and when we got outside, I saw Ady standing, with Shane on the floor between her legs. She was staring at the moon when Shane got up. He grabbed her chin and told her to look at him while he took her," Gabe shudders.

"I was frozen until Alpha Ethan rushed over and pulled him off of her," Gabe says and looks at Alpha Ethan.

"So... you're saying that Adea is Alpha Ethan's... mate?" Alpha Joshua asks, looking at Alpha Ethan.

"Yes, she's mine," he says in a low tone that sends tingles down my back.

Mavy looks at me and then looks at Gabe, and bites her lip.

Alpha Joshua takes a deep breath and exhales. "Congratulations on finding your mate Adea," Alpha Joshua says. His eyes are cold as he looks at me. Luna Rose gives me a small bow.

"I punished your pup and he's been on lockdown in his hospital room because I needed to inform you about his crime," Ethan says coldly.

Alpha Joshua slumps, "He is my heir."

"He touched what was mine," Ethan bristles. "He dared."

"What will… what will you do with him?" Alpha Joshua asks and Luna Rose turns and grabs onto her mate. Unable to hold them back sobs wracking her body.

"He will receive 100 lashes and you will exile him from your pack. If you don't agree to exile him, I will kill him. I should kill him but I'm offering this mercy to you, Alpha Joshua, so we can end things on a positive note between our packs," Ethan tells him.

Luna Rose and Mavy are crying and their Beta takes them outside. "I was protecting what's mine. Not only has your son touched what's mine but he's also been abusing her under your nose."

Alpha Joshua turns to me and looks me in the eyes. "I want to apologize in Shane's place. I'm sorry, that you've been suffering Adea. I'm sorry your …. abuse went unnoticed." He gives me a deep bow before turning back to Ethan.

"Will you let us say our goodbyes to him?" Alpha Joshua pleads.

Ethan looks at me and then looks back at Alpha Joshua. "Yes."

When Alpha Joshua and Luna Rose leave, Olivia walks over to Gabe and grabs his hand leading him out. I'm left with Beta Odis and Ethan.

"You're dismissed Odis," Ethan nods to him.

"Alpha, Luna," Odis says bowing to us before leaving, closing the door on his way out.

I'm left alone in the meeting hall with Ethan. I reach out to him when he raises his eyes to look at me. I can't explain the emotion swirling in his eyes.

"Come here little one," he murmurs, grabbing my hand and pulling me into his lap.

STARBURST

Adea

I'm sitting on his lap and his hands run down my shoulders, caressing my arms until they land on my hips. My head comes up to his chest and I feel his hands grip my hips.

I feel tiny in his arms and I can't help but look at his large hands.. "I've been trying to be a good mate, little one," he says as he leans down until his lips are by my ear.

I feel his hard length pressing into my ass and I try to wiggle away. He lets out a groan, "Stay still."

After a few minutes of silence, he presses against me. "It's hard to sit here and listen to what another man has done to you," he growls and I can feel his voice rumble in his chest.

Ethan nips at my ear and I feel my legs start to shake. I know I'm not ready to have sex with him but my body has a mind of its own. I can feel the wetness pool between my legs and I squeeze my thighs together to try and relieve the pressure.

"I'm going to give you a safe word and if it's too hard to remember then you need to let me know," He says.

I can't trust my voice so I just nod for him to know that I understand.

His hands leave my hips and pull a tie from his pants pocket. "I'm not going to hurt you, baby girl," he says while he slowly ties my hands together. "I just need control, and I can't hold back anymore. I can't have you touching me. Do you trust me?"

I swallow, "Yes." And I mean it.

When my hands are tied together his hands find my waist. He picks me up and sets me on the table in front of him. Lifting the tie wrapped around my hands up in the air he brings my hands above my head and lays me down on the table.

Ethan ties me to the end of the table and his hands wander down my chest stopping at the deep plunge of the v-neck, his fingers continue wandering down until they reach my belly button. His hands unbutton my denim shorts and he slowly pulls them down my legs until they're clean off.

I'm trying to fight the panic making its way into my chest. His hands slide up my legs and grip my thighs. I'm wearing dark red underwear and he hums in approval.

Leaning down until he's eye level with my hips, "Your safe word is 'starburst', okay, little one?" He says looking up at me.

I swallow and nod. He pulls my legs apart and his eyes drop to my center. "I won't take you… but I need to make you mine. I can't wait any longer," he murmurs.

His hands reached up and lifted my shirt above my breasts. The red matching bra sprang free and my breasts were bare and open to him. His hands stroked along my breasts and hips.

His warm tongue licked up my folds and I bucked my hips. His mouth wrapped around my pussy and he sucked. I arched my back and pushed into him. His fingers moved the fabric to the side and I felt his warm tongue lather up and down my aching core.

His mouth disappeared and before I could protest he bit the inside of my thighs. His hands kneaded my breasts and the feel of his rough hands made my head fall back. His mouth was back on me but this time he was sucking on my clit.

I let out a moan and bucked my hips. This couldn't feel any better, or at least that's what I thought until two fingers pushed into my pussy. I saw stars as his fingers thrust into my core, I let out another moan and arch my back.

He flicks my clit with his tongue and licks circles around my clit. Ethan fills his mouth with my pussy and hummed, causing me to clench around his fingers.

"Ethan…" I cried breathlessly and I tried to touch his hair but my wrist met with restraint from the tie. I let out a small frustrated breath.

"You're so beautiful Adea," Ethan murmured. "Having you here, underneath me, withering against my touch," he kisses me wet folds and I can feel my orgasm building. "Remember my kisses," he licks my clit, and I push into his fingers. "Remember my touch," he licks up my folds and I'm so close. "Forget anyone else," his fingers gyrate into my wet pussy. "Your body, your soul," his mouth sucks on my clit and I'm lost. "Belong. to. me." He growls and I come undone around his fingers.

"Ethan!" I scream as my pussy clenches and convulses.

I look at him and he's watching my pussy clench his fingers and he slowly continues finger fucking me. Withdrawing his fingers, he drops his head to my aching folds, he sucks me into his mouth and sucks up my release.

"You taste as beautiful as you look, little one," he says as he looks up at me. It's so hot watching a man lick and suck you while holding eye contact.

"Did you enjoy yourself?" He says when he sits up licking his lips.

I can't help but blush, "Yes, Ethan."

"Look at me," he murmurs and I look at him.

"I could take you right now," he says and I can feel myself freeze. "but you're not ready yet. Thank you for letting me touch you, little one."

He pulls my shorts back up before untying my wrists. He lifts me up and pulls me into his chest.

"I can't promise to always be gentle with you, but I can promise that I'll never intentionally hurt you."

I shiver and his arms wrap around me. I've never felt so safe before.

FAMILY

Adea

When Ethan puts me down, I have the urge to crawl back into his arms but I fight it. I'm overwhelmed with what just happened and I'm not sure what's going on between us. If I think from my wolf standpoint, he's my mate and I belong here now.

"What do you think of him?" Korra asks me and I know she's fishing. She wants me to like him as much as she likes him. But I just feel pressured by her and the mate bond.

"How did his touch make you feel?" She continues as Ethan takes my hand in his.

I bite my lip ignoring the warmth and fighting the tingles shooting up my arm gives me.

"I don't know, Kor… He makes me feel…" I shake my head before I can finish the sentence.

"Come on Adea, what about what just happened?" She pries.

"I didn't hate it… We just did something… and I enjoyed it. I liked it," I tell Korra as my cheeks heat up.

"And what did you think about Ethan after," she whispers.

I think for a few moments and I look at our hands intertwined.

"I didn't hate him after," I admit. I honestly wasn't sure what I was expecting. Korra moves to the back of my mind but I can feel her smiling as she goes.

***

My face heats as we walk through the kitchen door. Sasha is busy cooking and doesn't look at us. Odis is sitting at the table and smiles when he sees us. I notice Gabe is seated at the table next to Olivia. My heart warms and I can't help but smile at him.

"Ady!" Gabe calls out to me. "Fancy seeing you here," he says and wiggles his eyebrows. He makes me chuckle.

"Hello Gamma," I say to her before Ethan pulls out a chair for me. They both sit across from me. Odis sitting by Ethan's side. Olivia and Gabe next to Odis.

"Good evening Luna," she says and my eyes flicker to Ethan.

He doesn't seem to hear or he ignores it. Odis starts talking to Ethan and I hear something about rogues.

Turning my attention back to Gabe and Olivia I feel giddy. "I'm happy you found your mate, Gabe," I look at him and Olivia. Gabe blushes and Olivia gives me a knowing look.

"Thank you, Ady. Gabe tells me you guys are very close," Olivia says with a genuine smile.

"Yes, he's the closest thing I've got to family," I tell her hoping she knows that's all we ever were.

"I know we're your family now but I'm glad to hear that you will have someone so important here with you. It's thanks to you that we were able to find each other," she tells me.

Worries of her not being happy about our friendship are lost and a sense of relief washes over me.

"Does that mean that Gabe will stay here?" I ask, trying not to sound too hopeful.

"Yes, we briefly talked about it and we both agreed that I would stay here," Gabe says. His eyes twinkle with happiness and I dab quickly at the tears.

"That's great to hear!" I laugh.

Sasha walks over pushing a tray of food. Stopping next to Ethan she grabs a plate and leans down slowly in front of him. Serving him before grabbing another plate. She turns to Odis and he shakes his head.

"You will serve our future Luna her plate next," Odis tells her. I watch as irritation flashes in her eyes and she strides over to me. She gracefully puts the plate in front of me and turns back to the cart. Ethan doesn't bat an eye but I have to bite down the frustration I'm feeling. I watch as she heads over to Gamma and serves her plate before serving Gabe his plate. I watch as he keeps his eyes on the table until she leaves. Sasha continues to serve the Deltas as they walk through the door.

It feels weird not to be prepping dinner. I wonder if Gabe feels the same way. It's only natural for us to prepare and cook the meals for everyone. Being served my food is definitely going to take some getting used to. I wonder if Ethan will let me help prep meals? I watch Sasha as she walks back to the kitchen and starts cleaning up.

"Is she going to keep working here?" Korra bites.

"Is there a reason she can't?" I ask her.

"What do you mean? She's been with our mate!" She huffs.

"How many women do you think Ethan's been with? Are you going to get rid of all of them?"

She bows her big white furry head and I almost pity her.

"We don't know how our relationship with Ethan will turn out… Let's not think about Sasha, okay, Kor?" I plead.

She whines but doesn't say anymore.

I look down at the food and realize I haven't eaten since breakfast. Sasha's prepared rib-eye steak, garlic mashed potatoes, and buttered string beans. My mouth waters and I pick up my utensils and am prepared to dig in. Before I can start cutting my plate is lifted up in the air and switched with Ethan's.

"Wh-" I start but stop when I see that the steak in front of me has been cut up into little pieces.

I bite my lip. That's so sweet of him and I feel touched.

"Thank you, Ethan."

He looks at me and I watch as his lip curls slightly before he looks back to his plate and starts cutting.

The rest of the dinner flies by with good food and light conversation. If the rest of my life continues as today did. I would consider myself lucky and I think I could be content here. I wouldn't have to worry about Shane around every corner... Mavy knows now... so I won't have to lie to her about what's going on. I look at Ethan and for the first time in a while, I let go of the breath I didn't know I was holding.

I KNEW

Gabe

Alpha Ethan's Beta opens the door and we walk into the meeting room. I'd be lying if I said I wasn't nervous. There's a petite she-wolf with piercing grey eyes. She shoots me a smile when the smell of freshly cooked waffles fills the room. The black-haired vixen still and smells the air. Her eyes lock in on me and she lets out a low growl, "MATE."

A smile spreads across her face and her eyes start to glow. I feel my dick stand on end as her eyes trail down my body until she brings them up and searches my face. I don't know what to say. I never thought I'd find my mate… I sure as hell didn't think I'd find her here at Desert Moon…. and definitely not in this meeting room. I'm frozen in place as thoughts of what I'm going to do flit through my mind.

The angel with the tight body stands up and glides over to me slowly. She's staring at me like she's got a million questions on her mind. Before I know it I've got her pinned up against the wall.

Thoughts of where I am, why I'm here have been thrown out the window. I can't help but lean down and breathe deeply. She offers her neck to me and my wolf, Felix, takes over. I'm unable to fight the urge as he licks her neck.

My canines are starting to slide out as someone coughs behind us. We both turn around distracted by the sound. Alpha Ethan is standing in the doorway looking at us. I blink and look over to their Beta and see an expression I can only explain as jealousy on his face.

When I blink again, the emotion is gone, and if I wouldn't have seen it I wouldn't have known it was there. She's got my full attention when Ethan coughs a little louder.

"Gamma," he demands.

My mate's eyes open wide and she looks around to her Alpha. A light blush spreads across her cheeks and I want to see if she's red anywhere else. I'm grinning down at her when she looks back up at me.

"As hard as it is for me to say this, this," she motions between us and I feel her press against me, "will have to wait until later." She lets out a little giggle and I let her go.

"Later," Felix and I repeat.

When her feet touch the ground, she pats her hair and smoothes out her clothes. Fuck. Alpha Ethan said Gamma.

"What are you doing here? Ethan asks Ady.

"She said she needed to be here, as future Luna," Beta Odis says with a small bow.

"If you don't want her here, I can escort her out, Alpha."

"Please let me stay for Gabe," she pleads and I feel my heart drop for her.

A small growl has me turning my attention back to my mate.

"Sorry, I don't know what came over me," she says with a shaky voice and I can't help but groan internally at her blushing cheeks.

"It's okay, she'll stay," Alpha Ethan tells his Beta.

"Shall we begin?" Beta Odis asks with his business face on.

**

Everyone sits down and the trial begins.

Alpha Ethan looks at me, "I asked you here today as a witness of what happened last night."

The guilt is back and it's eating at my chest. My heart hurts as I remember my failure.

"Alpha Joshua and his Luna will be here in a few minutes with their Beta and their pup."

I know it's hard to follow through with punishment without a witness, especially when it's between two different packs.

I look Alpha Ethan in the eyes, "I will tell them the truth of what happened. I have to do something to help Ady." My eyes flit to Ady's for a few seconds and I try to give her a reassuring smile.

"I knew... something was going on between them and I didn't say anything. I'm partially to blame for what happened last night, Alpha. When the trial is over, I will take whatever punishment you see fit."

I've just found my mate but after my failure, I don't deserve to be happy. I fucked up. I hear Ady gasp and avoid her gaze. Instead, I look to Alpha Ethan and watch as his jaw tenses and twitches.

I say what I mean and I mean what I say. I feel a stab in my heart but ignore it.

"I think that we should ask him what happened," my sweet mate says. There's a tremor and I know she fears for me. "Or go over what he plans to say," she says firmly.

"Where were you?" Alpha Ethan asks but I can see the blame in his eyes.

Ashamed, I can't bear to look at my mate, I dropped my eyes to the desk and exhale. "I was with Sasha," I say and raise my eyes back up to look Alpha Ethan in the eyes.

I hear and can almost feel the pained cry coming from my mate and I can't look her in the eyes. I know Sasha gets around so I'm sure everyone in this pack knows. I hate that I haven't even had a conversation with my mate and already I've hurt her.

"We snuck into one of the bathroom stalls and she was giving me head. When we were finished, we walked back to the dance floor. That's when I noticed that I couldn't find Ady," I say unable to hide the emotion and my voice cracks.

"I promised her I would be by her side tonight but I let temptation sway me."

Don't pussy out now. "I searched for her when I saw Alpha Ethan going outside, I followed him. When we got outside, I found us in the gardens, and I scanned the area… That's when I saw Ady looking at the moon and Alp-Shane was on the floor. He stood up and grabbed her chin, when he pulled his cock out, Alpha Ethan roared and pulled him off. I went straight for Ady, she was almost completely naked, and I ripped my jacket off. I called her name and it was like she didn't hear me… didn't see me."

I'll never forgive myself. "I plan on saying the same thing when Alpha Joshua gets here and I'll repeat the same thing when Shane is put on trial."

The door swings open, Alpha Joshua and Luna Rose walk in, followed by Mavy. I can't focus on Mavy and her pain. I have to focus on Ady. I won't let her presence here distract me from helping Ady.

CONSEQUENCES

Gabe

Alpha Joshua spotted Alpha Ethan first and he walked over to greet him. Alpha Ethan stands and greets him. I've never seen Alpha Joshua look so tired and I feel a pinch of pity for him. Luna Rose looks just as tired and her eyes are puffy and bloodshot.

They all looked confused when they spot Mavy. "I've called you here today so we can discuss what has happened and what the consequences are going to be," Alpha Ethan says addressing my pack leaders.

"Do you know what he's done?" Ethan asks Alpha Joshua.

"I don't know what my son has done to deserve such a beating, Alpha Ethan. We came here as guests hoping to enjoy the ball. My son has been in the hospital for 2 days now and I would like to know what he possibly could have done to warrant being treated as a prisoner when he's injured," Alpha Joshua says. He's angry and confused and I don't blame him. They didn't know what Shane was like.

Alpha Ethan cracks his neck before answering, "Your son has attempted to rape my mate." Alpha Ethan's voice is calm but I can hear the anger he's trying to conceal.

Alpha Joshua and Luna Rose's eyes go wide. Everyone knows that his crime is punishable by death. Mavy lets out a cry and I ignore the tug on my heart. I watched her grow just as I watched Ady grow.

"Alpha... I know my son... he may be... difficult at times... and headstrong but he... he wouldn't-" Alpha Joshua chokes out before Ethan cuts him off.

"He would and he did attempt to," Ethan tells him. "My Beta and I both witnessed it but I know it can be hard to believe people who aren't from your own family. Thankfully, we have a witness who happens to be from your pack."

That's when all eyes turn to me. Sitting at this table by myself makes me feel that much more alone. I square my shoulders and tell myself I'm not afraid. I ignore the thought of not getting to be with my mate.

I bow respectfully to Alpha Joshua and Luna Rose. They took me in just as they took in Ady. I'm determined, I will tell the truth.

"I witnessed it, Alpha. I promised Ady I would be by her side tonight because she had been having issues with Shane. She was afraid of being alone with him and since Mavy set her and Shane up, she had no choice." Mavy lets out a cry.

"Last week during breakfast, I saw Shane touching Ady under the table and that night I made a mental note to ask Ady about it but changed my mind because I figured she would talk to me about it. That night at dinner she was a mess."

I don't want Alpha Ethan to misunderstand but I need to tell him I went to her room. Felix groans. "You're going to get us killed."

I swallow before beginning, "I went to her room that night to check on her. I took liquid courage so she would hopefully feel relaxed enough to tell me what was going on. She didn't say anything about what happened and instead cried in my arms."

"We made plans for me to escort her to the Ball here at Desert Moon but Mavy set her up with Shane somehow and she let me know when we arrived here. I ignored my gut feeling and escorted Sasha instead. I didn't notice when Ady disappeared because... because I was in the bathroom stall with Sasha. When we went to the dance floor, I couldn't find Ady."

"I let temptation sway me. I searched for her and joined Alpha Ethan when I saw him go outside. I followed him and when we got outside, I saw Ady standing, with Shane on the floor between her legs. She was staring at the moon when Shane got up. He grabbed her chin and told her to look at him while he took her." I can't help but shudder when I think about it. So disgusted with myself for being unable to prevent it.

"I was frozen until Alpha Ethan rushed over and pulled him off of her," I finish and look at Alpha Ethan.

"So... you're saying that Adea is Alpha Ethan's... mate?" Alpha Joshua asks, looking at Alpha Ethan.

"Yes, she's mine," he says in a low tone that has me sneaking a peek at my mate.

Alpha Joshua takes a deep breath and exhales. "Congratulations on finding your mate Adea," Alpha Joshua says. His eyes are cold as he looks at Ady. Luna Rose gives her a small bow.

"I punished your pup and he's been on lockdown in his hospital room because I needed to inform you about his crime," Ethan says coldly.

Alpha Joshua slumps, "He is my heir."

"He touched what was mine," Ethan bristles. "He dared."

"What will... what will you do with him?" Alpha Joshua asks and Luna Rose turns and grabs onto her mate. Unable to hold them back sobs wracking her body.

"He will receive 100 lashes and you will exile him from your pack. If you don't agree to exile him, I will kill him. I should kill him but I'm offering this mercy to you, Alpha Joshua, so we can end things on a positive note between our packs," Ethan tells him.

Luna Rose and Mavy are crying and their Beta takes them outside. "I was protecting what's mine. Not only has your son touched what's mine but he's also been abusing her under your nose."

"I want to apologize in Shane's place. I'm sorry, that you've been suffering Adea. I'm sorry your... abuse went unnoticed." He gives Ady a deep bow before turning back to Ethan.

"Will you let us say our goodbyes to him?" Alpha Joshua pleads.

Ethan looks at Ady before looking back at Alpha Joshua. "Yes."

My chest feels a little lighter now that I've done something to help Ady. My mate walks over to me, grabs my hand, and leads me out.

When we get out into the hall, she doesn't say anything to me. I'm focused on the electricity shooting up my arm. When we get into the elevator, she still doesn't look at me. I hang my head... where do we go from here?

I WANT TO PLAY

Gabe

When we get upstairs, I expect angry glares and spiteful comments. I wouldn't be surprised if she rejected me. I have no right to ask for her hand. We're on the top floor and she pulls me into her room.

She closes the door and locks it behind me. She walks over and sits on her bed, pulling her legs up to her chest, and wrapping her arms around them.

Instead of anger, I see pain. I walk over and sit next to her. I brush the loose strands of hair off of her face and put them behind her ear.

I've been with a lot of women but she's the most beautiful woman I've ever seen. Her cheekbones are perfectly defined, her lips are soft and plump. Her nose is small and symmetrical. Her black hair is short and frames her face perfectly. She's tiny, but her little body has curves that would make a priest blush.

She's the picture of perfection and all I want to do is cherish her, mark her, love her. I don't know if I will have her in my life after today.

I want to say something, I want to make her feel better. Felix is incredibly frustrated with me. I wish I could make her feel better and make her understand why I have to go through with the trial.

I grab hold of her hand. "My name is Gabe and I'm your mate."

She stares at my hand and I give in to Felix's demands and intertwine my fingers with hers.

"You fucked her," her little voice breaks my heart.

I've never regretted any of the women I've been with and I never thought the day would come when I would. I've played around not thinking about my mate.

"Yes."

I regret them now. I regret Sasha. I hate myself for putting that look on her face.

She wraps her arms around herself... shielding herself... from me. Felix whimpers.

"I didn't think I'd ever find you." I hope she can hear the honesty in my voice.

I watch as a tear escapes and slowly drips down her cheek.

"I don't know what to say," she whispers.

"Have you been with anyone?" I ask her, afraid of the answer.

"No," she tells me.

"I've played around but I've never given myself to anyone," she whimpers.

"Is there a future for us?" I can't look at her.

There's a long silence while I give her time to think... to answer.

"If you can promise me that there won't be any more women, I think I can try. That means no more Sasha, no more girls from your pack. None," she says firmly. Daring me to disagree.

I get down on my knees in front of her and I look into her sad grey eyes. I lean in and can smell her sweet scent.

"I promise you will be my one and only going forward. I won't look at Sasha, I won't do anything to make you feel insecure, or doubt me. I'm yours and only yours," I vow to her.

Her grey eyes look into my soul and I'd do anything to know what she's thinking. She blinks and then leans forward.

My mate's grey eyes flicker to yellow, "Olivia might forgive you but I'm not so easily swayed," her wolf seethes. "If you hurt her, I will rip your balls off and feed them down your throat," she growls.

She blinks and my mate's grey eyes are back. I gulp. Well.

"Isn't she divine?" Felix murmurs.

Yeah right. I laugh. "She's scary…" I tell Felix.

"I'm sorry, Cam is protective of me," Olivia tells me.

"I finally know your name," I say more to myself than to her.

"My name is Olivia and I'm the Gamma of Desert Moon," she tells me proudly. "Alpha Ethan is like a brother to me and Odis. It's only been the 3 of us for a long time."

"It's the same for me and Ady. I care for her a lot, and I hope that we can all be close."

"Will you stay here with me?"

"I'll do whatever you want me to do, darling," I tell her and I mean it.

"Do you have family back at your pack?"

"Ady is my family."

"Mmm… so it worked out in the end, didn't it?" She asks me with a smile.

I smile faintly at her. Her eyes darting to my lips.

She leans down and briefly kisses my lips. I'm parched and her lips are like water, I need more.

My hand reaches up and wraps around her neck, pulling her back to my lips. Our lips touch and I shiver as tingles spread and run down to my belly. Our lips glide against each other and I smell her arousal.

When we separate, I look into her eyes, "I want to mark you."

Her eyes widen and she leans back. Shaking her head, my little mate looks back at me.

"I can't let you mark me. I don't know if I can trust you yet," her honest words prick at my heart.

I glanced away, hating her answer but knowing she was right.

"Giving in would satisfy me but my wolf wouldn't be happy. We are one and the same and I can't do this without us both being ready."

I nod.

"But I do want to touch you," she whispers as her hands lay on my chest and my dick jumps. My eyes flutter, my breathing slowly picks up, and the butterflies in my stomach are flapping their wings pretty fucking fast.

I don't dare move. She leans forward pressing her chest against mine and Felix is salivating. Her lips are soon on my neck and she gently kisses where her mark will go, adding fuel to the fire.

Her hands slide down to the hem of my shirt and pull them above my head. Her fingers wander across my abs and I bite back a groan.

They start to lower, "I wouldn't do that, darling."

"This?" She asks as her fingers slipped lower.

I gasp and squeeze my eyes shut. "I won't be able to sit still if you keep going," I warn. Looking into her eyes, a small smirk pulls at her lips.

"I want to play."

PERFECTION

Gabe

"I want to play," Olivia murmurs. I have her full attention and I swallow the lump in my throat.

Watching her look up at me. All the different things I could do to her and Felix practically purrs in agreement.

I lean back against the chair and thrust my hips up. I watch as my mate's body jerks up and her hips start grinding against me. Lifting my hips again my mate's hips start rolling against me.

I continue my rhythm and watch her cheeks flush and her mouth slowly drops. She's lost in the feeling I'm giving her when my hips stop. I bite my lip to stop the laugh that threatens to escape.

Her eyes snap open and a look of confusion spreads across her features. "Why did you stop?" Her lust-filled eyes stare back at me.

I touch her chin, my fingers trailing her lips. "As much as I want to keep going. I'm going to sit here, and you're going to ride me."

She opens her mouth and I hold a finger to her lips. "You're going to take what you want, Princess. Noo, you're going to take what you NEED from me."

She's quiet for a few seconds. "But what about you?" She asks with those perfectly thick lips.

"I'm going to watch you chase your orgasm. I'm going to watch you take it, and I'm going to enjoy the look in your eyes when you cum all over me."

My cock is pressing against my pants as I think about her riding me into oblivion. My mate looks unsure but I grip her hips and give her a smile. I jerk my hips up as my hands pull her flush against me.

Her eyes close and her head drops back. Pulling away from me a little bit she moans and her hips start to slowly grind against my pressing wet tip. "She's perfect," Felix groans.

I lift her shirt up above her breasts and let out a groan when I see there's a clip in the front. Thank Goddess!

I unhook her bra and her breasts fall freely in front of my face. Her breasts are perfectly round and her nipples are cute little hardened tips.

I watch as they bounce for me, sliding back and forth as my beautiful mate chases her orgasm. My dick pulses as her moans bounce off the wall. I wrap a hand around her waist and let my hand follow her rhythm. She leans forward and her breasts are so close, I lean my head forward and take one in my mouth.

She whimpers and I circle her nipple with my tongue. "Gabe…" My mate moans out and I don't know how, but my cock got harder.

I lightly bite her nipple and use my tongue to flick over her nipple. Her hips start grinding faster against my dick and I suck on her nipple and breast.

I can feel her wetness soaking my pants. "Oh, fuck," she groans out and she's so close. My grip tightens on her hips and I move her a little faster. Her hips speed up, "Look at me."

She looks down at me and she thrusts back and forth a couple of times. I bite her nipple and she rubs against me a few more times before her hips buck.

"Gabe!" She screams my name while I stare into her eyes.

Olivia collapses against my chest and I cradle her in my arms as she comes down from her high. "Perfection," I whisper.

She giggles and nuzzles against my chest. I gently stroke her hair as her breathing slows. "I'll have some Betas bring your stuff up to our room," she murmurs. I like the way that sounds.

"Our room, huh?" I chuckle. "We're not moving too fast?"

She responds with a glare. "You're my mate, it's normal for newly found mates to move in together."

"I don't mind," I say and kiss her temple. "I'll pack and bring my stuff up though. I don't have that many things."

"If you say so," she says with closed eyes.

I didn't know someone could be so beautiful, so breathtaking.... so perfect for me. I don't know what I did for the Goddess to bless me with Olivia, but I'll treasure her and protect her for the rest of my life.

Thank you, Goddess...

Her breathing slows and when I'm sure she's fallen asleep, I slip out of our bed and quietly close the door. Taking the elevator downstairs, it opens with a ding. My room is the closest to the elevator so I walk over and head in.

I head over to the wardrobe and start packing my clothes into my suitcase. The light flicks on and I turn around to see Sasha standing by my bed.

"What're you doing here Sasha?" I'm not in the least bit happy that she's here.

She's wearing a dress that's way too short and I know why she's here. Sasha saunters over to me and I shake my head.

"You can't be here,' I tell her. "You need to leave."

Felix is growling and I'm trying hard to hold him back. She drops down to her knees in front of me and bows her head submissively.

"I've found my mate, Sasha," I whisper.

Sasha places her hand's palms up on her thighs. I know her eyes are closed and she offers her neck to me.

This is so wrong. I step back and close my eyes. Inhaling deeply and exhaling out. My time with Sasha has been pleasurable and memorable. If I hadn't found my mate, I would have kept her by my side while I stayed here for Ady.

I steel my resolve before I open my eyes.

"Get up," I order.

She hesitates before looking up at me.

"Please," she begs.

I swallow.

"Get out."

Her tears fall and she stands up. She looks at me one last time before walking out of my room.

MAVY

Adea

Getting in the shower, I washed quickly, eager to cuddle with Ethan. Not being near him was driving my wolf and my senses crazy. When I got out of the shower, I wrapped the towel around me before sticking my head out of the bathroom door.

He was laying on the bed next to the clothes I had pulled out to change into. He looked up and smiled when he saw my hesitation. Lifting my chin up, I walked over and picked up the clothes.

His eyebrow lifted as his eyes trailed down my body. Breathing in, I inhaled his intoxicating scent. My nerves felt like they were on fire, every fiber in my body trying to pull me to him.

Magnets pulling towards the other. I couldn't stay away from him. Dropping my towel, I got dressed quickly, and ignored the groan behind me. Ignored the way he made me feel. I walked into the bathroom to brush my teeth and after about five minutes, the door opened.

Ethan's head popped in, "Come to bed."

When I walked back into the room, he was wearing briefs and he was shirtless. His hair was a bit of a mess but my fingers twitched.

I wanted to run my fingers through his hair. His gaze was soft, not his usual intense gaze.

Moving closer, I went to place my hands on his chest and ask him about Gabe's trial. But he moved so quickly, my heart skipped when he grabbed hold of my wrists tightly. The sparks from his touch turned me on and I needed to bite my lip to avoid making any embarrassing sounds.

What did he see when he looked at me? What thoughts were in his mind as he looked at me? He went to say something but then stopped. I reached for him and his grip on my wrists tightened.

I wanted to touch him, ask him questions, get to know him more, but the look on his face looked so calm I didn't want to disturb him.

Before I could even reach out and touch him, he was on top of me, his legs pressed against my thighs, his head pressed to where my mark would go.

His warm lips pressed against my neck and shivers ran down my spine. "Goodnight, little mate," he murmured as he lay down next to me. Ethan pulled me into his chest and I listened to his breathing as it lulled me to sleep.

***

When I wake up the next morning, I could hear his light snoring. Groggily, I open my eyes and peer around the room. His room looked like something you'd see advertised on Insta. All of the furniture was made from real oak, the carpet was the hide of a black bear.

Getting up, I noticed right away that he didn't have any photos. His room was twice if not three times the size of the room I had downstairs. There was a fireplace and a long sectional.

Peering back at Ethan sleeping, I didn't have the heart to wake him. My stomach growled and I needed food. After I wash up, I quietly slip out and get into the elevator.

When the doors open, I walk out and spot Mavy sitting in the sitting room looking a little lost. She's wearing a red floral spring dress that falls below her knees and her hair is braided in one french braid.

Despite what Shane's done to me... she's been my best friend for the last four years. I wanted to keep what was going on hidden from her.

I never meant to hurt her or cause her family so much pain. I don't know why he did those things to me... and I don't know how to explain what was going on to her.

Were we dating? No... Did he sexually touch me? Yes... Did I let him? No, but did I do anything to stop him?

"Was there anything you could have done?" Kor asks me.

I don't have an answer.

"It wasn't supposed to be like this. We were supposed to find her mate and she was going to live happily ever after," I say. I know it's not her fault but I'm upset.

Mavy's lower lip quivers and I feel that tinge of guilt again.

I walk over to her and tap her shoulder before she notices me.

"Hey Ady," she mumbles.

"I asked daddy if I could stay behind yesterday and talk to you. He didn't want to risk it......" Mavy sighs.

"I would have talked yesterday. But I get it. I wouldn't want to make your dad uncomfortable."

She looks at me and smiles weakly. Her eyes are red and puffy from crying and she has bags under her eyes. She probably hasn't been able to sleep since...

I close the distance between us and wrap her up in a hug. She stiffens but returns the hug. We pull apart and there's a moment of silence where we sit side-by-side...

"The sitting room is a little too… public for us to talk. We can go somewhere else if you don't feel comfortable, Mavy."

She looks around and I follow her gaze. The sitting room is empty but there are a few people walking into the kitchen.

She shakes her head and smiles at me. "This is fine, there aren't that many people here."

"Where's Nikki?" I ask.

"She's sleeping in. I was hoping to speak to you alone," Mavy says, folding her arms in front of her chest.

I nodded, unsure of what to say.

"How long has this been going on?" She asks me.

"Honestly, it wasn't this serious at first. He never… things escalated this past week or two," I tell her.

"I wanted to tell you at first, but I was afraid of losing you," I say, and my voice cracks.

"When did it start? Where, how?" She asks flustered.

"The first time was at breakfast when you first mentioned the Ball," I start.

"Wh-… In front of everyone?" She asks and her eyes grow wide.

Sigh.

"Yes. And the second time was after school. Nikki drove us home and I was late to the car. He asked me to meet him after school. I had this feeling I shouldn't have gone… but I did…"

She closes her eyes and nods.

"After the meeting yesterday, we heard what happened and Alpha Ethan declared Shane's punishment. It changed things. I will be taking over for my dad in the future… but I… I know what he did to you Adea and I'm so sorry."

Mavy's crying now and her hands are shaking. "I'm sorry he hurt you and did this to us. But he's my brother… my twin brother. I don't know why he did those things but I'm... I'm wrecked. What do I do without him? How do I go every day without him? He's my best friend."

Reaching out, I grab her hands. "No matter what happens, I'll always be your friend. So don't feel bad for me. Shane did this to me, not you. I don't want it to be awkward between us. I love you."

I take a deep breath. "Things will be different now but please know that I have your back. Always. Shane's banishment doesn't mean that he isn't your brother anymore."

She sniffles, "But he can't come home, ever again!"

"I know but you can plan to meet up with him outside of the pack territory. That way you're not breaking any rules. I know it sucks and it's not the same but you'll be able to see him at least, right?"

She nods and wipes at her tears.

We hug.

"You guys didn't talk about what happened to you," Kor points out.

"I know we didn't talk about what happened and honestly, I'm grateful she didn't ask. I don't know if I can talk about it right now."

Our conversation was short and ended when more people started coming down for breakfast. We promised to keep in touch before she headed back to her room.

My heart ached but I was happy I was able to clear the air between us.

SHANE

Doors slammed and Ethan held the door open for me. The walk to the trial was eery and quiet. Beta followed behind us, with Gamma Olivia and Gabe trailing closely. The trial was taking place at the same place the ball was held.

I held my breath as we walked into the building hand in hand with Ethan. His touch gives me the comfort I need. Before I dropped my head, Kor urged me to lift my head as we walked over the threshold.

One long mahogany table is lined up at the far end of the hall and smaller mahogany tables line up adjacent to the long one. Ethan squeezes my hand before heading over to the long table where he sits on the largest of six tall wooden chairs. Wooden vines swirling up towards a wooden crown at the top of the chair. Two wolves on each side of the crown and the armrest changing into claws.

His hand pulled me down into the chair beside him. After we were all seated, Alpha Joshua and Luna Rose came in and took their seats at one of the smaller tables. Mavy and Nikki walk over and sit at one of the smaller tables.

The lump in my throat was too big, too dry to swallow as the Deltas walked in with Shane. My body stills, my eyes unable to look away. His black hair hung in his face; his shoulders slumped. Shane's face and his body were riddled in bruises. His hands were bound together by the wolf's bane-laced handcuffs. Burn marks peeked from under the cuffs and I felt a stab of guilt.

I know he has to be punished. I know this but does he deserve this?

Kor growled. "He deserves death," she seethed.

"Don't let your heart soften for our attacker Adea. Justice will be ours and we won't feel guilty over it!" She almost howls.

Shane is thrown on his knees and he grits his teeth. Two Deltas stand on both sides of him. My stomach jumps into my chest when I see tears stream down Luna Rose's cheeks.

Pack members from Half Moon and Desert Moon shuffle into the hall. Beta Odis stands up and addresses the room. He looks around and waits for silence to fill the giant room.

"Today's trial is in regards to an attack that took place in Desert Moon on the night of the Crescent Ball. That night, Alpha Ethan found his mate. Everyone present was witness to this and saw when Alpha Ethan went out into the garden with his mate to exchange a few words in private."

His eyes lock onto Shane, his gaze filled with disgust. "When Alpha Ethan came back into this very hall, many congratulated him. No one noticed when Shane of the Half Moon pack slipped outside into the garden after Alpha Ethan. He watched their exchange and waited until Alpha Ethan left the garden to corner our Luna."

My chest heaves as I take a breath, I didn't know I had been holding. I feel Ethan's worried eyes look at me searching for what, I don't know. I can't take my eyes off of Shane as Beta Odis continues speaking.

"During this time, Shane expressed his dissatisfaction with Luna on being with Alpha Ethan, her Goddess-chosen mate," Odis bites.

Ethan growls beside me.

"Shane then proceeds to sexually assault and physically abuse Luna Adea," Odis finishes. "Do you deny this?" Odis questions Shane. My eyes travel to Mavy where I see her sitting with her head up, her cheeks stained.

Shane lifts his head and flecks of gold swirl in his eyes and I know his wolf is present. His eyes lock on me and his lips part, "She was mine the night we came here."

Ethan's shoulders tense and he lets out a warning growl, "Watch yourself." Ethan's eyes are locked on Shane but Shane's gaze never leaves me.

"You've taken what is mine," Shane says and his lips curl over his teeth, eyes almost glowing. I feel that familiar tinge of fear and the need to obey creep up my back. I can't hold back as a shiver racks my body. I hear a gasp from the crowd.

Shane tries to get up but the Deltas at his side grip his shoulder and push him down. Odis speaks again, "As soon as she found her mate, she was no longer yours."

"Thanks to your parents, your life has been spared," Odis says, his voice laced with disappointment.

Shane's eyes flicker to his parents before finding mine again. Odis gives a slight bow to Alpha Joshua and Luna Rose before sitting down. Alpha Joshua stands and addresses Ethan and the rest of the room.

"We are beyond grateful to Alpha Ethan for sparing our son's life. We know his sin is worthy of death and The Half Moon pack is in your debt." Alpha Joshua takes in a deep breath before speaking again.

"In return, I, Alpha of the Half Moon pack, pass judgment on my heir. "Shane, from here on out, you are exiled from Half Moon. Never to cross pack lines, never step foot on my territory again. Your title, your right to Half Moon has been forfeit, and you have been disowned."

Luna Rose breaks out in sobs, her hands reaching up to her face, her shoulders shaking. Shane howls as his link to his family breaks and the pain of being severed from his pack causes him to collapse on the floor.

A high-pitched pain-filled howl pierces the air and my eyes flash to Mavy. Her head is down and her hand is on her chest. She lets out a whimper and slumps into Nikki's arms. I recognize Devin as he comes forward and lifts her into his arms. He looks at Shane, bows, and turns away. Nikki follows and my heart is filled with the need to chase after them.

Ethan squeezes my hand and when I turn to look at him, he shakes his head. Turning to Alpha Joshua and Luna Rose, "I am satisfied." They both bow.

"This trial is now over," Odis calls out before sitting down.

LET HIM

It's been a couple of days since the trial. The Half Moon pack and all of their pack members left, not including Gabe. Mavy and her parents left after the trial; I didn't get to say goodbye but I think it's better that way. I know things won't be the same but that doesn't stop my stomach from churning.

Ethan is busy during the day but we get to share dinner together. At night we cuddle, we haven't done anything yet. I've started getting used to seeing him when I wake up in the morning. I know he wants me though; I feel him every morning.

Kor wants me to jump his bones and ride him until kingdom come. I haven't seen Gamma Olivia and Gabe though. Odis is around but he keeps his distance. I'm not sure what he's thinking but I would like to get to know him better.

"Adea?" Kor asked, her tone sounding lighthearted.

"Yes?" I questioned, doing my best. to try and hide my emotions from her. I could feel her intention, taste it on my tongue.

"Why haven't you completed the mate process yet?" Kor asked, causing a wave of knots to settle in my stomach. Keeping my thoughts at bay, I took a. deep breath and prepared. myself to answer.

"I-" I started, but Kor cut me off. I wonder if she even cared about my feelings.

"I know what you want to say but I honestly don't believe that that's the reason." She shook her head and her fur sway with the movement.

"I don't want to have to relive my time with Shane to try and make you understand me."

"You can't heal from this if you don't even try Adea." Kor sighed and I could feel her irritation and sadness seep through our bond.

"Sometimes Kor… people don't heal. It hasn't been that long and you're rushing me to jump into bed with Ethan!"

"He's not some random person Adea, he's our mate, our Goddess-chosen mate. He won't hurt us like Shane did. He cares for us and it's unfair. What you're doing to him is unfair."

She takes a deep breath. "Mates complete the mating ritual and mark each other within the first day of finding each other!"

She's pissing me off. Isn't she supposed to be my other half? She's supposed to understand me.

"You're supposed to understand me, Kor. I won't screw Ethan just to complete the mating ritual. It'll be when I'm ready!"

My mind wanders to simpler times when all I needed was a run through the forest to be happy. Feeling the ground beneath my feet, and the smell of the trees to help me through the day.

Something soft yet firm shifted against my stomach, fingers brushing against my bare stomach. The sparks spread like wildfire across my skin. The sensations were overwhelming. The sparks tried to soothe me, reaching over my nerves, gently caressing.

I swallowed and for a brief second, I welcomed the sparks and let my mind wander. Kor's thoughts blending with mine. My toes curled and a needy sigh fell from my lips.

The feelings of affection, awe, sexual tension, pulling at my soul begging for me to return the feelings. I pulled myself from his grasp and sat up.

The emotions were encouraging me to lay back down and to give in to him, give in to the mate bond. I stood up and looked at the bathroom door, I've never felt something so strongly before.

"I can feel you fighting it," Ethan's low gravelly voice came from behind me. His big rough hand closed around mine and I closed my eyes trying to steel my resolve.

"Just let him, love us," Kor pleaded.

"I can't, Kor," I tell her. "I don't know how to be loved, how to let myself be loved."

"Just sit back down, and feel what he does to us," her voice begged.

"He wants to take care of us, let him," Kor says, her voice pained.

"You said the other day that you didn't hate what happened with him. You told me you liked it, please don't backtrack. Go forward, keep going forward." Kor says more confidently.

"Give him a chance, if not for you, at least for me. Please, I want to meet my mate," Kor confides.

I'm doing this to Ethan, to her but I'm also doing this to Ethan's wolf. I open my eyes and lower myself back to the bed.

"I'm not trying to fight you, Ethan, I'm…" I trail off.

"I know this is a lot but you are mine, and I, yours. You don't have to explain anything to me right now. Just please, don't pull away from me," he says as he leans forward and kisses my neck.

His warm lips on me cause a shiver to run down my body as his hand slides up my arm. His tongue caresses my neck as his lips slide down my neck. I turn around and wound around his neck, and my fingers toy with the hair at the back of his head.

His muscular arms wrap around my body, holding me against him as if he needs me as much as he needs air to breathe. Every inch of skin that met his felt like fire within my soul.

I wrapped my legs around his torso and our chests were pressed together, my breasts squished against his. He kisses down my throat, and I tangle my hands in his hair, unable to stop myself from moaning.

His hand glides up my stomach and slips up through my bra, my nipples straining against him. His hard cock is pushing against my stomach and he lets out a grunt.

I reach down when his hand stops me, "I can't have you touch me right now, I might not be able to stop."

"We can do other things…" My voice is thick with lust and I'm surprised by how bold I'm being. I put my hands on his shoulders and slowly push him back until he's laying flat on the bed.

His brown hair is messy and it only multiplies how hot he is. He's looking up at me in surprise and I feel confident, strong. I feel in control and maybe that makes this easier with him.

MAKE ME FORGET

His hand traveled between us, traveling lower and lower. The urge to rock my hips was excruciating. I wanted nothing more than to see him come apart under me. Could I bring him there?

His fingers rubbed the length of my slit with his fingers. Thick wetness on his fingers would have allowed him to slide his finger into me effortlessly if it weren't for my underwear.

Our eyes locked on each other as he quickened his movements and my insides squeezed. His fingers pulled the thin fabric to the side and before I could protest his fingers glided into my wet pussy.

He didn't give me any time to adjust as he thrust his finger inside of me. He was merciless and his eyes clouded with lust. My eyes were locked on his sexy chiseled face. I reached for his briefs and pulled him out. His eyes watching me, waiting to see what I'd do.

Pre-cum glinted at the top of his thick fat cock. The pleasure was building as his finger continued sliding into me. I touched the pre-cum and lathered my inner palm with it before I wrapped my hand around his tip.

His eyes flickered down to my hand and I couldn't help but smile. I was affecting him. I slowly dropped my hand down his tip and slid my hand up off his tip. His breath hitched and I repeated the action.

My hand slowly going up and down his tip, slowly going down his length, inch by inch. His rhythm in my pussy matched my hand and I lifted my hips up to bounce a little on his fingers.

I leaned forward and spit on his tip. I watched as it dripped lower before my hand slid up and down and I watched as his cock glistened. My hand slid further down his length, the lower my hand got the less my hand was able to fit around his girth.

His hips thrust forward and I felt powerful as I stroked his length. I picked up the speed and moaned when a second finger slid inside of me. Arching my back as his fingers pumped into me, deeper, faster, harder.

I could feel the pressure build in my core and I squeezed his length as I continued stroking him. He got faster and I matched his rhythm, his hips thrusting faster as his fingers pushed in and out of me. It was pure ecstasy and I saw stars as I came crashing around his fingers. A muffled and breathless moan left my lips.

I rode out my orgasm before looking down at him, desire and longing in his eyes. "You are so fucking beautiful, Adea." I scoot down and lowered my head to his length.

Looking up at him, I peered into his eyes and lick my lips. His eyes darkened as my hand stroked his length. I sucked on the fingers on my right hand and lowered them to his balls, I know they're sensitive so maybe he'll like this.

I started tracing his balls with my right finger and knew it felt good when he let out a low groan. "Fuck A-" he stopped when my lips wrapped around his tip and I sucked. My left hand continued stroking his length and my right hand traced up and down his balls.

My left hand going up and down on his length in almost a circular motion while I slowly slid down his tip to his length. My tongue sliding out and as I sucked. His hand gripped my hair and his eyes on me made me feel so powerful.

His lips parted and a low moan was like music to my ears. I was doing good; he was liking it and so was I. I quickened my speed on his length, jerking him faster, gripping him tighter. I could feel his cock getting harder and I sucked on his soft tip while my tongue flicked between the middle.

His thrusting became harder and I knew he was close. "Oh, fuck Adea. Oh fuck," he half moaned. "You're doing amazing." I continued my efforts and felt his thighs tighten as he roared. He came and I continued sucking, licking, stroking him until he was empty.

His fingers in my hair almost hurt but made me feel good. I moved my hands away and sucked him a few more times before sitting up and wiping my mouth. His eyes twinkled and he wore a satisfied, tired smile.

"That was…" He said.

"Yeah," I laughed.

His hand reached up and wrapped around my neck pulling me down to him. His lips touched mine softly. Kissing him was like soft sensual dancing, I couldn't get enough. His kiss deepened and his tongue found an entry to my mouth.

When we pulled apart, I was a panting mess but so was he. My pussy was throbbing and I wanted more. I wanted to look into his eyes and feel his length inside of me. As if he could read my thoughts, he flipped me around and grabbed my waist.

He pulled me up towards his face and I shivered when I felt his hot breath on my thigh. He trailed rough kisses along the inside of my thighs and I whimpered impatiently. I can't believe I want this after what happened to me but I do.

"Make me forget," I whisper.

My body jumped when his tongue flicked against my wet lips. A moan escaped my lips when his arms wrapped around my thighs, yanking me down onto his mouth. His wet lips caressing my lips.

My already sensitive lips had me moaning loudly as his mouth took what he wanted. Fear gripped me for a second when I thought of Shane. His mouth devoured my pussy, he was skilled and I lost all thought about Shane as his tongue flicked over my clit.

Waves of pleasure washed over me as my hips rocked against his face. The pleasure was building in my core and I was starting to lose it when his tongue dipped into my pussy, tasting my arousal.

I continued riding his face, his tongue as my head fell back, and my back arched. His tongue lapped at my clit and slid into me as I began to come on his tongue. I whimpered as I came undone around him and I screamed in pleasure.

He didn't stop, he kept licking me and lapping up my juices until there was nothing left. When his tongue left my pussy, he pulled me down to his waist and sat up.

"All you have to remember is that you are mine."

THE LAKE

Ethan pulls me into his side as we walk out of the elevator. He's warm and the feeling of his hand around my waist is sparking a fire in me. I blush, yes, another fire. The hall is busy and I notice everyone is here. I see a lot of faces I know and a few that I don't.

Some are sitting together and some are walking around. Everyone seems happy here, safe. Someone has some slow jams playing, which makes me want to dance.

Ethan's hand trails up my waist and I know my face has betrayed me when he lets out a low chuckle. When we walk into the kitchen, I stiffen when I see Sasha turns around and sees us. Her long red hair is in a braid down her back, she's wearing a mini skirt and a low-cut blouse.

She gives a low bow when she greets us and turns to get our plates ready. Ethan doesn't pay her any attention and leads me to the table. Odis walks in and Ethan flashes him a smile. Beta Odis smiles back and even though he's smiling, he's intimidating.

Olivia walks in and even this early in the morning she's beautiful. She's wearing an oversize tye-dye white and brown tee that reaches her knees and she's wearing athletic shoes that work with it.

After Olivia is sitting, Gabe walks in and kisses her head. We all settle in and Sasha serves us our plates. Olivia is bubbly and talks with her hands as she explains how they have been fighting over their room decorations.

"Luna, I'd love it if we could have a girl's day or girls' night out soon. I know we don't know each other well but I thought it would be a great chance for us to connect," Olivia says with a smile.

"I think that's a great idea. We can plan something soon," I responded.

Throughout the rest of breakfast, the conversation is light and easy. Beta Odis doesn't say much other than to answer Ethan's questions or remind him about meetings. Gabe gives me a hug before leaving with Olivia and my heart swells for him.

After breakfast, Ethan and I go for a walk. We stand outside for a few minutes when Odis comes out and hands Ethan a small bag.

"Got everything?" Ethan asks.

"Yes, Alpha," Odis tells him.

"Thanks Odis," I tell him.

We turn to leave and we walk for a few minutes, simply holding hands and enjoying this moment in time. It feels comfortable and I am loving how comfortable I am with him.

We walk a little farther and I've realized we're behind the buildings that are the packhouse. We're faced with a trail that winds into a shaded forest area. We're walking down a dirt road, and the farther we walk the deeper we get into the trees.

Suddenly there is an opening and I stare in amazement as Ethan walks ahead of me. I thought we'd keep walking into the forest, but we came to a small lake.

"When I first found this place, I would come here by myself and swim. I always thought it would be cool to bring someone one day that could enjoy it with me." I'm staring at the see-through blue water and I cannot believe that this little oasis was hidden here in Desert Moon.

"It's beautiful, Ethan." A huge grin spreads across his face at my words.

He steps towards me, his hands cupping my face, "Not as beautiful as you."

Ethan leans down and gently places a kiss on my lips. The kiss was so soft, so light I wondered if he'd really kissed me. I inhale his scent and kiss him back.

My wolf is itching to have some time with his wolf, but I haven't shifted yet, so it'll still be a while before they can spend time together.

"Come," Ethan coos. His hands sliding down to my waist, "Swim with me."

My eyes dart to the lake. "It's not as deep as it looks," Ethan reassures me.

I giggle and let him lead me to the lake. I've been staring in wonder at the lake for a minute or two when something drops. I look over to him and see that he's in nothing but his briefs.

He's watching me as my eyes drop the length of his body. Shooting me a smile, he takes off into the lake. When he's waist-high he turns around to look at me.

I swallow.

I have no reason to be shy, I scold myself. I take off my clothes slowly and walk towards him. Holding my chin up, pretending to be confident. When I'm less than a foot away from him, I reach out and touch his chest.

Hands shoot out, wrap around me, and lift me up. "Ethan!"

He laughs and throws me into the deeper end of the lake. I laugh as I go under and swim back up to the surface with a mouth full.

When I open my eyes, he's laughing and starts to swim closer. He's eyeing me like a predator eyes his prey.

His arms wrap around my waist and he picks me up and pulls me towards him. I wrap my legs around his waist so I can be closer. I'm rewarded when I feel his hard length pressed against me, hard and throbbing. His hands cup my ass, and I can't help but give a little wiggle, and his hands squeeze hard.

I wonder if he can smell how aroused I am, even though we're in the water. He starts kissing down my throat, and I run my fingers through his hair and tug. His hands slowly massaging my ass as his lips trail down my neck.

We spend the rest of the afternoon making out, grabbing each other, and swimming. We ask each other questions to get to know each other and I tell him stories of when I was a little girl.

It's comfortable, and we touch each other and enjoy exploring each other. After our swim, Ethan opened up the bag from Odis and pulled out a picnic blanket for us and two towels to dry off.

We cuddled under a blanket and got to know each other more before dinner. A thought crossed my mind. If every day was like today, I could find myself falling in love with him.

THE ATTACK

I was sitting up in bed the next morning, thinking of my day with Ethan yesterday. The bed dipped, "I could get used to this," Ethan said before he kissed my shoulder.

Off in the distance, screams filled the air. Every single one of my hairs stood on end, and my eyes shot to Ethan. His eyes glazed as his mind-linked someone. When the link was cut, he jumped from the bed and hurried to get dressed.

"What's happening?" I asked him, hurrying to his side.

He shook his head, as he threw a shirt on and hurried to put on some shorts. The screaming only grew louder.

"I need to know what's going on, Ethan!"

"Stay here!" He told me, looking into my eyes before he ran out the door.

"Ady!" I could hear Gabe's voice yelling my name.

"Adea, I think we should go see Ethan," Kor sounded as frantic as I felt.

"He told us to stay here." I snapped at her.

"Do you know what's going on Gabe?" I asked him as we hugged.

"There's been a rogue attack," Gabe says, his face painted in worry. "Olivia linked me. There are rogues at the pack school. I wanted to go to her but she told me I can't because only pack warriors are allowed to defend the territory," he says and I can hear the frustration in his voice.

"Don't you dare Ady," Gabe gripped my arm, his eyes staring into my soul. "I know that look."

I shook my head, "I need to see what's going on. Don't worry."

"You'll stay with me." He snapped.

I shook my head, using my strength to pull his fingers from my arm. "I can't leave him out there, Gabe."

"I know how you feel, really I do. My mate's out there too," he says and closes his eyes.

"I'm the future Luna of this pack, I should be there with him."

I shook him off and pressed the button on the elevator, glancing back at Gabe. When we get outside, I waste no time in running towards the screams. We barreled through the crowd of parents trying to find their kids.

"Where are we going?" Gabe yelled, managing to keep up behind me.

"I need to find Ethan!" I yelled back.

My heart was a fast and loud thumping. in my chest when I spotted a familiar head of black hair.

"Olivia!" I yelled and Gabe's head snapped to her, relief painted his features.

"Luna! What are you doing here." Olivia's face was flushed as she tried to get people to leave the area.

I notice a man lunge at Olivia and I try to warn her but something in my eye must have tipped her off. She whirls around, her claws out, her canines bared as she grabs the rogue and throws him to the floor.

She stands directly in front of him as he gets up on his knees and tries to get up when she grabs his neck and twists it with a. sickening crack. His head turned at an awkward angle as he falls to the ground.

Olivia looks up to me, "You two should leave. It isn't safe here."

"I -" Gabe starts before she cuts him off.

"She is your soon-to-be Luna, babe. I need you to focus on Adea's safety. We need her safe." Olivia leaves no room for discussion.

"Take her back," she says before focusing on the people.

I swallow.

She's right, I should be focusing on helping the people and the children. I look around and see people running, parents searching for their kids, kids crying. I need to be here.

"They either found a way in or they have someone on the inside," I tell her.

"If you're going to stay, Gabe, you need to protect our Luna. I'm trying to get everyone to go to the hall. You guys can gather up the children," she tells us.

Gabe and I rush to gather the children to start heading. to the hall. In the corner of my eye, I see another man, too skinny, his eyes almost completely sunken into his face. He was slithering towards a child that was hiding behind the bushes against the school.

I felt my feet take me forward, pushing strength into my core as I lunged at the starved rogue.

He was a mere inches away from the boy when I landed on his back. My claws extended from my hands as I reached in front of the rogue. I dug them into his chest as deep as I could.

Kor whined to get out but I hadn't shifted in the full moon yet. Somewhere in the farthest part of my mind, I was freaking out. I've never hurt someone, I never thought I would ever kill someone.

Back at Half Moon, my training consisted of my first 2 years on the territory. I never thought I would need to attack, or even kill someone.

The rogue screeched and thrashed under me, fighting against my hold. I could feel his arms thrashing around trying to reach me. A warm and wet sensation dripped down my arm.

My hand clenched his heart and wrenched it out of his chest. His thrashing ceased and his body stilled, collapsing to the floor.

I wanted to fall to the floor and cry, but something stopped me. I turned to the child on the floor and reached out to him. He was scared but his little arms reached out for me.

I stretched out my arms for this child I had just saved and pulled him into my chest.

Something flickered in me, and I found myself staring at Gabe. His eyes were wide and he stood there in shock.

"That was… that was badass Ady!" He exclaimed in awe. We had gathered about 10 kids, including the little boy in my arms. "We can't keep looking for Ethan, let's get the kids to safety," Kor pleaded.

She was right, we had no time to waste. We don't know if we're clear or if there are more coming. I held the boy tightly as we made our way to the hall.

OH-DEE

We got to the hall safely and the kids shuffled over the threshold and inside. There were a few people inside the hall and relief washed over me when crying children were united with their parents.

"Are you okay?" Gabe asks.

I nod.

"I am. That was… I wasn't expecting to kill anyone today or ever." I say nervously.

He wraps me in a hug.

"You did good Ady. You protected yourself and this little one. You're going to be a great Luna," Gabe says and I blush a little at the compliment.

"I'm going to check how many people are here and see if there are any injured," Gabe tells me before heading off towards the crowd of people.

The child in my arms trembled and my eyes met green eyes. The little one in my arms had blonde hair and sun-kissed skin.

"Do you see your mom here?" I asked him, trying to get him to look around.

"I don't have a mama," his quiet voice murmured.

He reached up and touched my face, "I have an Oh-dee."

"Oh-dy?" I repeated.

He nodded enthusiastically. A small smile spread across his face. "Oh-dee takes care of me," he looked around.

I don't know what I'm looking for but I scan the room with him.

"What's your name?" I ask him.

"I'm Paul."

The doors open, and Beta Odis walks in looking around. He's disheveled and I don't think I've ever seen him look so not put together.

"Beta!" I run to him.

He doesn't look at me, he keeps looking around the room.

"Has the situation been taken care of? Is Ethan okay? This attack doesn't seem like a random rogue attack, there were a lot of rogues out there today. Rogues don't attack in numbers, this had to be planned."

After Odis scans the room, he looks at me and starts to answer when his eyes drop to Paul.

"Oh-dee! Oh-dee!" Paul cries and his little hands reach out to Odis.

Odis leans in and sweeps Paul up into his arms. Hugging him he looks at me, "Thank you, Luna," his voice choking.

"I don't know how to repay you, thank you for keeping him safe."

"Oh, it's nothing, Odis. I had to do something..." I trail off and I think about the rogue I killed.

Noticing the blood on Paul's clothes he searches him and then sees blood on my hands.

"Forgive me for a second, Luna," he steps towards me and grips my hand. Flipping my hand around he searches my arm. When he's satisfied, he lets go and his gaze searches my arms.

"Are you hurt, Luna?" He asks.

"No, there was a rogue, he tried to attack Paul and I... I killed him."

He nods before looking back down at Paul, who's cradled in his arms.

"There were a few rogues left when Ethan dismissed me when we realized that Paul wasn't at the school. I had to come and make sure he was okay. The-" he stops and his eyes cloud over and I know he's mind-linking someone.

When his eyes clear, he looks at me, "Ethan has the situation under control. Thankfully, he didn't kill all of them. He's taking a couple of the captured rogues to be questioned."

Gabe runs up to me, "So, luckily the injured weren't injured deeply. Most of the injuries are scratches and bite wounds."

"Thank goodness, it could have been so much worse," I say, thinking about the way the rogue had slowly made his way to Paul.

I shiver and the door opens and a small crowd walks through. The remainder of the kids rush up to their parents and I feel relieved.

"You did well," Kor compliments me.

I can't help but smile. "I did alright," I tell her and let out a small chuckle.

"I wonder what their story is," Kor says, her focus on Odis and Paul.

"It's not our place to ask," I tell her.

"We are NOT asking him who Paul is to him," I tell her.

We watch them for a few minutes. Paul is curled into Odis' chest and my heart tingles as I think about what he said about his mom.

"We could ask our mate," Kor purrs and I roll my eyes internally.

The doors bang open and we all look to see Alpha Ethan walk through the doors. His eyes are fervent as he scans the crowd until he finds me.

He strides over and pulls me into his arms. His touch tingles and his chest presses up against my face.

"What were you doing there?" He growls at me.

"I-" He cuts me off.

"I told you to stay in the room Adea! I needed you to be safe." He says in frustration.

"I know what you said but I needed to be there," I try to reason.

"I told you to STAY in the room," he says as his eyes flicker between and his wolf.

"Aren't I the future Luna? I needed to make sure they were safe and… I needed to make sure you were okay, Ethan." I was scared. I was scared of losing him.

He's silent as he looks down at me. I brace myself and when I look up, I'm surprised when I see a smile curve at one side of his lips.

"What?" I ask. Confused as to why he's smiling when he just growls at me.

"That's the first time you called yourself Luna," he says nonchalantly.

"I-I that's what you're focused on right now?" I say with a laugh.

"You are my Luna, and this is as much your pack as it's mine but I need you to listen to me. Do you know how I felt when I smelled you out there?" He closes his eyes and stills.

"You haven't gone through training here with the warriors and… you just got here. I was afraid of losing you."

Ethan turns to the crowd I'd forgotten was there. "The threat has been eliminated. Somehow, rogues made it onto our territory and got far enough to attack the school. I swear I'll get to the bottom of this.

In the meanwhile, please return to your homes and spend the day with your families."

He turns to Odis and Gabe, "Meet me in my office for a meeting."

ETHAN

I'm sitting on Ethan's lap, Gamma Olivia and Beta Odis are standing across from us on the other side of Ethan's desk in his office. Gabe stands by the door, unsure if he should be here.

Silence fills the room and all I want is to get away from his lap. His hands tighten around my waist as if he can hear my thoughts. He leans forward, his chest touching my back, his forehead leaning down on the top of my head.

"Beta, do we know how they gained entry onto the territory?" Ethan asks and I just know he's trying to keep his feelings in control.

"No Alpha, they weren't seen until they got closer to the school but I have a hunch that there's been foul play," Odis reports.

"As in?" Ethan asks.

"I think someone is working with the rogues but it's just a hunch right now and I don't have any proof. I'm sure I'll know more after I spend some time with the captured rogues," Odis says without breaking eye contact with Ethan.

"How's Paul?" Ethan asks.

Odis clenches his jaw and I can see his jaw muscles flicker.

"He's safe, thanks to Luna," he says.

Ethan nods. "I'm happy to hear that."

Ethan turns to Gabe, "Why didn't you stop her?"

Gabe bows his head, "I-... Forgive me, Alpha. She couldn't be stopped, as Luna, she had every right to be down there. I failed."

Ethan is quiet and I wonder what he's thinking. "We lost 5 members from our pack today. Odis, I will need you to ensure that their family is well taken care of. We will hold their burials as soon as possible and we will take care of the cost."

"Yes, Alpha," Odis says with a slight bow.

He looks at Olivia and Odis. "Despite the attack, you two fought well today. I'm proud to have the two of you by my side."

I can tell by the look on Odis' face that he's caught off guard while Olivia is smiling. Gabe is now by Olivia's side and is holding her hand.

"Gabe, we will need to hold a small ceremony to welcome you to the pack," Ethan tells Gabe, and Olivia's smile widens. She squeals and wraps her arms around his torso.

"Beta, I'll see you in the morning for the interrogation."

"Yes, Alpha," Odis agrees.

"If there's nothing else, I think we're done for today."

"Goodnight!" Olivia and Gabe call over their shoulders as they head back to their room.

With one last bow, Odis turns and walks out leaving Ethan and me alone in his office.

"What am I going to do with you, little one?" Ethan murmurs before standing up, lifting me up with him. He carries me out of the room like I'm a sack of potatoes.

"Mm... you could... put me down?" I say and blink more times than I thought possible in a minute.

He chuckles and I decide to enjoy his arms wrapped around me. I stare up at him as he carries me, his jawline begging to be licked and his neck ready to be marked.

My eyes shutter as I'm lulled by the way my body sways as he walks. I stare at his face, thankful for his safe return as I welcome the blanket of sleep that has made its way up my body. I drift off in his arms, the most comfortable I've ever been in my entire life.

***

Adea

I feel like I've been running forever. When I get to the bottom of the stairs, I push with everything I have on the door. Please, please, please, I think to myself. I step back and push my shoulder into the door and it opens for me.

I was blinded. All I could hear was the ringing in my ears. The wolf's bane grenade had gone off. I squinted as the fog cleared. Everything was moving in slow motion as I tried to find him. Tried to smell him.

I couldn't hear Mavy. I stumbled over a body and stared in shock as I found the head of the body belonged to Gabriel. I didn't have time to mourn. I rushed past the arms, legs, and heads of familiar faces. Fumbling and moving trying to find him.

I saw movement in the corner of my eye. I turn and see a pile rise up and fall as a shape pushes up through the bodies. I can see his black hair and my heart swells as I watch him search for me. When his eyes lock on mine I see the relief flood his face.

Ethan. My mate. The love of my life. The reason I breathe lives and breathes. He's okay. He's alright and I can feel my heart well up inside of me and I could cry.

I know what's going on. I know what's happening. I've been here before. This has happened already. I know what's about to happen but I can't help but feel the excitement and need to touch him push me forward.

He stands up and I can feel the need to touch him grow and almost explode as he starts towards me. I can feel his need and his relief. I feel his shock... Shock fills his eyes and I frantically try to see what's wrong. I look down at his chest... his beautiful chest...

The mate bond snaps and my world is cold and I'm all alone. All I can feel is a numbing pain as I fall to the ground. I can't breathe, the world crashes down on my shoulders but I can't look away from my mate. I can hear his footsteps coming closer. He drops something near my head and grabs my hair. He starts dragging me and I hit my head on a rock.

The last thing I see is the empty eyes of my mate before I lose consciousness. The last thing I feel is cold.

WHAT DO YOU WANT

I wake up feeling like I'm being doused in ice-cold water. I inhale a deep breath that my throat restricts against. I can't believe it. I don't know what's going on with my dreams but I've never seen anyone I know in them before.

I was crystal clear on what I saw, or who I saw. What does this mean? Maybe it's a coincidence, maybe with everything that's going on I'm starting to see people I actually know in my dreams… but it wasn't just seeing people. His face was finally clear when I would have the dreams before, I couldn't see the person's face clearly.

I'd see his hair, his jaw, his lips but never really saw him. Last night… last night I watched Ethan as his heart was ripped out of his chest.

I bit the inside of my cheek hard enough to draw blood. What would Alpha Ethan think if I told him about my dreams? What would he think if I told him about what's been happening to him in my dreams?

"Our mate won't judge us. He will listen and want to help with the dreams. We can talk to him." Kor nodded, "He's on our side."

Kor didn't know what she was talking about. It's crazy but I feel my dreams are trying to tell me something. I'm not sure what but I know Ethan is part of this now.

"The full moon is coming up soon, Adea. We will be able to shift," Kor says a little excitedly.

I flopped back down in bed, feeling defeated now that my mind is filled with thoughts of shifting. I've been told the first few times hurt, your bones crack and move as your body tries to change into wolf's form.

"I don't know if I'm ready for that Kor," I whisper.

"I'll be with you the whole way Adea. I'll lend you strength."

Even though there was a small part of me that knew she was only trying to comfort me, I was still mortified. I'm going to go from walking on two feet to walking on four paws.

I took a few calming breaths, trying to calm the storm raging in my mind. In order to mind-link someone, you had to be a part of the pack. Even though Ethan and I are mates, we haven't discussed the Luna ceremony or the Mating and Marking process.

"Are you ready to be Luna?" Kor asked.

"I know you're ready but I don't think it's something that I'll ever be ready for. I do understand that this is my home now. It's just a lot, not only have I found my Goddess-chosen mate but I'm also going to be Luna."

I looked around the bedroom and realized I was in my room. Ethan wasn't in the bedroom and he wasn't in the bathroom.

A soft knock sounded on the door, and when I opened it, I was face-to-face with Ethan. Closing the distance between us he picked me up and placed me on the bed.

I watched as he stood up and removed the belt he was wearing, putting my hands together, he secured them with the belt. He shoved me back onto the bed and pulled me towards the headboard.

Ethan pulled me towards the headboard and hooked his belt to it, forcing my hands up, and leaving my body exposed to him. My heart was in my chest and I didn't know if I was angry with him for being forceful or if I was insanely turned on. Maybe I was both.

He slowly prowled towards me until he was right across from me. He slid in between my legs and I watched as he shredded my underwear and tossed it to the floor. I could feel his hot breath on my lips, and I couldn't help the shiver that ran down my spine.

Ethan looked up at me knowingly. I watched as he leaned down and his tongue darted out and slid down and up my lips. My hips bucked, and I let out a small moan.

He growled in approval, "You're all wet for me." His tongue licked me unabashed and mercilessly, the pressure in my pussy grew tighter, and his fingers entered me while he sucked on my clit. Ethan moved two fingers in and out of me at a slow agonizing pace.

My hips lifted up, needing more. Ethan's eyes lifted back to mine, he chuckled before sucking my clit again. "You're so responsive to me."

His head bobbed up and down slowly as he licked up the inside of my lips. His fingers are still sliding in and out of me at the same pace. "What do you want?" He murmured in between licks.

"I want…" My mind is foggy and I can't think straight. "I want to cum," I whisper.

He chuckled, while his fingers sped up, pushing in and out of me. My body reacted to him, craved him.

"Good girl," He snarled, as his lips latched onto my clit and sucked. His fingers fucking my pussy. I was close, so close. He sucked, and his fingers slammed deep inside of me until pleasure racked through my body.

He continued licking and sucking while my hips rode his face. When I finally came down from my high, he was watching me with a smirk on his face. He kissed my sensitive lips before rolling over and laying down beside me.

I wanted him inside me. The thought crossed my mind again but this time I didn't shy from it. I wanted him inside of me, I wanted him to fill me. I wanted to orgasm from him filling me.

The thoughts running through my head sent a hot blush rushing to my cheeks. I prayed he couldn't tell. Darting into the bathroom, I turned on the shower and stepped in, and sighed when hot water cascaded down my body.

When I finished showering, I had a devious thought cross my mind.

"Oooh, I like the way you think, Adea." Kor laughed.

"How about a little surprise?" I laughed.

Dropping my towel, I braced my shoulders and lifted my chin. Maybe I'm a little crazy, maybe I'm not but seeing his shocked face would be worth it. I opened the door, channeling confidence I didn't know I had, I strolled into the bedroom ready for his reaction.

I locked eyes with Beta Odis, his eyes widening as he took in my nakedness. He cleared his throat before looking away from him.

"Shit, shit, shit."

FUCK

Ethan

I can't believe I did that. I know what she's been through but I couldn't help myself. A howl fills the sky. Excuses. How different is what I did from what he did to her? What is the difference between him and I?

I've shifted and I'm running through the hills through the territory still close to the packhouse. A run was desperately needed to clear my thoughts.

"The difference is she is ours," Elijah reassures me.

"He thought of her as his too!" I growl in response. "We took what we wanted from her as he did to her that night and Goddess knows on what other accounts."

The earth bends beneath me as I thunder across the lands like lightning strikes through the sky. Wind pushes past me as I press forward.

I shudder when I think of that night and what I saw out there in the gardens.

"Mate wanted it just as much as we wanted it. She would have told us no," Elijah argues.

"Would she? After what she's been through, that night, did she tell him to stop? I didn't hear it. I saw our mate broken, looking away from him, her eyes were void of emotion."

My heart feels heavy and my chest feels stuffy.

"We didn't do that to her. There's no way we could have known what she was going through," Elijah says.

"We need control. I need to take her and make her mine. How do I change what I am?" I ask.

"We won't change who we are and I won't feel guilty for being who I am. We are Alpha, we are one and the same. We should not, will not feel shame for touching what is ours," Elijah says and I can feel his anger.

"We're going to go back upstairs-"

I cut him off. "I couldn't stay there after what I did. I had to get out of there. How can I face her?"

"WE DID NOTHING WRONG!" Elijah growls. "I'd slap you if I could. SOMEONE needs to slap you out of this stupor you're in. Snap out of it. We did nothing wrong. If our mate didn't want it, she would have told us."

"And if you need to talk to her about how she feels about being physical then do it but I will not hold back from touching what's MINE," Elijah says and I know he's right.

"Alpha." Odis mind-links me and I can hear the tremor and uncertainty through the link.

"What's wrong? Did something happen?" I ask a little too anxiously.

Odis hesitates before answering, "No. Nothing is wrong but… I think we should talk."

"I'll be right there."

I come to a stop and turn back towards the packhouse.

***

Odis

"Beta," Alpha's strained voice calls me through the mind-link.

My body is instantly on high alert.

"Yes, Alpha," I answer.

"Please come to her room. I need you to stay here with her."

"Is something wrong Alpha?" Confusion is evident in my response.

"No."

When I get to her room, Alph is sitting on the bed looking distressed. His head is in his hands and he takes a moment to speak. I don't know what happened but it's none of my business.

"I need a run and I don't want her to come out of the shower without me here. Guard her until I get back. I shouldn't be long," he says without looking up.

"Yes, Alpha."

Ethan gets up and doesn't bother putting a shirt on. He leaves without another word and I can tell he's itching to shift. Being in wolf form gives the human counterpart the ability to detach from their problems and just focus on their wolfie tendencies.

"I hope you find relief," I say to the empty room.

The shower is still going and I decide to stand and wait for her to come out. I look around the room and fight the urge to tidy up a bit. She's not a slob but the call to pick up the clothes on her chair is strong. A few of the dresser dwarves are slightly open and her shoes are tossed next to the door. My fingers twitch with the need to arrange them.

"Deep breaths, Odis," Troy chuckles.

I fight the urge to roll my eyes. Troy thinks my preference is laughable.

"Her room is clean," he says.

"I didn't say anything," I told him.

He laughs.

"You don't need to."

This time I roll my eyes and loosen my tie. I don't usually go into the guests' rooms and I never thought I'd be called to Luna's room. If she was here I wouldn't have the time to look around her room.

The showerhead shuts off and my thoughts are thankfully interrupted. I let out a deep sigh. All too soon the bathroom door opens and Adea steps out and I'm left breathless.

My jaw drops and Troy growls low. I see her long legs first, my eyes travel up for what seems like forever. They glisten with water and I gulp when my eyes reach her thighs. She's got a thigh gap. She's bare and she has a small love mark that sits right above her pussy. My throat is dry as Troy sucks in a deep breath. She's got the perfect hourglass shape and my eyes run up quickly past her plump breasts.

"Oh, fuck," Troy moans. I can feel what he's feeling and I cannot be feeling that right now.

His voice snaps me out of it and I clear my throat and cast my eyes to the ground. "Excuse me, Luna," I say hoarsely.

There's silence as she shuffles and when I look back up her body is covered in a towel. Her face is flushed and the red reaches down to her chest. I snap my eyes away.

I swallow.

"Forgive me, Luna. Alpha asked me to come and stay with you until he got back."

Her forehead scrunches up and her button nose looks cute. "Forbidden thoughts," I correct myself and say to Troy.

"Is he okay? Is something wrong?" She asks. Her eyes widened and I'm glad she's got her mind off of this particular situation.

"Nothing is wrong Luna. He went for a run. He said he'd be back soon."

She swallows.

"Alpha," I mind-link Alpha.

"What's wrong? Did something happen?" He asks.

I hesitate before answering, "No. Nothing is wrong but... I think we should talk."

"I'll be right there," he responds before cutting the link.

"I'm sorry about... this," she whispers her eyes avoiding my gaze.

I lick my dry lips. "Nothing to apologize for Luna. You didn't know I was out here."

There's silence for a couple of minutes.

"I apologize for not letting you know I was here," I told her.

She gives me a slight smile. "I'm going to get ready..." she says.

I nod. I turn and start for the door.

"You don't need to go out, I'll grab my clothes and go into the bathroom," she tells me.

When she disappears into the bathroom, I let out a long exhale. Unsteady hands reach up and tighten my tie. I straighten and clear my mind of the images there.

Troy laughs.

"Shut up," I mumble.

KNOW YOUR PLACE

Adea

What. the. actual. fuck. I'm mortified. I could die. I could just die. Oh, my goddess. What was I thinking?!?! I'm so stupid. Naked, Adea? Really? Why did I think that was a good idea?

"He saw a little skin. You're fine," Kor laughs.

Ugh. Wolves.

"I heard that," she says.

"It's not a habit for me to flash my body Kor! Of course, I'm flipping out."

"Well get used to it. After we shift, we're going to run with the pack and they'll eventually see you naked. It isn't as big a deal as you think," she assures me.

"Yeah?" I ask hopefully.

"Yes, now stop worrying about it."

I slipped on some jeans and a blouse, threw my hair up in a bun, and took a few deep breaths. I hear the door open and close by the time I've slowed my heart rate.

There's a crash that causes me to shriek. I rush out into my room but before I can ask what's going on I see Odis on the floor, his head bent to the right, his neck offered in submission.

Ethan is standing directly in front of him. He doesn't even look at me, his eyes are focused on Odis. I realize he's angry.

"Ethan?" I call out quietly.

He doesn't answer. "Is there a reason I should doubt you?" He asks Odis.

"Never." Odis answers, his eyes on the floor.

"I would never," he says.

I swallow.

"Ethan?" I called again.

His eyes snap to me before looking back to Odis.

"Stand." He demands and I can feel him using his Alpha voice.

Odis stands, his eyes never leaving the ground.

Ethan takes a step forward and I feel my hair stand on end. I watch his chest rise and fall as he stares at Odis. The muscle in his jaw ticks and he closes his eyes and I relax as his chest starts to slow.

"Beta," he says this time without his Alpha voice.

Odis raises his eyes to meet Ethan's.

"You're excused," Ethan tells him.

"Yes, Alpha," Odis says before bowing and heading for the door.

I wait for him to leave before I step closer to Ethan. His eyes lock with mine and my breath catches as he strides over to me.

He reaches for me and I flinch.

He freezes for a second, "I'd never hurt you, little one. You don't have to fear me."

"I know," I whisper.

"He didn't do anything wrong." I need him to know he didn't do anything inappropriate.

"I walked out completely naked. It wasn't his fault. I didn't know he was out here." I take a breath before continuing, "I thought… I was trying to surprise you. I thought I could shock you if I came out completely naked."

"Well, it was a surprise."

He wraps his arms around my waist. "I'm not angry with you. I would have liked the surprise."

Ethan leans down and gives me a brief kiss on the cheek.

"Why are you angry with him?" I ask.

"I'm not angry that he saw you naked, as surprising as that sounds, I'm not angry because of that. I'm angry because he was aroused. He was turned on because of you. And that is why I'm angry."

I bite my lip. What do you say to that?

"I mean… maybe it wasn't his fault? There was a naked woman in front of him. I'm not trying to make excuses for him but he's not a saint," I tell him,

I watch as he clenches his jaw. I lean up on my toes and plant a kiss on his lips.

"I mean, look at me," I say jokingly.

He cracks a smile and I relax a bit.

Ethan lets out a sigh.

"When it comes to Odis, it would be hard for it to not mean anything."

"What-" I say but he cuts me off.

"Not today, little one," He grabs my hand.

"Let's get some food into you," he says and he leads me downstairs.

After brunch, Ethan tells me he has to go and interrogate the rogues from the attack. When they leave, I start picking up my plate and stack the other plates to take them to the sink.

"You can leave them there," Sasha says curtly. She's wiping the counters and doesn't spare me a glance.

My fingers instinctively freeze.

"Bitch!" Kor growls.

"I don't mind putting these away," I tell her and continue stacking the other plates that were left on the table. I lift a stack and take it to the sink, ignoring her glare as I turn around to grab the rest of the stacks. I finish putting the rest of the stacks into the sink when she throws her apron onto the counter.

"I don't know what he sees in you but it won't last long," she says with her hands on her waist.

"I don't know who you think you are," I say emphasizing the 'you'. "I am your future Luna," I say and square my shoulders. I won't let her make me feel inferior.

"He always comes back to me," she says matter-of-factually, and I'd be lying if I said it didn't hurt to hear that.

"Or didn't he tell you?" She says looking down her nose at me.

"He's told me about his past with you, and that's what it is. The past."

"You mean the past, as in the week before you?" She says maliciously.

"Rip her throat out!" Kor says through bared teeth.

"What happens between us is none of your business. I hope you know your place... and that's not between me and Ethan."

Her beautiful face screws up in an angry scowl. I don't even see it but her hand cocks back and slams forward. The slap resonates in the room and I stare at her as I clutch my face. I'm shocked.

She takes a step towards me and leans in.

"Enjoy him while you can, bitch."

Sasha turns on her heel and stomps out of the kitchen, her red hair bouncing on her way out.

MINE

The day passes quickly in a blur. I'm not sure what I should do about Sasha or if I should mention anything to Ethan. Knowing that he's got the rogues to deal with and possible future attacks. I decided to handle it myself.

I lay in bed thinking about how to handle Sasha. I try not to let my insecurities bubble up as I replay Sasha's thoughts in my mind. He didn't say he was going to come after the interrogation but I find myself waiting for him as I drift off to sleep.

***

Adea

The air in my lungs feels like ice as I struggle to keep running. "Run, Adea," my wolf encourages weakly. I get to the end of the hall when I swerve down the stairs scraping my shoulder against the stone wall.

I wince in pain but all I can do is propel my feet forward. The sound of growls and meat ripping can be heard from outside. I reach the bottom of the step and I can feel my wolf's urgency.

Feeling the wolfsbane still in my system, draining my wolf's strength, I push my feet to move faster, fighting the vomit from coming up.

I feel like I've been running forever. Bracing myself for the locked door I crouch down and notice the white of my dress getting dirty on the floor. I charge for the door and smack into the tall wooden door pain erupting through my shoulder.

"Please, please, please," my wolf and I say at the same time. I turn around and walk back to the stairs. Stealing my resolve, I inhale deeply as I face the door, gathering what little strength I have left. I charge for the door.

To my relief, the door smashes open. I was blinded. All I could hear was the ringing in my ears. A wolf's bane grenade must have gone off as the door opened. Squinting through the fog, everything was moving in slow-mo.

"Find him," my wolf pleaded. "I'm trying Korra, I'm trying," I whined. I lifted my nose into the air but the wolfsbane still lingering in my system dulls my senses. I try to mind-link Mavy but I couldn't hear her anymore. I'd forgotten I couldn't talk to her anymore.

I stumbled over a body and stared in shock at familiar eyes. I realize the eyes belong to Gabriel and my wolf howls in agony at the loss of a dear friend. I open my mouth to scream but nothing came out. Gabriel looks like… Gabriel looks like Gabe. My heart shatters and I reach out for him.

"Leave him, Adea. There's no time to mourn right now. We must find our mate." I close my eyes and pull myself away, I rushed past the arms, legs, and heads of more familiar faces. Fumbling in my weakened human state, I tried to find him. Ethan.

In the corner of my eye, I saw movement. I turned and saw a pile rise up and fall as a shape I recognized pushed up through the bodies. Seeing his black hair my heart swells as I watch him search for me. When his eyes lock on mine I see the relief flood his face.

Ethan. My mate. The love of my life. My mate here. My mate now. My mate forever. The reason I breathe lives and breathes. He's okay. He's… my eyes scan his body, he's unharmed. My heart filled with emotion and my shoulders sagged in relief. I could cry.

Stop it. Stop him. Help him. My voice pleads.

He pulls himself through and I do a quick once over, he's naked. His body is painted in blood, his chest and abs beautiful as ever and unharmed. His eyes lock on mine and I can see the relief flood his face.

He stands up and I can feel the need to touch him grow and almost explode as he starts towards me. I can feel his need and his relief. Korra is… Korra? My Korra. Korra is here. Time doesn't stop, Korra's mentally wagging her tail and urging me to run to him when I feel his shock… Shock fills his eyes and I frantically try to see what's wrong. I look down at his chest… he's ripped open… his beautiful chest is…

The mate bond snaps and my world is cold and I'm all alone. All I can feel is the numbing pain as I fall to the ground. I can't breathe, the world crashes down on my shoulders but I can't look away from my mate.

There's fresh blood seeping from his chest and my heart grows cold when the mate bond snaps. Korra howls in agony. Pain. I feel a gut-wrenching pain as I fall to the ground. I can't rip my eyes away from my mate. He falls to the ground as I crawl to him.

I hear footsteps moving away from him. Korra is whining in my head. We're too engrossed to notice when the footsteps get closer.

There's a sound near my head as he drops something. I feel a slight tear as he grabs my hair wrenching me along with him.

He drops something near my head and grabs my hair wrenching me along with him. Korra retreats to the farthest part of my mind.

The world is quiet and still. My mate is just out of reach when he starts dragging me away. Goddess knows where to. I can't pull my eyes from the empty eyes of my mate, My Ethan. My love. I hit my head, the last thing I feel is cold, and I welcome the cold consciousness that takes me.

***

My body is moving back and forth. I strain against the darkness that's trying to keep me under. I fight against Korra trying to keep me down. My hands are restrained and I try to open my eyes. I can hear heavy breathing and feel a hot breath against my cheek.

I'm being pressed back and released. Something wet along my neck. Panic sets in when I hear grunting. "Adea," a familiar voice moans.

Sharp teeth clamp down on my bottom lip drawing blood. My body still keeping that rhythmic motion.

"I've waited too long for you." My eyes open and I see long black hair above me, his eyes aren't looking at me. They're focused down on something between us.

What is… my eyes trail down his bare chest, his abs flexing, and his hips thrusting. I watch as his hard cock pulls out of me.

No… he's not my… His eyes close and he moans as he thrusts into me to the hilt making my body jerk back. Repeating the movements he starts moving faster. A loud ringing in my ears threatens to split my head open.

My hands are still restrained. "Korra?" I whisper to her. I can't hear or feel my wolf. Kor… Kor… please… I call out to her. I whimper when I feel his hard cock thrust into my warmth causing pain. His eyes snap open and I feel his hand clench my throat as his cold lust-filled eyes locked onto mine. I know him… why can't I… The warmth I once saw there was completely gone.

"I chose you then and I choose you now." He murmurs. He leans down, trailing his lips along my neck.

Without my mate… without Kor… Having no fight left in me I close my eyes, his grip on me tightening as he continues ravaging me. I hear his canines extend and feel them poised at my neck.

My first mark is still there, weak but it's still there. He sinks his canines deep into my neck, and I scream, he doesn't let go as his thrusts quicken. He comes undone and licks my wound to seal his mark. Ethan's mark disappears and I feel his seed fill me as he growls, "Mine."

I WANT THIS

I woke up to birds outside. I stayed in bed, running through my dream.

"What do you think of it?" I asked Korra.

"I'm not sure. I have no memory of past partners Adea," she murmured.

"But that was?" I asked.

"Yes, that was... my voice you heard," she said.

It took a few minutes to shake off the shock of seeing Gabe and hearing Kor in my dream. I was left with the burning desire to see him. I needed to see him pulling out my phone, I texted him.

Where are you?

I watch my screen as a texting bubble pops up. I wait patiently for his reply.

In my room. What's up?

I drop my phone and go into the bathroom to freshen up. I grab a bra and throw on a shirt. I grab a pair of shorts and underwear. I stop and look down at the underwear in my hands as a smile spreads across my face. Kor purrs as I drop the underwear back into the dresser drawer.

I rush to his room and when I run in, I'm met with Olivia and Gabe. Olivia looks at me knowingly and I scan the room until I see him. The world stops and I inhale a deep breath and exhale in relief.

The room, the world, and life as I know it stands still.

"I think we're going to… step out… for something…" Olivia pursed her lips, her gray eyes flickering between the two of us. "Give the two of you some time, to uh, talk," Olivia told me as she grabbed Gabe's hand and led him past Ethan.

I didn't hear her as she left, nor did I see her. I was sucked into Ethan; my mate was safe in front of me. As soon as the door shut, I flew across the room to him. My chest smacked into his as his arms wrapped around me. His scent swirled around in my head. A sweet cinnamon smell envelops my senses.

Ethan and I stood there, staring into each other's eyes. I could feel the mate bond pulling me to him and I wondered for a second how the mate bond would feel after the process was completed. His dark brown hair was tousled from the wind, his skin flushed.

He towered over me, his build huge and intimidating. Every cell in my body felt like a live wire. His fingers slid up my arm and I felt the familiar feel of electricity sparking in their wake.

My body yearned to get closer to him. Touching him wasn't enough. His eyes roamed my face, questioning what was going on, wondering what brought out this side of me. His lips were full, plush, and pink. Had I kissed him yesterday? I wouldn't waste another day without his lips on mine.

I slammed my lips to his, shock registered on his face for a split second before he matched my rhythm. His large hands traveling up to my neck, he held me as he deepened the kiss. Having him here in front of me overwhelmed me, the image of him still at the front of my brain, brought tears to my eyes.

"Ethan I-" His name on my lips tasted like honey, "-I need you."

He searched my face, looking for what, I don't know. All I wanted was to get lost in his touch, feel his skin on mine. I reached up to kiss him when he murmured, "Are you sure, little one?" I clung to him; I needed this closeness. Tomorrow wasn't guaranteed, maybe I was being dramatic over the dream but what I did know was that I wanted this. I wanted him, I didn't want to think of what someone else did to me, or what I've been through. I wanted him.

"I want this," I murmured.

I shook my head, finding a boldness I didn't know I had, I leaned up on my toes and pressed my lips to his. His lips responded immediately, melting with mine.

A low growl rumbled from his throat, vibrating against my lips. Ethan's large hands moved from my neck, grazing my chest and sliding to my back. Ethan gripped my hips tightly, lifting me up, I wrapped my legs around his waist.

He walked until we were in front of the bed, and I sunk into the bed as my back hit the bed. He hovered over me, staring down at me, he leaned down until his lips were pressed against my neck. His mouth opened, and his teeth grazed against my skin.

I inhaled deeply, trying to commit his scent to memory. My skin felt like it was on fire under his touch. His lips were like gasoline, only adding to the fire. My fingers played with the hem of his shirt before I lifted it above his head. My fingers ran the length of his abs. He was beautiful, scars, tattoos and all. He reached out and grabbed my shirt, ripping it from my body. His fingers touched my stomach and slowly slid up my torso.

"You're so beautiful," he murmured.

"Please," I begged, praying he could feel how badly I needed him, how badly I burned for him.

"Please, what?" He asked. A small smile playing on his lips.

I lifted my hips and pressed myself against him, needing to feel him. I whimpered as I looked down and watched myself rub against him. I wasn't ashamed of the fact that I was acting like a dog in heat.

He was deadly, yet beautiful and I sighed in content as I stared at what was mine. Ethan's eyes stared a hole through me, he reached down and ripped my bra from my body. My nipples hardened against the cool air and I watched as he slipped my shorts off. I wasn't wearing any underwear and I smiled as he growled in approval. Wetness pools between my legs and he groaned as he smelled my arousal.

Ethan got up and he reached down and roughly parted my legs. His eyes are taking in every inch, every crevice of my body. I could feel my stomach and core tighten as his face moved lower.

I let out a small moan as my head leaned flush against the pillow in pure ecstasy as his warm lips pressed against my pussy, his tongue dipping in and out. His hands gripped my thighs as he licked at my clit and tasted my juices.

Ethan pulled me against his face and I unabashedly grind against him. I watched as he devoured me with his tongue. He brought me to the edge, and pushed me over it, lapping up my juices.

YOURS

He continued his merciless rhythm on my sensitive pussy despite my wriggling to get away from his tongue.

Sinful obsidian eyes stare up at me as he murmurs, "I'm not done with you yet."

Ethan continued to lick me, my mews falling on deaf ears. His tongue slid slowly up my lips.

He groans, "I'll never get enough."

My mate lifts himself up and stands in front of me. It's his turn to drop his pants and I watch as he takes his time taking them off. My pussy clenches as I take a good long look at how badly he wants me.

"Goddess," I pant. How was he going to fit?

Kor purrs at the sight of him. I could only hope that pleasure would follow the pain sooner than later. I wanted all of Ethan, every single inch.

Ethan licks his lips and the bed dips as he makes his way back to me. When he makes his way up to me, his breath on my cheek, he gives me a kiss.

"See how sweet you taste," Ethan growled against my lips, his tongue entering my mouth. His lips were sweet and his tongue coaxed my tongue out. Our tongues danced as I tasted myself on him.

When we separated for air Ethan closed his eyes. When his eyes opened, I knew Elijah was present. His hands reached down and spread my legs. I watch as he places himself between them. Ethan looked between us as he positioned himself over me, he leaned down and kissed my neck.

"Try to relax, love, it'll hurt if you're not."

He grabbed his cock and positioned the head against my opening, rubbing it up and down over my swollen clit. I moaned as my wetness wet his tip.

He let out a tortured groan as he continued sliding his tip along my lips. Ethan looked me in the eyes as he entered my pussy.

He pushed a few more inches in when my nails dig into his back, he stills. Ethan closed his eyes, taking a few deep breaths. When he opened his eyes, he looked pained.

"Fuck, you're so fucking tight," he breathed.

I was lost for words. I lifted my head, my lips searched his neck. I kissed him as he pushed in further, making me feel full.

I've never felt so full. He had to be all the way, I tried to look down between us. He lifted away from me and I started to panic when I realized he wasn't even halfway.

Before I could have a full-blown panic attack, he thrust inside of me to the hilt, and I felt like I was being torn in two. It hurt.

He didn't move, he let me adjust to his size. He peppered reassuring kisses on my head, on my cheek, on my lips, on my neck until I was ready. I nodded letting him know I was okay.

Ethan slowly pulled out of me and I flinched when he pushed himself inside of me slowly a few times. The pain started to etch away and was replaced with... pleasure.

His pace quickened and my moans became louder. I've never felt something so filling, his cock buried inside of me made me feel so... full.

It wasn't enough.

My legs wrapped around his waist and my nails broke skin as I moaned, "Harder." I thought I was full before. He thrust his cock inside of me mercilessly, his pace painfully increasing.

"Oh, fuuuck," he says as he pulled out and thrust into me. I could feel something building inside of me with each thrust.

I cried out and arched my back as his thrusts brought me closer and closer. The sound of his flesh slapping against my own had me near the edge. His grunts only fuel my fire.

"You're," thrust, "so," thrust, "fucking," thrust, "perfect." He growled as he grabbed my breast.

I looked up at him as he fucked my pussy. I watched as he got closer and closer. He was getting closer and I watched as he started to come undone.

"Please, don't stop." I whimpered as his hands gripped my waist.

"Don't stop," I moaned as he pumped in and out of me.

"I won't," he said breathlessly.

"I can't," he promised.

My pussy clenched around his cock.

"I love you," his voice was rough and I could hear the hesitation in his voice.

"I love you too, Ethan," I moaned.

"I love you so much," I cried.

The pressure in my stomach had built and threatened to explode.

His thrusts were harder, faster. His hard cock lay claim to my body.

"This is mine."

Thrust.

"You are mine."

Thrust.

"You belong to me."

Trust. Thrust.

"All of you."

Thrust.

"Say it," he demanded.

Thrust.

"I'm yours," I cried.

Thrust. Thrust. Thrust.

"I'm yours," I repeated.

Thrust.

"Come for me, princess. Let me see your face as I make you come." I stiffened and then I moaned as I came all over his cock. My back arched, my toes curled, as my hand curled in the sheets.

"Fuck!" He growled.

Ethan closed his eyes and slammed his cock into me. My eyes rolled back as pleasure pulsed through me as his warm seed filled me.

My pussy continued clenching his thick cock, milking every last drop as he came inside of me. I stared up at him in awe as he came undone. I couldn't believe this man was mine.

He thrust a few more times and growled before he opened his eyes. A small smile playing on his lips.

His eyes twinkled as he leaned down and placed a sweet kiss on my lips.

"Mine," he murmurs before placing another kiss on my neck.

I flinch as he pulls his still-hard cock out of me and I feel my eyes widen. He chuckles and pulls me into his arms. We snuggle up and I feel exhaustion settle in my bones. I feel content as darkness takes me.

REGRET

I woke up as light poured in through the window. My fingers twitched on the sheets and I stretched and let my hands search the bed. Flailing my arms around, Ethan was missing and the bed felt cold.

I sat up and confirmed that my mate was not in bed. Looking around, the room empty, I hear running water and relaxed when I realized he was in the bathroom.

Feeling pain for the first time, I grimaced, my face heating as I remembered what transpired the night before.

Kor stretched and wagged her tail excited to do it again. "I'm in pain, I don't think I can go again right now Kor!"

She snickered and mentally nudged me, "Trust me, we could." I shook my head at her as I heard the water turn off.

I swallowed and my heart started to beat a little faster.

I looked down at myself and realized I was still naked. Kor squealed as we saw the hickeys forming on my chest and small bruises darkened on the inside of my thighs. No low-cut shirts or shorts for me this week.

The doorknob turned and my eyes widened as Ethan stepped out with nothing but a towel. Would his chest ever get old for me? The v-shape dipping low below his towel, the hard outline obvious.

A cough had my eyes slowly drag up his body to his eyes. A knowing smile on his face, "Good morning, baby girl," Ethan says as he makes his way over to me.

"Morning," I say quietly and blush, I can feel the warmth spread across my cheeks.

Sitting on the bed, his back facing me, red marks start near his shoulders and run down to his lower back. I watch as he raises a towel to his hair and starts drying his hair. When he's happy with his hair, he puts the towel down and turns around at the waist to peer back at me.

My stomach explodes with butterflies flying around wildly with the way he looks at me.

I didn't bother trying to hide my nakedness from him. Ethan's eyes wander down my body and I'm rewarded when his eyes darken.

I watch as Ethan gets up and drops his towel, his firm ass in front of me has me giggling like a schoolgirl. He turns around and my laughter dies as I'm face to face with a raging hard-on.

"Looking at you, with my marks on your chest, pleases me so much I could burst right here, right now," Ethan says before he gets on the bed.

"Tell me you don't regret it, tell me you don't regret last night," he says, eyes closed as he comes to a stop an inch away from me.

Reaching up, I close the distance between us. His eyes flutter open and we stare into each other's eyes. His dark brown hair is darker now that it's damp from the shower.

"I thought you were too sore," Kor chides.

My body needed him again, needed his touch, his kisses... I needed him. Hadn't I had enough? I was sore but looking at him made my heart ache for him. I leaned forward and touched my lips to his, his cool lips moved against mine, searching, claiming.

My lips tingle and a low growl rumbles in his chest. The growl sent shivers down my back and I squeezed my thighs together.

Separating from him, I lean my forehead against his before opening my eyes. "I don't regret it, Ethan, how could I? Last night was... more than I've ever dreamed of."

His arms wrap around my waist and my hands circle his neck as our lips reconnect and he devours me. My brain shuts off and my mind is filled with thoughts of Ethan.

Ethan lay down next to me and pulled me above him. I sat on his muscular stomach and he pulled my knees until they rested on both sides of his torso. His cock stood up on its own and his tip pressed against my belly button.

Holy shit.

"I want you to take what you want from me," Ethan murmured below me. "I want to watch you as you grind yourself on my cock. I want to watch you as you get closer and closer and I want to watch you move above me as you cum around me," he said, his voice laced with lust.

"Ethan, I've never done this, I don't know what to do..." I trail off, my eyes focused on the sheets spread around us. Insecurity spreads like poison as I start to worry, I'm not good enough for him.

His fingers wrap around my chin and pull my face towards him, my ass lifting in the air as I lean down. His hair falling down to the bed, away from his face.

He's breathtaking and I'm under his spell. My eyes trail to his lips and I realize he's saying something.

"-you hear me?"

I shake my head.

"No, Ethan, I didn't," I say and blush.

"You don't have to worry about knowing what to do, or about anyone else," Ethan says while he looks into my eyes. "You, Adea, are all I want. You're everything I've ever wanted. I never expected a mate, I never expected to feel the way I do about you."

He leans up and kisses my lips, "Knowing that you've never done this with anyone else, only makes me want you more, it makes me happy knowing this is mine. Can't you feel me?" He asks and I look down and see pre-cum slowly dripping down his hard tip. I feel his cock twitch against my stomach and feel the right side of my mouth curl up in a half-smile.

"There's my girl," he says. "Don't worry, I'm here with you. I'll help you if you need help. I just want you to take what you want from me. "This," Ethan says as he grips his length. "Belongs to you, I belong to you," he says confidently.

"I'm yours," Ethan says as his strong hands grip my waist.

ADEA

"I'm yours," Ethan says as his strong hands grip my waist and lift me up on my knees. His tip sits at my entrance and his grip on my waist lessens as he lets me take control. His hard length stands at attention pressing against my lips.

I sway my hips back and forth against his tip and Ethan sucks in a sharp breath as my wetness coats his tip. Slowly, I sit down and feel his tip push past my lips and my legs shake.

"Surprise him and sit down, bury him inside of you to the balls," Korra whispers. I look down at Ethan below me and bite my lip. Keeping my eyes on him, I brace myself and sit down, letting his thick length open me up. I continue until his cock is deep and I feel full, his balls pressed against my ass.

"Fuck," he groans.

"Ethan I-…" I'm at a loss for words. I drop my head back and bask in the feel of his length buried deep in my cunt.

I'm breathless, speechless, and irrevocably his. The new spots his member is reaching, are searing his name inside of me. He's touching parts of me no one has ever touched before.

Lifting my ass up, I feel my cunt sucking in his cock even as his cock pulls out of me. His tip still inside of me, I push halfway down his length before lifting up until I'm on my knees and pushing down, clenching my pussy as I slide down.

"Adea," he murmured breathlessly.

"Ah, you feel so good Ethan," I moan, "so fucking good."

I bounce up and down his length, squeezing my core as my body moves up and down, riding his cock.

"Oh, Adea," he groans. My fingers run up and down the length of his abs below me. My hands gripping him, trying to hold on as I bounced up and felt every inch of him pull out of me before I dropped down on his thick hard cock. My skin was on fire where he gripped my waist but I felt light, so light.

My breathless moans filling the room, the squelch of my pussy taking him completely driving me closer and closer.

His grunts encourage me and I speed up slightly needing him, needing the friction that's taking me closer and closer.

"You're so fucking beautiful, Adea," he groans as he watches my tits lift up and down as I continue bouncing. His hands moving along with my hips, helping me find that pace we're both looking for.

Ethan lifts his hips and thrusts further into me as I continue bouncing. His dick reaches deeper, touching that part of me that shakes my core.

"Ethan, oh Ethan," I moan.

"Right there, please, right there," I plead and he continues thrusting up into me, his eyes locked on where we meet.

I look down between us and watch as his thick hard cock dives deep and disappears into my warm wet folds. I stare in awe at his length as he pulls out of me, even his dick looks muscular.

I laugh and he thrusts up into me and it turns into a moan. He's thrusting deeper, faster, and harder into me and I try to keep up, grinding back and forth on him.

The slaps of when our bodies collide bounce off the wall and my toes curl as I come around his cock. Ethan keeps going, giving me more than I can take. My pussy clenches as he fucks my sensitive cunt.

"Ethan!" I moan.

"Adea, oh fuck, baby giiirl," Ethan groans as his thrusts get faster, his release closer. I bounce once, twice, three times when he throws his head back and I feel his cum filling me.

"Fuuuuck," he moans lowly as he empties the last of it inside of me. My pussy milking every last drop before I crash against his chest.

Ethan leans up and kisses my forehead, his arms wrap around me as he pulls me down to his side.

"You're so beautiful, Adea," he murmurs as he reaches down and we share a quick kiss. Our breathing is still fast, our chests expanding and shrinking as we try to calm down.

When we've come down from the high we were just in, he turns on his side and rests his hand on my side. His eyes searching my face, his hand slides up and down my arm.

"Not that I have any complaints," Ethan chuckles, "but I want you to tell me what spurred that on."

His fingers slide up to my neck and I welcome the warm tingles that spread from his fingertips.

"What's going on Adea," he asks.

I take a deep breath and exhale. I don't even know where to start. Oh, I have these dreams where I'm someone else but still myself and I watch you get your heart ripped out? But that's not even the weirdest thing. What's odd about the whole situation: the weirdest thing is I've been having these dreams since before I knew you?

"I think we should tell him," Kor says.

"What would that even do?" I ask her as I feel his fingers dip into my hair.

"Maybe it was a vision," Kor says.

"A vision? What are we? Psychic?" I sigh. "And a vision of what? The past? Because it was us but it also wasn't Kor," I tell her.

"I don't know Adea," she mumbles.

"I'm not mad at you Kor, I just don't know how to tell him or anyone for that matter about my dreams. I just need more time…"

I lean over and kiss him lightly on the lips before snuggling up to his chest. "Just a bad dream," I mumble into his chest. And that's what it was… just a bad dream…

ALWAYS

The moon is high in the sky when I wake up. My stomach is growling but I need to go and get clothes for tomorrow. I refuse to do the walk of shame in the morning when everyone's awake. I'd die of embarrassment if I saw Olivia and I was wearing the same thing I was wearing yesterday.

Looking over at Ethan, I watch as his chest rises and falls with his breathing. I'll go and get some clothes and maybe whip up a late-night snack for us and be back before he'll even notice.

Sitting up slowly, I hold my breath as I listen to see if he's stirring. Ignoring the pain between my legs, I creep towards the edge of the bed.

I throw my legs over the edge, plant my feet firmly on the ground, and pull myself up as gracefully as I can muster.

A light breeze raises goosebumps on my arms, I steal one more glance at Ethan laying in bed, his muscular tanned skin slightly covered by the white bed sheet, his eyes still closed.

I let out a breath of relief as I tiptoe around the room. Finding one of his shirts I slip it over my head and pull it down over my body. The material hangs down below my thighs and I pull my hair up in a messy bun.

When I get to my room, the idea of a warm bath calls me. After the night or day, we've had I need one but I love smelling like him. I inhale and freeze when I smell an unfamiliar scent.

Alarm bells start going off and I scan my room. This is my room so it should smell like me. This smell…. this smell doesn't belong to me or to Ethan.

Nothing is out of place, I search the dresser and my chair, my eyes stop on the deckle-edged paper sitting on my bed.

The paper feels flimsy in my fingers but my heart is hammering like it's trying to jump out of my chest. Peeling the seal off I unfold the letter and open it.

I love you so much that I can barely stand to breathe without you. I'm sorry if I was rough with you but you have to understand Adea. You fucked up.

Even though I hate that you destroyed my life and made me lose everything that was rightfully mine, I love you.

Is it easier without me by your side? Do you miss me as I miss you? Without me, you're nothing… but don't worry, soon, you'll return to your place.

It makes me sick thinking of you by his side. I hate it. I hate this. Don't worry though, you won't be by his side for long.

Don't forget where you belong. Don't forget who you belong to.

-Always,

Yours

My hands are shaking by the time I've finished reading the letter. I swallow the lump in my throat. A shiver slides down my spine and I grip the bedside table to stop myself from collapsing.

How did this get here? Who put it here? Was he here?

Oh gosh…

"Kor?" I squeak

"Yes, Adea, I'm here. Don't worry. We need to tell Ethan; show him the note and he can help us. We don't know how the note got here, if he brought it himself or if he has someone spying on you for him," she instructs me.

I nod.

"I'll have to show Ethan, won't I?" I ask.

"Yes, and he'll help us. He loves you and he won't let anything happen to us. He's our mate, our partner," she says and I can feel the warmth of her words.

"I know," I whisper.

"I'll tell Ethan," I say uncertainty lacing my words, and doubt spreading in my mind.

Looking down at the letter, I raise my right hand to my lips and nibble on my thumb. I need to get out of here. I can't stay here any longer.

I throw my clothes into a bag and head out of my room. I need to feel his arms around me, I don't want to think of Shane or his hands on me. I don't want to think of what he'd do to me if he had me to himself. I don't want the images of what we've done before in my head.

Tears break free and run down my cheeks. I look down the hallway and make my way to Ethan's room. My hands are shaking and I fist them to try to stop the shaking.

I see a small light from under his door and I hope he isn't awake yet. I could use a few minutes to calm down first. When I open the door, the room is dark, and I let out a breath of relief when I see Ethan's still in bed, sleeping.

Putting down my bag of clothes, I walk to the bathroom, I slowly twist the handle and open the door. I slip inside before carefully closing the door. There's no light streaming in from anywhere and I flip on the lights.

I take in a breath and walk over to the shower, turning it on hot. I pull Ethan's shirt off and fold it nicely before putting it on the counter. Walking over to the shower, I reach out my hand and test the temperature.

It's hot as I step in under it. The water trails down my back engulfing me in heat.

My fear from earlier in my room is still there, but also a touch of anger. I've never felt angry about my situation before but I feel a tinge of it now.

I hate myself.

I hate what Shane does to me...

I hate the effect he has on me.

Why is he doing this to me?

This isn't love. Why can't Shane see that? I can't stop the sobs that wrack through my body. I'm so tired of this.

It's been so long since I've felt so free... so good. I don't think I can remember the last time I felt this way. Ethan makes me feel.

The letter only reminded me how dirty I am. Do I even deserve to be by Ethan's side?

MARK ME

Adea

Ethan was still asleep when I opened the door, I crept back into his darkened bedroom, his naked torso separated from the sheet as he lay sprawled across the bed.

For a moment, I forgot what I needed to discuss with him, forgot Shane, forgot the note, and I just admired the powerful muscles on his back, every detail on display under the moonlight, his hair a tousled mess from sleep.

Biting my lip, I can't help but fidget as I make my way to him. I continue to the bed each step harder, heavier.

I place the letter on the bedside table before I turn to face him. I slipped into bed beside him and curled into a ball away from him.

The bedsheets were now cold and a line of goosebumps rushed down my arm. How do I tell him I've brought another problem to his pack, to his life, to us?

Looking at the note I wonder if I should keep it to myself. I don't want to ruin this right now. I lay in bed contemplating what to do when Ethan stirs beside me.

It's his turn to still when he feels me behind him before he flips over to face me. His arms wrapping around me and pulling me into his embrace.

"Mmm," he sighs, his chin dipping into the curve of my neck.

"Good morning," he says, his morning voice is gruff and lower than usual.

"Morning, Ethan," I respond.

Closing my eyes, I take a few deep breaths trying to push myself into facing him and telling him about the letter.

After a few moments, I turn around and scoot in until my body is pressed against his. What I see leaves me breathless, my whole world stares up at me. How can someone who is feared all over the country and kills ruthlessly look at me with genuine gentleness in his eyes?

"Adea?" He murmured. I could hear the slight frown in his voice as his eyes take in my expression.

His eyes flit left and right as he searches my face, "What's going on?" He asks.

I gulp, trying to figure out how to come out with the letter.

"I found something, when I went back to my room," I start. "I don't know if it's something we really have to worry about right now or if I could handle it on my own. You're someone who's important in my life and I would want us to talk about any troubles we're having or problems we go through."

Ethan's eyes never leave my face and I know without a doubt that he's got my back, that I matter to him, that he would do anything to protect me. I hate making him worry.

"When I went back to my room, there was a letter for me," I say. I watch as confusion paints his features. Confusion melts into worry which changes into anger.

"A letter from who?" Ethan asks, in a deadly voice.

"I—" I start before he asks his next question.

"Where is it?" He asks before sitting up.

Turning towards the bed, I pick the letter up and hand it to him. He eyeballs the letter and sniffs it, what he smells makes his eyes darken. I wait as Ethan opens it and starts to read it aloud.

"I love you so much that I can barely stand to breathe without you. I'm sorry if I was rough with you but you have to understand Adea. You fucked up…" He trails off and I watch as his facial features harden and his breathing grows deeper as he reads the rest of the letter.

Squishing the letter in his hand before raising his eyes to mine. "Shane," he growls. I don't know if he's asking me or saying it to himself. He stands from the bed, the sheet dropping to the floor and I watch as he paces back and forth.

I can feel his anguish radiating from his body in waves. I can hear a low rumble in his chest before he stops and turns his head to look back at me.

Ethan walks over to me and drops to his knees. I don't know what's going on or what he's going to do before I know it his hands are gripping my hips, his lips claiming my mouth.

My mind goes blank as his tongue darts past my lips and I let out a breathless moan. One of Ethan's hands leaves my hip and makes its way up to the back of my neck. Holding me in place as he continues kissing me and I press my body against his, feeling his chest.

When he releases my lips, I'm a breathless mess of putty in his hands. My lips are tingling and I can tell they're swollen from his dominating kisses. Ethan's eyes on my lips slip down to my unmarked neck. His eyes flicker from black to yellow and I know Elijah is just as angry as Ethan is.

My bottom lip trembles and I bite my lip, I feel vulnerable but I don't regret the choice to tell him how about the letter.

His grip on the back of my neck tightens just enough to sting a little. "Is this the first time he's reached out to you?" Ethan asks me. There's anger in his voice and I have to remind myself that he's not mad at me.

"Yes," I whisper, and Kor's shoulders hunch, her head bowed. I know she hates this as much as I do. Ethan shuts his eyes and his chest starts to slow as he gains control over Elijah.

His hand on my neck disappears and he drops his head to my chest as he leans into me. His arms wrap around my waist and I lift my hands to run them through his hair.

"This is my fault," He murmurs into my breasts. "Because of my shortcomings, someone got into your room. If you were to have walked in on them…" he stops.

Squeezing his hair in my fingers, I pull down and the action raises his eyes to mine. "Don't blame yourself for this. This is happening because of me…" I say. "This is my fault, Ethan."

I look into his eyes, and I hate myself for the pain I see there. I'd do anything to make it go away. I wish there was a way for Shane to know there was nothing he could do to make me his, to show him that I was indefinitely Ethan's.

My eyes widen as I realize there is something I could do, something we could do. Not because of Shane but because of us, for us. Something that could bind us together, forever for always.

Kor's head snaps up in attention, her tail wags as she realizes where my thoughts are going. Leaning down, I pull Ethan's head to the side before kissing his neck.

"Mark me, Ethan, make me yours, completely yours."

OH, PLEASE

Ethan

Her fingers in my hair pull down on my hair until my scalp tingles. I stare into my little mate's eyes as she stares down at me with a vulnerability that stabs at my heart. She's deep in thought and her eyes dilate, her eyes widening.

She pulls my head to the side, reaches forward, and I feel a sweet kiss on my neck that sends tingles down to my dick. I buck my hips against the bed and my brave mate looks into my eyes and the next words out of her mouth make my dick stand and harden for her.

"Mark me, Ethan, make me yours, completely yours," she says the words with absolute confidence. Like there's nothing else in the world but for us to become one.

I want nothing more than to make her mine, to see her walking around with my mark on her neck, my scent blended with hers. Knowing that no one else can have her, that everyone who sees her will KNOW she's mine. I moan as liquid seeps from my tip at the thought. Fuck, the thought alone has my cock pressing against the bed.

I'm naked on my knees in front of my Queen, my Luna. I grip the hem of one of my t-shirts she's got on, and in one swoop I pull it off of her. She's naked underneath and I grunt in approval.

It's all Elijah's wanted since the moment we first laid eyes on her. Her legs wrap around my waist and I slide both hands to cup her perfect ass. Her arms reach around my neck and her tits press against my chest. I nip at her neck as I lift her as I stand.

Her head drops back and she lets out a whimper I feel all the way down in my cock. She's so fucking perfect and she's all mine. My length pushes up against her ass and she starts grinding her tight cunt against my lower abdomen.

My naughty little minx. She's driving me mad while Elijah chuckles in approval, excited to leave our mark on our little mate. I drag my tongue up her neck before sucking on the sweet spot made for my mark.

Adea thrusts her hips against my torso with a thirst that needs quenching. I turn and walk to my ceiling to floor windows. Pressing into her, she gasps as the cold glass touches her ass.

Her fingers are in my hair again and she pulls my face down until my lips crash against hers. I groan, and the taste of her only sets me on fire. Her eyelids flutter closed, the heat and adrenaline rushing to my cock.

Pulling my hips back, my cock poised at her entrance, I glide my tip against her lips.

She pulls back, her hands fisted in my hair, "Ooh," she whimpers.

Dipping my head, my mouth covers hers, seeking more, taking more. A beautiful flush paints her cheeks and slides down her chest.

Her tongue is hot and demanding, my tongue hugs and plays with hers, and she pulls my hair again as she bites down on my bottom lip.

I make my way down to her neck, leaving kisses down her jaw and she arches her back against the glass as she offers herself up to me.

"Fuck," I gasp, unable to close my eyes as I stare down at her, my brows etch in ecstasy.

I pant, desperate to be inside her. She grips my shoulders and grinds against my tip, searching for the friction of my tip against her, so close to her clit.

***

Adea

His tip pushed through my wet folds and pressed against my clit. Tingles spreading from my tip to my core. I grip his shoulders, bracing myself for his hard cock to thrust home when his eyes glaze over and I know someone's linking him.

Stilling, I bite my lip and keep my eyes on his, while I grip his length. His mouth opens and his jaw drops, and my hand pumps his hardened member up and down. Closing his mouth, he clenches his teeth and the muscle in his cheek throbs.

I love watching him lose focus because of me, because of what I do to him. It makes me feel powerful. Watching this man squirm because of me.

Every other pump of my hand, Ethan presses slightly into my grip, and his tip hits my clit. I see stars.

His eyes are still glazed so I know he's still talking to whoever linked him but I know he can still feel me and what I'm doing.

I can stay still or I can be a little bold. I need to feel him inside of me, I need him to fill me.

I don't know if I can stay still. Kor purrs when she hears my devious thoughts. I decide to go for it, and she hastily agrees with me.

Removing my hand, I look down at his thick cock.

I bite back a moan and watch him disappear inside of me as I slide down. My pussy clenches around his pulsing cock until he's buried deep inside of me.

"Ah," I whisper as I lean my head back against the glass and feel my pussy adjust to his size. I wonder if I'll ever get used to his length or his girth.

Ethan's hands are still gripping my ass, my hands are still on his shoulders, as he cuts the link. He looks down at me with a mischievous smile and approving eyes.

A smile pulls at the corner of his lip, he pulls out to the tip and thrusts hard until he's buried inside of me again. My body jostles against the glass, my head drops down locked on where we connect.

"That was Odis," he grunts as his hands slide up to my thighs. Ethan widens them, so he can get a good look at my clit. His eyes lock on my clit, his thumbs dig into the inside of my thighs, as he pulls out slowly of me.

I moan, his words go in and out of focus. I know it's important otherwise he wouldn't say it but all I can think about is the way his fat cock slams inside of me.

"Oh please," I beg.

SORRY

"Oh please," I beg. Ethan's grip on my thighs tightens and I can feel him pulsing inside of me. He pulls out of me and I feel his length as he slides his cock so it grazes my clit. My sensitive clit erupts in sparks at the friction and my body jerks.

"Odis informed me that the rogues finally cracked. They've shared information regarding who…" he pulls back before his hips thrust forward and push into me again. "… sent them," he grunts.

"We now know their motive and who they're working for," he says it like we're just having a conversation. Talking like this is a normal day and he doesn't have me pinned against the glass while he fucks me into oblivion. It's so hot, he's so hot, this position is mind-blowing.

He continues his onslaught of thrusts as I struggle to hold on. His thrusts are hard, almost angry. My moans fill the room one after the other and all I can do is continue taking him, taking his frustration, taking his anger, taking what he gives me.

"Ethan," I moan, it's almost too much, he's almost too much.

His thrusting speeds up, I can't help but shatter around his hard cock and then I'm floating on pure ecstasy.

This doesn't get any better, I think to myself, then I feel his lips on my neck.

Before I can come down from my high, canines pierce skin and push down into my neck. I see white, pain fills my senses before it's followed by pleasure. My pussy clenches down on his member.

Ethan lets out a low grown of approval, and I bite my bottom lip as he withdraws from my neck and licks the bite make to seal it. He continues to thrust into my wet, sensitive core.

He shows no mercy, his hips diving deep, my back and head banging against the glass. "Now everyone will know you are mine, every man who sees you will see that you belong to me, that I've claimed you."

I know he's close. Leaning my head into his neck, Kor comes forward, and together we bite into Ethan's neck. He grunts, his cock hardens almost painfully. He thrusts in and out of me until his cum fills me.

My tongue licks over the bite as he did to mine, sealing it. A beautiful blue half-moon appears on the raised skin where I bit.

I orgasm again and crash into his arms. A sense of pride comes over me as I realize we've completed the mating process. We've marked each other, and now, we are bound together.

Ethan kisses my forehead before carrying me into the shower. The shower turns on and water flows until steam fills the bathroom.

"I love you," Ethan murmurs as we slip into the shower and under the hot water. "I don't know what I'd do if something happened to you, my little mate," he tells me in a low voice.

"I love you too, Ethan," I whisper. He lowers me until my feet stand firmly on the ground. "I'm sorry," I say, my voice cracking.

"Sh sh, this isn't your fault. I don't want to hear that you're blaming yourself for this. You didn't do this. Shane and his sick obsession with you is the reason for this."

Nodding, I turn around. I grab the shampoo and squeeze some into my hand, lathering it into my hair.

His cock presses into my lower back, my fingers massaging into my scalp. I feel his hands reach around and cup my breasts. His fingers rolling my nipples in between his thumb and index finger.

I continue washing my hair, pretending to be ignorant of his fingers. His fingers pinch my nipples a little harder and my breathing picks up. One of his hands slides down my back along my spine and finger the dips above my ass.

His hand lands on my hip while the other is still twirling my nipple. "I don't like thinking of him claiming you as his," Ethan says.

"He can't claim me as his," I whisper. "You've marked me as yours, and I've marked you as mine," I say, the skin on my neck thumps, agreeing with me.

"It still drives me to madness, it drives us to madness thinking of another man talking to you, thinking of you, calling you his."

Soap-suds slide down my body, as he rubs his thick head at my entrance. His hand on my hip, encouraging me to dip lower.

I watch as the hot water washes the suds, they slide onto the floor and down the drain. His tip pushes at my entrance and in one stroke his tip, his length fill me.

"Ah," I cry out.

His hand on my nipple makes its way up my chest. Ethan leans down as his hand grips my neck. He pulls out before thrusting into me.

"Ah, Ethan," I whimper.

"I know, I'm an ass for not giving you enough time to recover," he murmurs as he withdraws and thrusts home. His balls slapping against my ass as his cock claims my sore cunt.

"Seeing my mark on your neck soothes me, but knowing that another man thinks he has a claim to what's mine… sets me ablaze," he says.

Ethan grunts as he pulls out of me, he's long, thick, and hard, so hard. I'm lost as he drives into me over and over again. The water splashing on the walls as his body slaps against mine.

"Oh fuck, Ethan," I moan loudly. "I don't, I can't," I cry.

His grip on my neck tightens slightly, my orgasm getting closer and closer. His cock slamming into me as he chases his own orgasm.

"I need to feel you convulsing around my cock, I love watching you lose yourself to the pleasures I give you, little mate."

His words push me over the edge and I cum again all over his cock as he continues to slam into me until he finds his own release.

"You are mine," he growls as his cum shoots into me.

ROGUES

Adea

We spent the rest of the day kissing, talking, and having our meals in bed. I was on the moon from all the attention and love he continued to shower me with. We had to get back to reality soon, with the rogues and the letter, we had to get things taken care of.

The next day after breakfast, we headed for the meeting room.

"As much as I'd like to stay in bed with you longer, I do have a pack to run," Ethan said. I welcomed the blush that spread across my cheeks, undoubtedly noticed by Ethan.

Beta Odis had linked Ethan to discuss the rogues and we needed to inform him about the letter. It was fun exploring each other and experiencing all these new things with him but we couldn't ignore the obvious issues we had to deal with.

Olivia came out of one of the rooms followed by a smiling Gabe. When she saw us, she flagged us down in the lobby and grabbed onto me, interlocking our arms. Gabe gives me a nod and I smile at him; I love seeing him so happy.

A smile spreads on her lips as she leans in and shared more than I'd like to hear of what her and Gabe had been up to since I last saw her. My ears heat at her words and she giggles gleefully.

I look over to Gabe and he just stares at her proudly. Like attracts like. Kor laughs in agreement.

"Oh, my Goddess!!" Olivia squeals, eyeing my neck. Her eyes widen with surprise that quickly melts into mischief. She starts bouncing on the tips of her feet.

"Congrats, congrats, congrats!" She hugs me tightly. Gabe comes over and gives me a hug.

Before we separate, he gives me a knowing wink, and I think I can die from embarrassment now. "I'm happy for you, Ady. Congratulations," he says before turning to Ethan.

"Congrats, Alpha," he says before reaching out his hand for a handshake. I watch Ethan smile and shake his hand firmly.

"Later, tell me everything!" Olivia whispers in my ear while we head into the meeting room.

We're all sitting at the same table when Odis walks in, his face tight, his mouth turned down. He's dressed in his usual attire, always professional. The gray suit was snug against his muscular build.

My shoulders tense and I ready myself for what he has to say. Ethan clears his throat ending our conversation. "Odis is here to update all of us on what he learned from the prisoners," Ethan says.

Odis remains standing as he loosens his navy-blue tie and runs his hand through his hair. I watch his adam's apple bob before he takes a step towards us.

"We were blindsided by the rogue attack, not only did they get past our borders but they got to our pups," he said, the muscles in his cheek straining. "I took my time … breaking down the rogues we captured. Turns out the recent rogue attacks were all connected. They were feeling us out," he growled.

Ethan nods.

"There are rumors of a new pack forming and these rogues have confirmed that they are a part of this "pack"," Odis says in disgust.

"The rogues were told to feel out our lines to see where our weak spots were. They're low leveled and have been rogues for a long time. The wolf in charge promised food and entry into the pack for every rogue who helped."

Odis walks in front of us as he talks. "They don't know the name of the human in charge but the wolf goes by Max. They say he's informed them of Desert Moon we have something of his."

"Now, they didn't know what it is, but they said he's adamant about crossing the border and taking it back and once one of the rogues cracked the other followed and confirmed."

"I don't mean to be rude, so please excuse my next question. I see you two have completed the mating process. Congratulations are in order."

I flush for the millionth time today. "Have you discussed the Luna ceremony yet? Do you know when you will be introducing Adea as our Luna, officially?"

"We haven't discussed the Luna ceremony yet but I know that as soon as we're ready we will announce it to the pack," Ethan says before looking at me.

I gulp.

"I still have my first shift coming up this weekend and I think I will need some time to adjust in my second skin," I say firmly, despite the overwhelming fear I have about my bones cracking and transforming.

Odis nods, "Pardon my forwardness but it would be best if we could hold the ceremony as soon as possible. For the pack, for the rogues who think that our Alpha is weak because he doesn't have a Luna by his side."

"First, we need to make sure Adea can easily switch back and forth between her human and wolf form. I'm positive they'll give us a date as soon as they know she's ready," Olivia tells Odis.

Odis is about to say something else when Olivia gives him a glare that shuts him up. Instead, he nods before turning to Ethan. "The rogues gave me a little bit of useful information. In exchange, I promised one of the two freedom."

"And what information was good enough to grant freedom, Odis?" Ethan growled, clearly upset about letting one of the rogues go.

Odis smiled but his eyes were cold, "They gave me a date of another attack." His eyes twinkled and Ethan let out a breath.

"That was good enough to grant one freedom. Did you get rid of the other?" He asks.

"I snapped the other one's neck as soon as I got the date. Would you like him to go free or welcome him into the pack?" Odis asks.

"Let him join, he's earned it," Ethan says.

SHIFT

The days passed quickly after the meeting. Ethan was busy but checked in with me whenever he could. The weekend of the Full Moon arrived and it was hard to hide my anxiety and fear about my first shift.

It's close to sundown and I'm feeling fidgety. "Don't worry," Olivia tried to soothe me, "after a couple of shifts it becomes second nature. This is what our body was made for." She squeezed my hand and I nodded trying to calm myself.

"I'm here and will make sure to make it happen quickly," Kor said.

"Thanks..." I say. "Are you ready to come out?" I ask nervously.

I can tell she's excited and I don't want to be selfish. This isn't all about me. For her, this would be something exciting.

"Yes! I can't wait to feel the grass below my paws and to feel the wind on my face but... what I really can't wait for is to finally meet Ethan's wolf. I can't wait until I can hear and see him."

Guilt washes over me in waves. I've been so cruel; she's been living through me with Ethan but she hasn't even seen or talked to his wolf yet. She's been suffering and she hasn't said anything to me about it. I've been so selfish.

"I'm sorry Kor, I haven't been considerate of you."

"Ethan is my mate too! You don't have to be sorry Adea. I enjoyed our time with Ethan, I just want to meet him wolf part too," she tells me.

"As soon as I' shift you'll be able to see him."

"I look forward to it, Adea. Ethan's wolf counterpart is your mate just as much as Ethan is my mate. So, you'll need time with Elijah too," she says happily.

I gulp.

"You're right," I say nervously. "I haven't really had the chance to talk with Elijah but I've noticed when he's been present when I've been with Ethan."

Kor purrs, "I know, I could feel him when he was present."

"Are you nervous about meeting him?" I ask, curious.

"It's not the same for wolves as it is for you and Ethan. I already know that he's mine and I, his. I'm not nervous… I'm excited. I can't wait to see him, to kiss him, to hug him… to fu-" I cut her off.

"Okay okay, I get where that was going," I tell her. I do not want to hear about what she wants to do to or with Elijah.

Kor giggles like a schoolgirl who's about to see her crush at school.

"We've got this, don't worry," she encourages me.

Olivia and I sit on the couch in the lobby as we wait for Ethan. She starts mind-linking and I just know that it's him. After she cuts the mind-link she turns to me, "It's time."

Standing up, I follow her outside, and orange and yellow paint the sky. She walks around the building to where the forest starts. I watch as Ethan emerges from the trees wearing nothing but ripped shorts.

"Are you ready, little mate?" He asks with his hand outstretched.

Not trusting my voice, I nod while I close the distance between us and grab his hand.

"Olivia will follow us until we're deep enough into the forest. She's going to give us some space once we get out far enough," he tells me as he turns and we take the first step into the forest.

I don't know when but we've started running, Ethan holds my hand firmly in his while we go deeper into the forest. Olivia isn't far behind and it's comforting knowing that she's here.

The sun starts dipping lower in the sky and I watch as it gets closer and closer to the horizon. "I'm here," Kor says quietly and I nod knowing that I'll be okay.

We'd been running for minutes, maybe half an hour when Ethan stopped and turned to Olivia. She then looked at me, ran over, and gave me a big hug.

"You've got this!" She whispered before turning and running back the way we came. I watched her until she disappeared out of sight.

I gulped before turning to face Ethan, too afraid to attempt to hide the fear. My eyes were wide with fear, my heart hammering in my chest, my hands sweaty as a cold chill ran through my body.

I clenched my fists to try and lessen the chill but it didn't go away, it spread to my arms and ran down my spine. I opened my mouth to call Ethan when the sun dipped below the horizon and the light from the full moon hit me.

A loud crack had a pain-filled scream fill the night air and I fell to the ground. Ethan's soothing words fell on deaf ears, I couldn't hear anything. The pain was unbearable, my head throbbed and I tried to breathe through it.

My body continued to crack, my arm twisted at a weird angle and it hurt so much, I couldn't move. My back curled, my spine lengthening and curling against my will, my shoulders spread out.

Minutes passed and the pain only worsened. Ethan stood above me, trying to soothe me, his hands at his side. "Eth-," I cried as another bone-shattering crack came from my legs. I pressed my head against the earth, begging for it to stop, pleading for the Goddess to end it.

"Please, please," I begged mentally.

"It'll be over soon, Adea," Kor cried. "Hold on with me, just hold on," she pleaded.

"Kor," I screamed hoarsely.

"You're almost there, you're doing amazing," Ethan encouraged me. "It's almost done, little mate, you're doing great."

"I don't know if I can do this," I told Kor mentally.

"We're almost there, Ethan's here, I'm here. Soon, I'll take it from you," she cried. I could feel her anguish as she watched me transform.

Beautiful white fur erupted all over my body and my nose protruded from my face growing outwards. My hands morphed into strong paws, a tail grew from my backside and hair fell from it.

The pain disappeared and I realized that I was inside, while I looked out through Korra's eyes. The transformation was over, the pain subsided.

GODDESS

Olivia

I felt guilty leaving Adea behind with Ethan, the wind feels amazing as I run through the forest. The first shift is always the most painful but I know that she can handle it, I just know it.

I don't know how long I've been running. When I hear a howl fill the air, I smile knowing that it's finished. I knew she'd be okay. She's my future Luna, after all, the Goddess wouldn't have chosen her if she wasn't strong enough to handle shifting, to handle this pack, to handle Ethan.

Look at how he'd been in the beginning, he wouldn't even talk about finding his mate, and now look at him. One look at his face and you could tell he was madly in love with her. I've wanted nothing but his happiness from the beginning.

Now that he's found her, he doesn't have to worry about other packs questioning his strength, or wondering if he's weakened. He'll continue to grow and be the Alpha he was born to be.

I owe Adea more than I can ever repay. If it wasn't for her, I'd never have met Gabe. The thought makes me tear up and I shake the sad thoughts from my mind. None of that. I think of Gabe, I get to go home to him.

My heart swells and I run a little faster. The past week has been amazing... beyond words. I was truly blessed to have him as my mate. He was my mate but he was also my friend. He'd been through so much and I'd been through... my own struggles.

I'll go home to him, make love to him over and over tonight. The fight earlier wasn't worth being petty over. It isn't his fault she-wolves look at him. I can't help the protectiveness... the ownership I feel over him. I'll apologize and tell him that it won't happen again, that I'll be better.

I don't see the shadows following me until it's too late. I was too preoccupied in my thoughts, too trusting of this forest in our lands. I let my guard down and it was too late to shift.

Four wolves come out of the shadows, three of them rogues, one of them was massive with gold glowing eyes, and stood above the rest. I was outnumbered, I didn't stand a chance. How long had they been following me? Did they see Adea and Ethan too?

Goddess, I pray they didn't. I stand still, I don't have a chance against 4 wolves on my own. I won't fight them, maybe they just want to ask me questions... maybe...

They've surrounded me and I wait for one of them to shift into their human form. When none of them do, I feel a chill run down my spine. They don't want to talk.

Shit.

"We're fucked," my wolf, Gem says.

I can't help but chuckle. "You're stating the obvious, Gem."

"We could run, make it harder for them," she says and I know she thinks we should put up a fight.

"I don't want signs of a struggle," I say thinking of Gabe. "He'll be out here to investigate and I don't want him to see a fight."

She stays silent, and I know she understands me.

"I won't fight you," I tell the wolves as I take a step closer.

The massive stares at me before shifting. When he returns to his human form, I can't help the fear that spreads throughout my body. I know him. I watched his trial; I know what he did.

Shane.

The Alpha's exiled son stands before me naked; his eyes rake up my body and I feel bile in my throat.

Oh, Goddess.

"Don't try thinking of a way out now, you were smart to stay still and give in. Don't be stupid," he laughs. "I may be a rogue now but I still have Alpha blood running through my veins. I'm still stronger than you, and faster."

I gulp.

"What do you want?" I ask, hiding the fear from my voice. I won't let him have the satisfaction of knowing that I'm scared.

He cocks, his head and stares at me, his eyes scan me and I can see gold flashing in them. His wolf is staring at me as much as the human counterpart.

"I can taste your fear," he murmurs. "I can taste it on my tongue," he says as his tongue darts out of his mouth and licks along his top lip.

I fight the urge to run, it would be useless. I stare him down and remain silent. Shane chuckles as he takes a step towards me. The three wolves around us watch my every move.

"What do you want?" I repeat.

He doesn't say anything.

"Why did you come here?" I try again. "You were banished from these lands. You shouldn't be here."

He takes another step forward, "Oh, little Gamma…" He's in front of me now, his hand reaches up to touch my cheek, "I want you."

My stomach drops.

"You see, your Alpha took something that belongs to me. Don't you think it's only fair that I take something of his?" He says sweetly.

I swallow.

"I don't belong to my Alpha," I say. Does he think that I have something going on with Ethan?

He smiles, "You may not belong to him, but he cares for you. The Beta and you are the closest to him. Is that not true?"

I open my mouth, "Don't lie to me now," he says in a low voice. "You'll only piss me off."

"Your Alpha took something from me, and I'm here to take something from him. You. He's taken what's mine and he's made it his. I think it's only my right," he growls, "To make something of his mine."

The way he says mine has another chill running down my back, I know what's going to happen now. I know I have no choice but to go with him.

DON'T PANIC

Adea

Everything felt new, smelt fresh, tasted sweet on my tongue. The pain I felt just a few moments ago was already forgotten. I was a newborn looking at the world for the first time. A shake took over my shoulders and the rest of my body followed.

Korra put her snout into the grass and sniffed, grass and earth never smelled so good. The bright fullness of the moon made us look up to the sky. The stars twinkled and a shooting star ripped through the sky.

"Beautiful," a voice says from behind us. A low growl caught our attention and I watched with bated breath as Korra turned her head to find the source. What we saw left us breathless.

A beautiful black wolf with broad shoulders stood before us. Beautiful glowing eyes stared back at us and I felt Korra's heart skip a beat before beating twice as fast when she realized she stood face to face with Elijah.

"Mate," she said mentally before she whimpered.

My heart soared for her. I've been selfishly happy living with Ethan this whole time. She finally gets to see Elijah.

"Mate," he repeats.

A powerful paw takes a step forward before he bounds over to us. She rushes forward and meets him in the middle. Her snout touches his before they embrace each other.

I'm overwhelmed by Korra's feelings, by Elijah's feelings, and by Ethan's feelings as they all slam into us at once. Elijah's love for Korra, and Ethan's worry for me during my first transformation.

"I love you," I say. I don't know if he can hear me but Elijah's eyes twinkle as he looks down into Korra's eyes, looks down into me behind her eyes.

Korra leans up and licks the side of his snout before taking off into the field across the way. She's playing coy and daring him to chase after. I hear the sounds of his powerful paws as he bounds after us and giggles at her excitement.

We get pretty far but when we look back at him, we can tell he isn't even trying. Korra stares at his strong shoulders and beautiful black hair. For a wolf, he's very attractive.

Elijah comes to a stop and freezes. He lifts his nose into the air and sniffs the air and a low growl pierces the night air when he smells Korra's arousal. In the blink of an eye, he's caught up to us, his teeth are at our neck and she whines as he bites down.

Korra has no choice but to slow to a stop now and still as his grip tightens. A low warning growl escapes past his lips and Korra's belly erupts in butterflies.

Elijah mounts us, his member pushes her tail out of the way, and in one swift motion, he thrusts deep. She struggles and pretends to get up but he bites down harder and pulls out of her.

Korra whimpers and Elijah thrust into her again and again. He finds a rhythm and continues making love to her. He pulls in and out of her, over and over again until her legs shake.

The rhythm picks up and he slams into her harder and harder. Korra gives into him completely and welcomes his movements. His strong belly touches her back and she arches under him.

She cums under the full moon and Elijah's thrusts become jerky as he hits that sweet spot deep inside of Korra's core. Letting go of her neck, he howls as he empties inside of her womb. I pull away to give them their privacy and welcome the darkness that takes me.

Olivia

I know I had no choice but to go with him.

"I wish…." Gem said quietly. I was about to respond to her when my eyes were drawn to where Shane's men led the way. I didn't recognize this path. This way didn't lead out to the entrance of the forest. Shane's eyes land on me, he gives a chuckle as we walk through a dark shaded area.

"You tracked me," I said, staring at the grass in front of me.

"I did," he confirmed in a dangerous voice that sent a shiver down my spine. He leveled his cold blue eyes on the men in front of us. Shane's hand touched the flesh on my lower back.

My heart rate doubled.

"Olivia," he said sharply, and the look he gave me made me want to shiver again. I balled my shaking hands by my side.

Shane's face gave nothing away. Could I hope for mercy? For compassion? For there to be no pain in the next hours if not days? But I knew the answer to that question. Shane was ruthless to Adea, someone he grew up with. He wouldn't be any different with me.

"You will get in the car and you won't try to mind-link Ethan or anyone else. You have not been blindfolded because I need to watch your eyes. I need to make sure you don't try anything stupid," he said in an emotionless voice, his eyes holding a clear warning.

I swallowed and nodded. Because it was all I could do. What else could I do? It wasn't as if I really had a choice. I feigned indifference; I don't care if he could smell my fear. I won't give him the satisfaction.

"When we get to our destination, don't try to run or do anything stupid, Olivia. I'd hate to have to hurt you."

I gave another nod and he let go of my lower back before opening the door for me. I stepped in without hesitation. When he shut the door, I drew in a shaky breath. My heart was beating out of my chest.

This isn't good. This isn't good. My conscience screamed. Being Gamma is always a risky job title and I knew how to handle this. I knew how to handle what was to come.

Don't panic.

Don't freak out.

One of his men slid in next to me while the other two took the driver's and passenger's seats. "He shouldn't have taken what's mine," he said as he looked out the window.

NEVER AGAIN

Adea

"Leave him, Adea. There's no time to mourn right now. We must find our mate." Pulling myself away, I rushed past the arms, legs, and heads of more familiar faces. Fumbling in my weakened human state, I tried to find him.

In the corner of my eye, I saw movement. I turned and saw a pile rise up and fall as a shape I recognized pushed up through the bodies. Seeing his black hair my heart swells.

He pulls himself through and I do a quick once over and notice he's naked. His body is painted in blood, his chest and abs beautiful as ever and unharmed. His eyes lock on mine and I can see the relief flood his face.

He stands up and I can feel the need to touch him grow and almost explode as he starts towards me. I can feel his need and his relief. Korra is mentally wagging her tail and urging me to run to him when I feel his shock… Shock fills his eyes and we frantically try to see what's wrong. I look down at his chest… he's ripped open…

There's fresh blood seeping from his chest and my heart grows cold when the mate bond snaps. Korra howls in agony. Pain. I feel a gut-wrenching pain as I fall to the ground. I can't rip my eyes away from my mate. He falls to the ground as I crawl to him.

I hear footsteps moving away from him. Korra is whining in my head. We're too engrossed to notice when the footsteps get closer. There's a sound near my head as he drops something. I feel a slight tear as he grabs my hair wrenching me along with him.

He drops something near my head and grabs my hair wrenching me along with him. Korra retreats to the farthest part of my mind.

The world is quiet and still. My mate is just out of reach when he starts dragging me away. Goddess knows where to. I can't pull my eyes from the empty eyes of my mate. I hit my head and welcome the cold consciousness that takes me.

My body is moving back and forth. I strain against the darkness that's trying to keep me under. My hands are restrained and I try to open my eyes. I can hear heavy breathing and feel a hot breath against my cheek.

I'm being pressed back and released. Something wet along my neck. I start to panic when I hear grunting. "Adea," he moans.

Sharp teeth clamp down on my bottom lip drawing blood. My body still keeping that rhythmic motion.

"I've waited too long for you," the voice says. My eyes open and I see long black hair above me, lips I've seen before, eyes that I'd recognize anywhere.

Shane. The fear doesn't hit at once, his eyes aren't looking at me but focused on something down between us. As my eyes trail down his bare chest, his abs flexing, and his hips thrusting. I watch as his hard cock pulls out of me.

His eyes close and he moans as he thrusts into me to the hilt making my body jerk back. Repeating the movements he starts moving faster. A loud ringing in my ears threatens to split my head open.

My hands are still restrained. "Korra?" I whisper to her. I can't hear or feel my wolf. I whimper when I feel his hard cock thrust into my warmth causing pain. His eyes snap open and I feel his hand clench my throat as his cold lust-filled eyes locked onto mine. The warmth I once saw there was completely gone.

"I chose you then and I choose you now," Shane murmurs. He leans down, trailing his lips along my neck. Having no fight left in me, I close my eyes, his grip on me tightening as he continues ravaging me. I hear his canines extend and feel them poised at my neck.

Sinking his canines deep into my neck, I scream, as his thrusts quicken. He comes undone and licks my wound to seal his mark. I feel his seed fill me as he growls, "Mine."

Shane's grip on my throat lessens and I feel his body weight press down on me as he collapses on top of me. His length still fills me and I wince when he moves, and I feel his seed drip out of me.

Staying still, I feel his chest rise and fall and when I pluck up the courage, I look at his face. His eyes are closed and I can hear light snores fall from his lips.

Moments pass and he rolls over on the bed. I stare at the ceiling and look at the window. The moonlight spills in. Does the Moon Goddess enjoy my pain?

I slip off of the bed and walk to the open window. Looking outside I look at the territory, the night is filled with an eerie silence.

Thoughts of escaping bring a smile to my face. No... I can't escape. Looking down, I feel the urge to jump. I could escape him in death but… that would be too easy. He doesn't deserve to live having everything at his disposal. He doesn't deserve to rule.

I turn my head back to him on the bed, ass out, hair messy. I once considered him the closest thing I had to family.

I feel a warm liquid slowly sliding down my thigh. Looking down I realize the liquid is blood. Looking back at the bed I see his clothes on the floor, next to his sword.

My fingers twitch and my feet lead me to the bedside. Slowly, my hand reaches down and grips the blade. I wrap my other hand around the blade and call on strength I'm not sure I have.

Raising the blade above my head, I look down at him lying in bed and feel the tears run down my face. All I ever wanted was to be loved and live by Ethan's side. But he's gone now, I'm alone, and I can't… I'm not strong enough to live in a world without him.

I bring the sword down on Shane's neck, the blade slices skin, blood splatters violently. I feel warmth wetness on my cheek and I raise the blade again, bringing it down again. This time it severs his head from his body.

The tears continue flowing without my approval. I drop the blade and turn to the window. I look up at the moon once more, "In my next life, I'll save him. I don't care how many times I'm reborn. I won't live this life again… Never again," I whisper to the Goddess before throwing myself out of the window. My body hurls to the ground and the world goes dark.

ABOUT THE AUTHOR

J*p Sina* Is a Samoan-born American writer of fantasy and romance. She is a book obsessed reader turned author. She started writing on GoodNovel in 2021 and published her first book the same year.

She currently resides in Auburn, Washington.

Her days are spent chasing her kids around the house, making sure her young-at-heart cat Yuri eats and reads when the sun sets. She writes when she isn't reading and reads when she isn't writing. Writing and coffee are her happily ever after.

ALSO BY JP SINA

MY ALPHA'S MARK

Kacie is used to keeping to herself. She has been a slave to Ken, the Blood Moon packs Alpha for the past year. She has no dreams of escaping but as the abuse worsens she prays to the Goddess for a way out.

Alpha Viktor is the Alpha of one of the largest packs and doesn't want or have the time for a mate. When he sees Alpha Ken's arms wrapped around her waist he sees red. Could the Moon Goddess be so cruel as to present his mate to him in the arms of another?

THE FORBIDDEN LUNA

Adea struggles with doing what needs to be done when best friend is involved. Can she make the right decision? Shane is still at large and has proven difficult to track. When the loss of a dear friend will she rise to the occasion and prove her worth as Luna or will she fail? Will Adea be able to change fate?

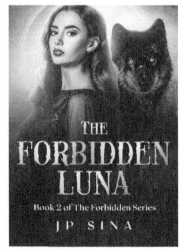